This Innocent Corner

This Innocent Corner

a novel by

Peggy Herring

OOLICHAN BOOKS
FERNIE, BRITISH COLUMBIA, CANADA
2010

Library and Archives Canada Cataloguing in Publication

Herring, Peggy, 1961-

    This innocent corner / Peggy Herring.

ISBN 978-0-88982-268-9

    I. Title.

PS8615.E7685T55 2010   C813'.6   C2010-906086-5

We gratefully acknowledge the financial support of the Canada Council for the Arts, the British Columbia Arts Council through the BC Ministry of Tourism, Culture, and the Arts, and the Government of Canada through the Book Publishing Industry Development Program, for our publishing activities.

Published by
Oolichan Books
P.O. Box 2278
Fernie, British Columbia
Canada V0B 1M0

www.oolichan.com

Printed in Canada on 100% post consumer recycled FSC-certified paper.

Cover photo by Shehzad Noorani.
http://www.flickr.com/photos/81504640@N00/

Mixed Sources
Product group from well-managed forests,
controlled sources and recycled wood or fiber
www.fsc.org Cert no. SW-COC-003438
©1996 Forest Stewardship Council
FSC

For

Michael and Devin

There is sound of fury on the land and in the water,
The innocent corner of the earth that I love
Has suddenly awakened.

—From "Durmor" by Sukanto Bhottacharya

Prologue

Hasan Chowdhury hasn't changed. Even after thirty years, even from behind the lights that glare on stage at the Shilpakala Academy, I recognize his bearish body. He lurches into the cavernous auditorium and stops halfway up the aisle. Though the proceedings have already begun, he pauses and surveys the stage and the rows of sour-smelling plush chairs as though they are his territory. Then he sits right in front, behind the row of VIPs. I remember him entering the dining room every morning with the same posture, throwing himself into the chair beside his father and peeling a steaming roti off the stack prepared by Shafiq and Kamala. He'd scoop up the bhaji, his hands like paws, and wash everything down with cups of cha.

His hair is still shoulder-length, and the grey looks incongruous. He's given up on the beard and the bushy side burns, thank god, but not the John Lennon glasses. The wire rims balance on the tip of his nose just as they did when we were at Dhaka University, another nod to the rebel he was then. Perhaps he loves that boy. More likely, he's just another lost man in his fifties clinging to the illusion of his golden youth.

I suppose I ought to try to be more generous seeing as it's his country I'm visiting and, after all, it has been thirty years. But I still find it hard to be considerate when it comes to Hasan.

I don't think he would have recognized me if I wasn't up on stage, my name on the silk banner suspended behind me, if I hadn't just been introduced by a woman in an olive saree printed with a dun pattern that reminds me of dried, bent earthworms. Though Hasan is nearly my age, time hasn't been as generous with my body. I've withered. My hair is completely grey and I've cropped it. He'd remember wispy hair the colour of apple scab, tied in a simple ponytail. I remember the ends incessantly loosening and curling themselves into corkscrews in the drenched heat. My smile sags now and I look unhappy most of the time, although that is not altogether true. And I have acquired a stomach, gifted by my baby, a droopy belly that I long ago stopped trying to conceal.

In front of the scratchy-sounding microphone, I wait for recognition from Hasan, but nothing. He looks right through me just as he did so many years ago whenever I asked what he thought was another ridiculous question. Questions like: why shouldn't Luna be able to choose her own friends? Why are Shaheed and Ruby avoiding me now? Why is the only suitable response to hatred and intolerance simply more hatred and intolerance? Hasan thought most of what I said was worthy of utter contempt, and though he's done and said almost nothing today, his mere presence and the attitude he carries set in motion an overwhelming and very familiar sense of injury.

The end of the applause leaves an expectation thick as the air before a monsoon rain. The woman in the olive saree has a tight, anxious smile on her face. Like a strange insect, she bobs her head and flutters her hands. A panoply of bangles on her wrists tinkle frantically. *Begin, begin*, she signals.

"Asalaam aliekum," I say. "Good afternoon and thank you for inviting me back to your country."

The crowd grows quiet.

"It's been about thirty years since I had the privilege to live in Dhaka –" My thin voice slips into the corners of the hollow auditorium and dissolves.

"Ektu jore! Louder!" Someone calls from the back. The woman in the olive saree gestures to a scruffy sound technician who wipes his palms on his shirttail, leaving behind two perfect, black handprints. He squats before a dusty, antiquated PA system just in front of the stage and turns some dials.

Hasan crosses his arms. I start again.

"It's been just over thirty years since I had the privilege to live in Dhaka – as an exchange student at Dhaka University –"

Paragraphs typed then deleted, notes scribbled on paper bags, grocery lists, napkins and even once on the border of a street map while I tried to find the passport office in Victoria. I don't know where anything is in that city because I rarely go there. Why should I bother? I have everything I need, and it's been that way ever since I escaped to my bucolic little island in Georgia Strait.

It's taken weeks to write this speech, most of it trying to remember what I'd written thirty years ago, the rest trying to understand why the Bangla-American Women's Friendship Society would find it interesting enough to invite me to speak. Transcribed onto a computer at the cyber cafe, rehearsed a hundred times in front of my bathroom mirror, and still, it's like I'm speaking in slow motion. Vertiginous spaces open between my words.

"Even though times were troubling and you were at the beginning of a struggle for your independence, you were always warm and kind." The sound improves but my voice remains insubstantial. I lean into the microphone and sigh. My exhaled breath comes like the roar of a jet. Everyone jumps.

"Sorry." I step back and clear my throat. "What I learned here encompassed so much more than what I was studying in class, which was, of course, your language, Bangla. At the TSC – the teacher-student centre – the library, the canteen, in many homes, I had the chance to listen and ask questions. Unfortunately, I was forced to leave early in the conflict when the American government called back its citizens. I departed with much sorrow not knowing what would happen to the close friends I left behind."

"Liar!"

Hasan. Now he looks at me – for the second time in thirty years.

The woman in the olive saree sits up. The audience divides as though choreographed, half looking to see who's spoken, the other half looking at me for reaction. But there is no going back.

"I watched you from afar. But there were no details in the news of the people I knew and how they were faring in the face of civil war, rationing, curfews and apparent unrelenting attacks. For months, I lived from newspaper to newspaper, from TV broadcast to TV broadcast, always looking for the names of the brave people I left behind."

"Coward!" Hasan is on his feet now. So is the woman in the olive saree.

"She is a guest from abroad. Kindly offer your hospitality. There will be a time for questions after." Her voice is lost beneath the growing murmurs of the audience.

"She's a collaborator!" People around Hasan stand. One man grabs Hasan's arm, shouts and pulls him toward the aisle. Two women in the VIP row wave their hands, flicking the tips of their bejeweled fingers as though to brush away houseflies.

"Listen to me!" Hasan is in the aisle. Others shout at him, at one another, all in Bangla now, and mine is so rusty from disuse, I can only guess what they are saying.

"Ask her what she thinks of the Biharis! Ask her how much money she gave them! Hard currency which they used to arm themselves to kill our brothers and rape our sisters!"

Hasan is dragged across the floor toward the auditorium doors. The sleeve of his red, homespun kurta tears as he resists. I remember well the passion of the Bangladeshis when it comes to discussing their independence, when it comes to offering at least the appearance of courtesy to a bideshi – a foreigner, when it comes to leaping headfirst into any sort of rousing scuffle. The woman in the olive saree nudges me away from the podium and takes the microphone.

"Sit down!" she shouts. There is a screech of feedback. The technician fumbles with the dials.

"Let her go to The Hague and be tried alongside Nixon and Kissinger and James Farland!" Hasan raises his arm. He points his finger as though it is a weapon.

"Remove that man from this meeting! Take your seats! Order!"

But her commands are absurd. There is anything but order in this auditorium. Chaos rules much as it had across the whole country thirty years ago. Some would say it was Sheikh Mujib and others would say no, Yahya Khan held the reins, or the Indian or Chinese or American governments, but it seems to me no one had control. And probably no one really has since, because that's what politics is all about, the illusion of control, although I couldn't say for sure what it is like today in Bangladesh. Moreover I've long since stopped investing much thought or emotion into politics.

The chaos grows in ridiculous proportions. Arms flail, fists clench, faces twist with hostility. The whole audience is drawn into it. And while Graham might have found humour here, I don't. Large, unruly crowds unsettle me.

I sit down and wait, but it is only for a moment, as another of the organizers taps my shoulder.

"Come, Apa." She calls me big sister, then leads me off the stage, down some steps until we reach a cramped dressing room.

We listen to the ruckus outside. Each of us smiles, remembers our manners, pretends nothing is happening. The girl offers me a biscuit. It tastes of coconut and cooking oil. She watches me brush the crumbs from my shirt. We both stare at the random pattern they leave in the lush crimson carpet.

She is the first to break the pretense.

"We are Bangladeshis. We are too much serious about our Liberation War," she says. I find her age hard to guess but am certain she was not even born when the war began. "Don't mind."

I don't. I mean, I do, I feel embarrassed, all those memories of that time thrown up in my face, and no opportunity to defend myself. Hasan's accusations are not true, not exactly, and anyway, if he has something to say, he should do it privately, at a time and place in which I would have a chance to explain, and find out what happened to Luna after I left, and Razzak, what happened to poor Shafiq, and, of course, Amma. Because I don't know what happened to any of them, and that's why I cannot say definitively that Hasan's accusations are complete lies.

In love, in war, truth is rubber that can be pulled and stretched into an infinite number of shapes.

But I do not mind the fact that the Bangladeshis still take their war seriously. They have to. In the same way that a person has to take seriously the shape of her hand, especially once she has lost her arm.

The girl whispers. "Mrs. Robin, you give money to the Biharis?"

"Please – just call me Robin. What is your name?"

"My name Falguni."

"How old are you?"

"Twenty-two years." I was right. Maybe her father was a freedom fighter. Maybe her mother cooked meals or knit socks and sweaters and sent them to the front. "The Biharis they killed many Bangladeshis, do you know? You must not give them money."

"I didn't." This is true, but it sounds defensive. I am unable to explain and again, wish my Bangla would return so I could tell Falguni what I could not say to Hasan and the crowd.

However, it is as though I have not spoken, as though Hasan's accusation has metamorphosed into fact. "But Apa, they were the collaborators."

Collaborator. That word again. Hasan has baptized me and I have been reborn as one of them.

But I'm not a collaborator. I did what I did from my convictions, after a lot of thought, and because Luna was the closest thing I ever had to a sister. I would have done anything she asked. Even though I believe in very little now, if I betrayed Hasan's family back then, I did so because I had faith in love.

But this, today, is not what I had intended, and if I had thought this might happen, I never would have accepted the invitation to come back.

All I want now is to go home.

"What do we do, Falguni?"

"What you want do?" Outside, there are still rumblings, although the voices are more distinguishable. Perhaps the crowd is dispersing.

I shrug. "Go back to the hotel?"

"Wait. I ask." Falguni leaves.

I am alone, faced with a plate of oily biscuits, a chair, the far off sounds of arguments, and a raft of memories.

Not really alone though. Never alone as long as I am afflicted with memory.

I bite into a second biscuit. Again, sweet coconut crumbles in my mouth.

1970

"You start with this. We use the chilis, you know. Maybe you don't like the chilis?" Mrs. Chowdhury loaded my plate with white rice, a single slice of fried eggplant and some tomato salad, and sat back in her chair; satisfied.

It was nine-thirty. I was exhausted by jet lag, but famished and determined to stay awake for my first dinner with the Chowdhury clan, my host family in Dhaka for the next year. Serving bowls and platters, laid out moments ago by the servants, Shafiq and Kamala, steamed impossibly in the heat of July. Aromas drifted in the air. Coriander and cumin, a waft of mustard, and I could smell cinnamon, cloves, and something reminiscent of smelly feet.

"Of course she doesn't like chilis," Hasan said. "No foreigner does." He took a raw chili pepper, green, waxy and the size of my baby finger from a serving platter and bit into it. He chewed deliberately and waited for my reaction.

"I'll try," I said. "I want to. Please."

Wary but curious, I really did want to sample. However, Hasan's unexpected pronouncement gave me a better reason for being enthusiastic about a vegetable I barely recognized. On behalf of all foreigners, I wanted to prove him wrong.

Mrs. Chowdhury offered me a second slice of eggplant. I took a chili, too, and set it on the rim of my plate.

Once Mr. Chowdhury began to eat, so did the rest of the family. They plunged their hands into their food. I expected this: right hand only, never the left. Hasan, to the right of his father, rounded his shoulders, bowed his head and shoveled in the food with accompanying garrumphs, an eating technique that would turn the stomach of the most thick-skinned diner. For that, I was not prepared.

I poked the tomato salad, pulpy and slippery. I decided to start with the eggplant. I picked up a whole slice. It wilted. A greasy piece detached itself from the charred skin and slid onto my lap.

Hasan guffawed. How he managed to observe anything with his face buried in curry was a mystery.

"I will not tolerate rudeness at the table," Mrs. Chowdhury said. "Use a fork, Robin dear. I am." Lady-like, she wiped her fingertips, which I noticed were barely smeared with food, and lifted her fork.

I decided to follow her lead, but for this meal only. I would practice in private. I would show Hasan.

I brushed the eggplant from my lap, then, with a fork, tackled what was left on my plate.

The meal was rich and oily, and spicy beyond anything

I had ever eaten back home in Lansing, Michigan. It was spicier even than the legendary chili con carne, slapped together and served up every Sunday night in winter by my father, with whom, just hours ago, I'd shared an easy farewell at an airport on the other side of the world. My eyes watered. My nose ran. But I would not give Hasan the satisfaction of seeing my discomfort.

"I have a question now for our newest exchange student," said Mr. Chowdhury. He rested his wrists on the edge of the table, and wiggled his fingers as though drying freshly polished nails.

"You ought to let our guest relax on her first evening with us," Mrs. Chowdhury said, "instead of peppering her with your questions." She turned to face me. "He is too curious. He nearly drove away our last student with his endless queries."

Their daughter, Luna, sitting at his side, giggled. She was in the middle of serving him big spoons of rice and vegetables.

"My endless queries, as you say, nourish our exchange students as well as ourselves. It is a mutually beneficially relationship," Mr. Chowdhury countered.

"I would be happy to answer questions," I said, "especially if I can help. I'm very thankful to be able to stay with you this year."

"No, no, no," cried Amma, "no need." She waved the air and I caught a whiff of licorice. "This is our duty to help the university. They always send us such polite and intelligent students."

Hasan stared, disbelieving at his mother, then at me, as though I were the one who had just finished an immodest speech about my superior intellect and well-mannered behaviour.

I reddened. "Please Mr. Chowdhury – what is it you would like to ask?"

"Well, Mrs. Chowdhury is right. I am the curious one, so please tell me. What are they reporting from our Bengal in your American newspapers?"

I knew. I'd been reading everything I could since I found out about my exchange. "Well, there's some about Pakistan. I saw in a news magazine last month…"

"No. I said Bengal."

I hesitated. Bengal was half of Pakistan. The eastern half. Wasn't it?

"But then that's what I expected," he sighed. "Luna, stop it. Give your papa some fish."

Luna ladled a fish head onto her father's plate, then followed with two spoons of sauce.

"That's my girl. You take good care of your papa." He murmured something in Bangla and she reached for another bowl. "This is one of our problems, you see. The western journalists are not interested in the story of Bengal. Space travel and the Russian red threat, anything to do with Vietnam – and there has been some interest in the British parliament of late. But young people from abroad know nothing of what is happening here, isn't it? Because your newspapermen do not even understand that we, in Bengal, are different from the people of West Pakistan." Mr. Chowdhury removed an eye from the fish head. "They are missing the best part. Mmm." He swallowed.

What he said was for the most part true. In fact, it was probably much worse than he imagined. Pakistan – East and

West – tended to get lumped together with India. So much so, that when I told my friends – whom I considered to be conscious that the world extended beyond the western hemisphere – that I was going to Dhaka for a year, many became puzzled and asked where. Others, with similar looks, asked why.

It's true, I could have chosen Burma or Thailand. Michigan State had close ties with universities in those countries, too. But I was drawn to Bangla, the language of East Pakistan. A fervent professor had led me on, speaking of Sanskrit, Prakrit, Apabrahmsa – ancient languages whose influence was felt in dozens of words in my own mother tongue. He showed me texts in Bangla and helped me begin to learn the letters. The alphabet contained so many letters they spilled over onto a second page, making our twenty-six look insufficient.

Still, it was odd for someone from Lansing to head overseas on anything other than a quick holiday, and that, usually, to the Caribbean. Most people were content to stay home, and the Canadian border marked the edge of the earth. Yet the peace movement, shuddering its way beyond the walls of the campus and into the town itself had opened up the world. Vietnam, yes. And what lay beyond that troubled place? I would find out.

Hasan finally lifted his head from his plate. "Abba, what about the Legal Framework Order? What did Bangabandhu say at Narsinghdi today?"

"The parliament must be supreme, otherwise the new constitution will be a mockery. Sheikh Mujib is wise not to change his opinion. The Awami League is adamant. This has been stated again before our assembly."

"But independence? We must go for it. Surely the AL will reconsider."

"You are rash, Hasan. Like all the boys." Mr. Chowdhury took a long drink of water. "The four caliphs will go too far. Mujib says first we will go for the six-point plan. Our autonomy within Pakistan is realistic, isn't it? Independence is not. But it will come. For now we must remain committed to the plan."

Hasan's response, in Bangla, was directed to his dinner plate. I heard the words "constitution", "election" and "Chairman Mao." But the rest, like the exchange I had just heard, made no sense. His father's face became progressively redder. My interest grew proportionately.

"You are speaking the rubbish. As usual. Just like Yahya Khan," Luna said cavalierly.

Hasan shoved his chair back from the table and stood. "Don't compare me to that criminal. Leave my sight. Go to your room." Curry gravy speckled the right lens of his glasses.

"That's enough!" Mr. Chowdhury spoke. "Sit down. And be quiet." Then he slipped into Bangla and continued until he seemed like a spring unwound by the effort.

Hasan sat. Mrs. Chowdhury spooned some fish onto my plate. "Be careful. There are many small bones in the chhoto mach."

Family politics, country politics – the simple mechanics of eating what was before me. I could make sense of none of them. It was like the hot light that sliced through the cracks in the heavy brocade drapes in the sitting room at noon, when I'd just arrived at their home. Enough so you'd notice, not enough to illuminate anything.

Then I bit off a tiny piece of my green chili. I let it burn into my tongue before swallowing. I refused to look at Hasan though I felt he watched and mocked me.

❦

I startled when the bicycle rickshaw ran up on the brick sidewalk and headed for Luna and me. The driver, head covered by a dirty, lacy topi, expertly steered through the crowd and came to a stop an instant before collision. I threw up my hands. He grinned at my reaction, his teeth stained scarlet as a Bing cherry by the betel crammed into his cheek.

Though she was tiny and, I thought, somewhat prim, Luna turned on him like a tornado. His bemusement seemed to inspire her, but finally, when through, she pulled me away. "He is always making mischief for the girls. Don't mind. Come."

I thought I heard the rickshaw driver laugh but I didn't dare turn to check for fear I would bump into the people we jostled against, or knock down one of the store displays that tumbled onto the sidewalk.

I had woken well before the hot summer sun rose. Jet lag was certainly to blame, but besides, it was my first morning in Dhaka – and I was itching for this first-hand look at the street life. Scenes had flit by the window of the car just yesterday, as I was taken from the airport to the Chowdhury home. I wanted to slow them down. To linger, and perhaps to begin to piece together some understanding of East Pakistan. I wanted to hear the language, be introduced to the customs of the everyday, as people negotiated their way through markets and livestock, heat and air dripping with moisture, and the burgeoning crowds into which everyone eventually dissolved.

I had to wait all morning though. Wait for meals to be served, baths to be had, clothes to be donned, and hair to be fixed. The list of chores to be given to Kamala and Shafiq. Schedules to be worked out – and reworked countless times – and all finally approved by Mrs. Chowdhury. "No shop will open until late morning anyway," she reassured. I suspected she was hiding the best part of the day, but I had no good reason to doubt her then. I chose to wait until she pronounced the family ready for their day – and gave permission for Luna to take me walking to the shops on Elephant Road. Hasan was to accompany us.

I stepped around a mangy pariah dog, teats hanging thinly to her ankles, attesting to her recent, though absent litter. Her snout was buried up to her ears in a heap of yellow rice. Good thing, too. I was afraid to catch her eye.

The street was filled with afternoon traffic. More rickshaws. Pedestrians. A horse-pulled tonga. And a large humpbacked cow that stood at the edge of traffic and reached for dusty leaves on a spindly tree in a planter. A few cars wove in and out. Although the intensity of noon had passed, heat still rippled up from the pavement and I sweated.

Hasan ably maintained a distance five steps ahead and never looked back. I resented both his presence and his distance, and could not understand why he had to be with us.

We passed a man sharpening knives on a pitted stone wheel. Another man polished dirty, creased shoes in a haze of solvents. A third man sat before an untidy heap of baskets. When he called out, I hesitated then met his eye.

"Come," said Luna, and pulled me forward before I could enter into any kind of negotiation. When the crowd grew too thick, I followed the long, thick braid that snaked down her back like a length of rope.

She stopped before the dark, greasy window of a small restaurant. "Look."

She cupped her hands around her eyes to block out the sunlight and peered through the glass. Her expression was pure expectation – clear, unselfconscious and radiant.

"He is not there," she whispered. I looked. Inside, a few people huddled around tables.

"Who?"

"Sometimes he is there. We take tea and sweets." I could barely hear her.

"Who?" I spoke more loudly this time.

"Shh." She looked over her shoulder. "Razzak – my boyfriend." She leaned close. "Apa, one time, he hold my hand. You think I bad girl? Please don't tell Amma or Hasan." In the days of free love in America, her innocence both astonished and moved me.

Luna was nineteen, less than a year younger than me; working on an undergrad in botany; interested besides in books, film and fashion. The university-supplied dossier on the Chowdhury family had provided this much information. At dinner last night, I'd filled in the blanks – a devoted daughter, a squabbling sibling. But this latest information intrigued me. Clever Luna also had a secret life.

Just then, a child in a dirty maroon dress appeared. One sleeve was held in place by a safety pin. Her face was smudged with dirt, the corners of her mouth crusty yellow. She held out her hand. Tears welled up in her eyes.

Luna pressed a coin into her palm. "Jao!" The girl disappeared among torsos. "Come – your first lesson in Bangla."

"What did you say?"

"I told her: go."

A few shops ahead, Hasan waited until we caught up. "Where were you? I have better things to do than loiter on the street like a vagrant and wait for you."

Luna looked at me and rolled her eyes.

"Do not misbehave or Abba will hear about this. Do not idle any longer."

"But we were just helping a starving little girl," I said, and pointed back.

The girl had emerged from the crowd – and was nuzzled up to a modestly-dressed young woman on the corner. There was no sign of tears now. The young woman spoke softly into the girl's hair before mussing it with the heel of her hand. She passed the girl a candy then steered her into the stream of traffic, nodding her head, urging the girl on. The girl skipped up to the window of a stopped car and knocked on the glass. Like an actor, her face wrenched suddenly and deliberately into a pitiful look as one hand moved up and down to her mouth, miming the act of eating, and the other rubbed her belly.

I didn't know what to say. I'd seen people begging in Detroit and Chicago, of course, for food, work, money, warm clothes. Shabby men and women whose entire lives were tragic. But no one begged in Lansing, and I hadn't put any further thought into it.

Now Hasan rolled his eyes and walked ahead.

"Apa, look!" Luna stopped before a tiny stall, no wider than my desk back home. Bangles – boxes, trays and cylinders of gold, silver and coloured glass were piled up rather precariously, nearly touching the fluorescent tube that appeared to be hanging from nothing more than a single red wire. It was hard to know where to look first. They were dazzling. But Luna immediately pointed to a pale green set of bangles that sparkled like cut crystal. They were displayed on a white plaster forearm that appeared to have been severed at the elbow from its mannequin owner. "So beautiful," she sighed. "You like?"

The shopkeeper slid the bangles off the artificial wrist and passed one of them to Luna.

"Shundar," she sighed again and held it up to admire it further. By some miracle, it caught a shard of natural light that had found its way into the stall, and splintered it into tiny rainbows that rippled on the wall and ceiling for an instant. But even in that brief moment, anyone could have seen how Luna's trick of light outshone the shop's bangles and made the beautiful bracelets suddenly appear tawdry. I marveled at how she accidentally engineered such a simple but wondrous sight.

The bangle seller's chin jerked up as we heard a commotion outside. Hasan's voice rose and blended with the shouts of others. Luna dropped the bangle and ran toward the ruckus.

Two doors away, in front of a shoe store, Hasan was face to face with a man who appeared to be the shopkeeper. A crowd had gathered, some also yelling at the shopkeeper, others bellowing at Hasan.

"Bapre bap," Luna said. "He is always fighting."

"What's happening?"

She listened. "You see the signboard?" she finally said.

On the window, a hand-lettered piece of paper hung askew. "It says *gent's shoes*."

"So?"

"It is Urdu language. Not our language. You know?"

"I know. You speak Bangla."

"The government in West Pakistan wants us to speak Urdu. Ever since partition they are saying Urdu is now your language.

"This shopkeeper he is maybe Bihari. He is speaking Urdu. Hasan is saying you stop speaking Urdu, you speak Bangla."

"Who cares what he speaks?" I didn't understand why such a trivial and crude notice would create such animosity. Then a scrawny man, his face ugly with rage, pushed his way in front of Hasan. He slapped the shopkeeper's face. The crowd roared. "Why did he hit him?"

"Razzak is Bihari, too. Apa, don't mind," Luna lowered her voice again. "Please don't tell Amma."

"Why? What's wrong with being Bihari?"

"Come. We go."

"Shouldn't we wait for Hasan?"

Luna laughed. "Hasan is not listening, Apa. He never listening."

Hasan tore the sign down. It was like gas thrown on a fire.

Luna took my hand. "Come. Amma waiting for us."

❧

Just as I itched to get out on the street, Mrs. Chowdhury yearned to introduce me to the only American in Dhaka with whom she was intimately acquainted. I shrugged at her suggestion of a visit – it was only my third day, and I was thinking instead of a nap to alleviate the jet lag and avoid the dense afternoon heat. "Beth will be your close friend in Dhaka," Mrs. Chowdhury said. "We must go now." I was puzzled by her insistence and even more confused by her assured pronouncement of my friendship with a woman I'd never even met, let alone one who was married with children. But before I could object, I saw Luna at the front door, smiling sweetly.

Her smile widened, her eyebrows rose – conspiratorially – and I saw in a flash that she understood exactly what I was thinking about her mother. Through a nearly imperceptible gesture, Luna sent me a survival message: save your breath. Any follow-up question or protest will be in vain.

Another sign of Luna's astuteness? I was most definitely intrigued now.

A servant led us to Beth's terrace. It was late afternoon, just slightly cooler since it had rained during lunch. Among the flowers and potted shrubs, the air was almost bearable. Mrs. Chowdhury sat on a cane armchair under a canopy propped up by bamboo, well out of the sun. When Luna sat on a swing suspended from an iron frame, I joined her.

"Beth loves her garden," Mrs. Chowdhury said.

Luna set the swing in motion. It squeaked, but soothed. We swayed in and out of the sun, and lapped up the breeze our movement created.

"I tell her: you need the mali, this is too much work for one person. But she is out here with the sunrise. Stubborn woman," Mrs. Chowdhury continued.

Pink bougainvillea clambered up and tumbled over a

wall. There was a smaller white one beside it, being trained to climb up jute cords that spun off in five or six directions. A windmill palm quivered as though caressed in the breeze. Two rows of pots stood empty along a wall, their clay waiting for seeds or seedlings to push up and colour that part of the terrace.

"You should see her dahlias in the spring," Mrs. Chowdhury said. "Like footballs. I tell her she is practicing sorcery to grow them so big."

"Salma," a voice said. "You must be baking out here. Why don't you come inside?"

"Oh no, it's so lovely and cool when one is out of the sun. You have the most beautiful terrace in all Dhaka city," Mrs. Chowdhury gushed. She rose and embraced the tall, lean woman, pecked both her cheeks. "This is Robin Rowe. And this is my good friend of many years, Beth Ahmed." She pronounced it 'bait.'

I rose, we shook hands, and she said a quiet hello to Luna. Her ivory saree, patterned with deep green twisting ivy, flowed with her movements. I thought of a fish swaying within a net, unaware of the filaments about to close in.

"I've been waiting to meet you. How are you?"

"Not bad. Hot." By now, there were several layers of sweat on my forehead. Beth smiled. "But Mrs. Chowdhury's bending over backwards to make me feel welcome." I glanced at Luna, but she was watching Beth and continued to rock the swing softly, and stir a breeze.

"No, no, it's my duty," Mrs. Chowdhury declared.

"Sit, sit," Beth said. "You have no tea? What is that boy thinking of, showing you out here and not a drop to drink? Hamid!"

A few minutes later, she served tea piping hot. "It cools the body, you know. It's simple physics." Mrs. Chowdhury nodded happily. "That's what they say in the desert." There were cookies, too and a fragile crystal dish of rice pudding with cloves, cardamom and chocolaty flakes of cinnamon bark. And squat bananas like fat fingers.

"So how are you finding our Dhaka city?" Beth asked.

"She is becoming accustomed," Mrs. Chowdhury said. "We begin Bangla lessons tomorrow." She beamed. I smiled back.

"I haven't seen much yet. But it's different from Michigan," I said to Beth. I looked over at Luna – who'd finally stopped swinging when the tea was served. She cradled an untouched bowl of rice pudding. I wondered what she knew about Michigan, about me and my life with my Dad, what she had already imagined and how I measured up to her expectations. Her face was impassive though, and she offered no opinion.

"We're almost neighbours then. I grew up in Cincinnati," Beth said.

"She married a Bengali boy," Mrs. Chowdhury said. "She met him at the university in Washington. He was an exchange student. Just like you. And now they are married eleven years. Two boys."

Beth laughed. "Thanks. That about sums it up."

"Do you like it here?" I asked.

She exchanged a smile with Mrs. Chowdhury. "Very much."

"What do you do?"

They laughed. "Oh, this and that. Just like Salma."

"So you're staying here forever?"

"Well, I don't know. Who could answer such a question?"

"What I mean is – you're not going back home?"

"This is home now. But if you mean Cincinnati, I go once a year. To see my parents. My sister has a family, too."

"You don't miss them?" I didn't miss my own father, and didn't really expect to very much, but I thought us different from most families.

"Of course. But my in-laws are my family now. We had a few – obstacles to overcome," she glanced at Mrs. Chowdhury, "but now, I think they accept me. Still, it's always good to go back for a visit."

"What obstacles?"

"I didn't know this would be an interview. Don't you think she should be answering my questions?" Beth asked Mrs. Chowdhury.

I shrugged, though I wanted to know what she'd faced. "Sorry. Please. Go ahead."

"Well. Let's see." She looked at the table beside me, where I had placed my empty cup and plate covered with crumbs and a banana peel. "What I would like to know is this: would you like more kheer?" She nodded at the rice pudding. I shook my head. "Then maybe a sandwich?"

"Thank you. No." I was stuffed.

"Luna? Ar kichu?" Luna, her head down, did not acknowledge that she'd heard which Beth seemed to interpret as a 'no.'

I found Luna's behaviour strange. She was like a shy child possessing neither thoughts of her own nor the ability to articulate them. Where was the voluble Luna I had glimpsed on Elephant Road? The perceptive Luna, at the doorstep of her own home? I had a niggling doubt – perhaps I was talking too much when I should be following Luna's lead – but I dismissed it quickly. Intelligent, young women do not dissolve into the wallpaper; they do not hide behind their dessert dishes.

"Well then," Beth said, "give me time. There will be plenty of questions as we get to know you. And we will get to know you well, I am certain."

She turned to Mrs. Chowdhury then. They talked about their families, people they knew, about the weather, the flowers, everything. I was attentive at first. However, as Beth told an elaborate story about her husband's cousin's child trying to get admitted to a good school in Mirpur, I lost track of the thread and watched Luna instead.

Except for continuing to push the swing with her toe, she was still and quiet. She didn't look particularly unhappy about it. I further considered her lack of participation, and wondered whether I had judged hastily. Perhaps she did not mind sitting on the sidelines. Maybe she was elsewhere. Maybe she had *chosen* to go elsewhere. Yes. She hovered over us, on a plane much more to her liking; surely that was why she held herself like an unopened flower. I wondered where she was – no doubt her clandestine boyfriend was there, too – and let the gentle squeak of the swing lull me into a daze. Until Beth said "election." Then I sat up.

"Not again. It's not possible," Mrs. Chowdhury said. "They wouldn't be so impudent."

"Oh yes they would," Beth said. "First it was October fifth, now the twenty-second. They'll postpone as often as they need to."

"But why? You cannot avoid what is inevitable."

"There's nothing inevitable about elections under martial law," Beth said.

"What you say is true. But the people. The people want it."

"They'll blame the rains. Floods. I can hear it now."

"Everyone knows the worst of the flooding is past by October," Mrs. Chowdhury said. "My husband says that is no excuse."

Beth shook her head. "There will be no election in October. Mark my words."

"What election?" I asked. They both looked startled, as though they had forgotten Luna and I were there.

Mrs. Chowdhury's brow furrowed, her lips pursed. "Beth, please help," she sighed. "I cannot explain to her everything."

"Our country has been under martial law for the past twelve years," Beth said. "We have been promised elections and a new constitution over and over again. But the President –"

"So-called president," Mrs. Chowdhury said. "Yahya Khan is self-appointed. No one has voted for him." I remembered the name – and the rancour it created – from dinner two nights back.

"I thought you couldn't explain everything," Beth said, amused.

"I just want to make sure you don't miss any important points," Mrs. Chowdhury said, a little hurt.

"Thank you, Salma. Please help me if I miss anything else."

Mrs. Chowdhury was placated.

"He seems reluctant to give over power. Just yet."

"This election is not about power. That is what Hasan says," Mrs. Chowdhury added.

"Hasan is correct," Beth said. "There are some who think this election is a referendum. On autonomy."

A black crow flew overhead and cawed twice.

"For East Pakistan?"

She nodded. "The whole partition thing – you know about that, right? – the whole thing was a mistake. How could Pakistan hold itself together with the big lump of India sitting in the middle like an elephant in your drawing room?"

"No, no, no," Mrs. Chowdhury jumped in. "It was not a mistake. The idea is a good one. The problem is the leadership. My husband says they do not listen to the people. Especially our people."

"The Bengalis are very different from their western brothers," Beth agreed. "Language is just the thin edge of the wedge."

The crow flew back and dipped close. *Whoosh.* Air passed over its stiff wing feathers.

"Hasan said at the Ramna Race Course meeting last week, the cries of 'Bangabandhu' would make one deaf."

"What does that mean?" I asked.

"*Friend of Bengal.* It's what Sheikh Mujib is called," Beth said. "You must read the papers while you are here. He's in the news every day. He is the leader of the Awami League – one of the major political parties in East Pakistan."

"No, no, no," Mrs. Chowdhury interjected. "I mean, yes, he is. But he is so much more." She turned to me. "He is the father of the movement for autonomy. He is the rightful, elected governor of this state. And he is a friend to every man, woman and child in East Pakistan.

"Bangabandhu is backed by everyone," she continued. "His charisma is such that absolutely everybody in East Pakistan has been drawn into the politics – even lowly housewives such as I."

"You're anything but, Salma Chowdhury, if indeed such a creature exists at all."

The crow returned, dipped down again, and lifted the banana skin off my plate. The tip of its wing brushed my cheek. I jumped.

"Pests," Beth said. "It's better to offer them something than put up with their thieving."

"We must go now," Mrs. Chowdhury said. "It's late." She peeled her body, now sticky with sweat, off the chair. "Come Luna." And although her daughter seemed to have been completely absent from the conversation, she heard this much and obediently leapt to her feet.

"You must call if you need anything," Beth said to me. "Anything at all. Anytime."

I nodded.

"I really mean it. Don't be shy."

I followed Mrs. Chowdhury and Luna back to the car. The sensation of that black crow's wing lingered on my cheek. The image of it sailing off into the flat horizon, carrying the limp, brown peel between its hooked claws remained with me the rest of the evening.

❧

"What courses are you taking?" Ruby asked. She flicked ashes off the end of her bidi cigarette onto the grass on campus where we sat between classes trying to shelter from the burning sun which, so far that day, had been undaunted by the monsoon. It was my first day at Dhaka University. Luna had just introduced me to her and Afsana, another friend.

The shade seemed thin. I sweated in my armpits of course, and on my back, between my breasts. Every pore on my face was wide open, and still it was not enough. I squirmed. I already knew how red in the face I was – as though I'd just run a marathon – and could only imagine how grotesque I appeared next to these three carefree girls who seemed not to move or sweat at all.

"I just had my Bangla tutorial," I said. "And I have 14th century Asian history this afternoon."

"Is that with Dr. Kabir?" I opened a notebook and shuffled through some papers to find my schedule. "Never mind. It is. He is not the best in his field, but as Yunus Khan is on sabbatical this year, you have no choice."

She offered me a bidi. I shook my head. I couldn't bear the thought of anything hot, even something as small as the burning tip of a cigarette.

Luna said, "She is learning Bangla. Amma is giving her lessons every – "She stopped, blushed and looked down. Afsana smiled and bit her tongue naughtily, then elbowed Ruby who looked over her shoulder, then exhaled the pungent smoke from her bidi cigarette and grinned.

"What's going on?" I asked.

"Shhh," Luna said.

Ruby tipped her head back into the distance. "Look. Razzak."

Tall and very thin, his hair was long and choppy in the

style of the day, similar to Hasan's. He wore a simple white kurta and a pair of jeans. Flat leather sandals flopped against his feet. He carried a book on his hip. He was alone.

He passed beneath a sprawling gulmohar, still ablaze with blossoms, and followed a brick path that led to the library steps which he climbed. After he disappeared into the building, they all giggled.

"You like him?" Luna asked me.

But he was like a cloud that passed overhead before anyone even noticed the sunlight was blocked. "I'm sure he's a nice guy. But I hardly know anything about him."

"He is too much poor, Apa," Luna said. "His father is beker. He have no job."

"They live in the slum, the basti in Mohammedpur," Afsana said.

"No, a house in Mirpur," Ruby said. "Next to my uncle's office."

"This is not true," Afsana said.

"You ask Luna then," Ruby shrugged. Afsana's back stiffened.

But Luna's eyes were downcast. "I cannot go to his house. His father will not accept me. Razzak is too much proud. He is not complaining." She blushed. "He not tell me where he is staying."

"I don't get it. Why won't his father accept you?" I asked. I couldn't imagine my own, easy-going father rejecting any of my friends – romantic or not.

"They are Bihari," Ruby sniffed and butted out her bidi. She wore a thick kohl eyeliner which, with her cigarette, made her look like a glamorous silent film star. "They do not mix with us."

Bihari. Again. "I still don't understand."

The girls glanced at one another and shifted. Then Afsana sighed.

"It's very complicated," she said. "You know about the partition of India in 1947?" I nodded. "There was a mass migration across our border. But the Muslims from Bihar – they have never been accepted by the Bengalis."

"Why not?"

"They are too different. They cannot understand our way," Ruby said. She was already digging in her satchel for another bidi.

"What way?"

"Our Bengali way." I wasn't sure what that was then, but it seemed too complicated to get into when all I wanted to understand was why Razzak and Luna's relationship had to be a secret. "Besides, they have Urdu-ized our language. You hear them talk? It is like a broken sitar – *twang, twang, twang.*" She laughed and pulled a fresh bidi from its package.

"Let me finish," Afsana said. "The next year, there was a famine, and thousands more came – with nothing. They have spent years trying to earn back what they have lost: homes, jobs, security. You can see the Biharis in the slums in Mohammedpur. And Azad Gate. Have you been?"

I shook my head, and began to scheme to convince Mrs. Chowdhury it was necessary to go.

"Now they have to decide," Ruby said, "which side to support in the independence movement."

"The wrong choice could jeopardize what they have earned back of their former lives," Afsana said.

"Unfortunately, most have made the wrong choice,"

Ruby said. She lit the bidi. "Those who collaborate with the West Pakistani administration will lose everything. And we Bengalis hate them."

"But that's intolerant."

"Intolerant? You do not understand. They are turncoats. They are spying on the leaders of the independence movement and reporting their activities to the army. They are the ones lacking tolerance." She pointed the burning tip of her bidi at me.

"So – you expect them to leave?"

"Some have been here since 1947. They have had their children here," Afsana said. "And what is left for them if they return? A desert. Houses and land occupied by Hindus who left our country. This is their home now."

"That's awful. Those poor people," I said.

Ruby pursed her lips. She was about to say something when Afsana hushed her. Afsana spoke quickly in Bangla. As usual, I listened closely. But of course I could decipher nothing.

An idea dawned. "You don't think Razzak is one of those spies, do you?" I couldn't imagine Luna with someone she suspected was a professional snitch, but Ruby's hatred seemed out of proportion.

"Razzak not collaborator," Luna cried. "Is not true."

Afsana touched her arm and whispered in Bangla. Again I did not understand, could interpret neither the words nor the body language. When, after a minute Luna was calm, Afsana held out a handful of hard candies wrapped in cellophane. "Here. Take."

I helped myself to a green one. "I can't wait to meet him. When are you going to introduce him to your parents?"

All three faces were transfixed by my words. Ruby broke the silence. "Hasan will murder him."

"Murder him?" I laughed. "Hasan's nothing but a big windbag."

"Excuse me? Apa? What means windbag?" Luna asked.

"He's full of himself. Who cares what he thinks?" The girls exchanged glances. "Do you want me to invite your boyfriend over? Hasan doesn't bother me."

"Apa, please –"

"But why should you have to keep your relationship secret?" I couldn't get it out of my mind how different this would be for her if she lived in America. If she were me.

"Apa, stop!" Luna was horrified.

"Are you ashamed? Why? It's totally normal."

Luna looked terrified, Afsana disbelieving and Ruby scornful. But I saw nothing unusual about my way of thinking. I just knew that it would be up to me to get Luna to see the truth and start standing up for herself.

❦

Mrs. Chowdhury and I sat together three afternoons a week. A teacher by training – "That was long ago, dear, before my marriage" – she was to help me transform my interest in the Bangla alphabet, brimming with dees, tees and esses, nearly impossible for my untrained ear to distinguish, into something functional. I was in a hurry. Without enough language to get by, I was at her mercy, and I had already developed the sense she was holding things back from me, things I would benefit from learning without her mediation. Necessity brought timely success, and by the end of a couple of sessions, I could manage a brief conversation; enough to introduce myself, say that I was learning Bangla, and ask for forgiveness if I made a mistake. I found this last part odd. The words did not sit well with me.

"Mrs. Chowdhury, would I actually say this kind of thing to – for example – a child?"

"We have formal and informal. Do you understand?"

"Tell me."

"There is one way of talking to your elders or other superiors – like your teachers or your supervisor – but also strangers – but not a shopkeeper or a rickshawallah. Then you use informal."

"But what if you have an old rickshawallah? Or one that's just about the same age as you, but you think he might be older. Won't he be insulted?"

"No." She had no problem understanding what was beyond my comprehension. She squared some papers before her. "And while we speak of this, I think it is time you addressed me differently."

After two weeks living under the same roof, and finally recovered from jet lag, I suddenly realized that unbeknownst to me I had been offending Mrs. Chowdhury. "I'm sorry."

"I am not accustomed to this. Even Shafiq and Kamala, they do not address me this way."

"Forgive me." The words came easily now, as I squirmed, not knowing still what I had said that was so impolite.

"From now, you will please call me Amma. All Hasan and Luna's friends do. It is normal. You must also."

Amma. Mother. I smiled. But it was more relief than any kind of familial feeling I had for Mrs. Chowdhury. I was grateful I hadn't been insulting my host. After consideration, I also felt touched that she included me among her children's friends. Perhaps I was settling in, finding a place in this close-knit clan.

Amma's sessions offered other valuable lessons. Though her explanations were almost always inadequate, she at least initially expressed willingness as she attempted to explain some of the more puzzling aspects of Bengali culture.

Ever since I'd arrived, I'd been wondering about the relationship between Shafiq and Kamala.

"They are brother and sister," Amma said. "Shafiq was married to Kamala's elder sister. But she has passed many years ago."

"So they're not exactly brother and sister." I thought for a moment. "Then they could – are they – you know – thinking about getting married?" I knew they shared quarters in a narrow building at the rear of the yard, but I couldn't bring myself to ask Amma if they were sleeping together.

Amma looked startled and slightly alarmed. "Kamala is married." But I had never seen another man in the house. "She has four sons." Four more boys besides? Where? "They stay in Hatiya on the coast. They are fishermen."

"Wow. That must be hard."

"What, dear?"

"Being so far apart like that – the whole family, I mean. I guess they could come here on holidays. Or she could go there for her vacation. I suppose they must write often…"

An expression I had just come to recognize settled on Amma's face. The expression normally followed a stream of things that came pouring from my mouth, one after the other, things I thought causal, linked, rational, though evidently, to Amma, they were not.

My curiosity about Shafiq and Kamala was still not satisfied. They were, after all, intimately involved in my life. They made my bed, cleaned my toilet, washed all my clothes, even my underwear, and made nearly everything that I ate. With my American sense of equality, I was certain they were just awaiting my overture before we became good friends.

A few days later, I asked Amma to help me approach them. "I was thinking I could maybe spend a day with them – you know, go to the market with Kamala – and Shafiq – well, I'm still not exactly sure what he does yet..."

"You are not alone in that," she murmured.

Amma resisted initially. "Robin, dear, they must get on with their work and they will not be – comfortable – if you are – you ask many questions, and they are simple people from their village."

"Then I won't say anything. I'll help them, too, so they'll be able to get their work done faster. I know how to make a bed after all – it's not an elaborate science." Amma appeared alarmed. I had never before seen her speechless.

But eventually, she taught me how to ask them – using the more polite formal form of address, at my request – if they would mind me hanging around with them for a day.

I entered their lair – the kitchen – the next day. Light slanted through a dusty, broken shutter onto the stained concrete floor. The room smelled of mustard oil, onion and phenol. Kamala and Shafiq were sitting on low stools, cups of tea balanced on their drawn-up knees. A prayer mat was rolled up in the corner beside the door.

"Salaam aliekum." I held out my hand and smiled.

They looked at each other. Then me. Kamala pulled the end of her saree up and over her head. It was like a beach ball had just benignly rolled into their kitchen. They didn't quite know what to do about it, or even whether any response at all was necessary. I couldn't remember then what I planned to say. So I backed toward the door. Just before I made my exit, Kamala burst into laughter, and for the first time, I saw her mouthful of stained, wide-gapped teeth. When I wrote my father about them the next week, I omitted the part about my attempted overture.

Once Amma became more comfortable around me, she spoke more and more often of Luna and the grief with which her daughter filled her life. Luna was, depending on the day, obstinate, inattentive, too restless, a poor student, disrespectful, and spoiled by her father. Unlikely to make anything of her life if she continued along the wayward path she was following. Because I knew a different Luna – a quick-thinking, intelligent, independent, perceptive one – I took Amma's words with little more than a grain of salt. Clearly, Amma was going through some sort of inner battle about her daughter's growing up, a sort of Bengali version of the empty-nest syndrome. When things got really bad, Amma'd pop a pill.

She'd bellow as though calling livestock, though from where she mustered the breath remained a mystery. "Kamala! Asho!" Come.

And Kamala, in her silent but attentive manner, as if she'd been waiting right around the corner, would materialize with Amma's medication, which she kept in a tiny draw-string pouch on a lace around her neck, and a small glass of water.

Teary-eyed, Amma would swallow the pill Kamala offered, then hold a hand to her throbbing head because for the third afternoon in a row, despite her coaxing, Luna had chosen to spend time with a friend instead of staying home. I suspected, but didn't know for certain that the "friend" was often Razzak.

"Daughters are far more difficult than sons," Amma said once. I tried to visualize my own father saying such things to a stranger, but it seemed bizarre. "You will understand when you start your family."

"I'd rather finish my degree first. And then I'm getting a job."

"But you will marry. And have children. Just like my Luna."

"Don't you wish for something better for Luna? You're her mother."

"But what could be better for a woman than having children? Your time will come. Don't worry." She assumed the extremely aggravating air of a wizened sage on a mountaintop.

"I'm not the least bit worried. Where I come from, women have fought hard to earn the right to choose. Why should a woman have to marry? Have children? Now women can do anything they want."

"What? As though they were God?"

"It's not like that," I reddened, but insisted. "But they have more control over their lives than…than they used to," I finished weakly. *More control than women like you.* That's what I had meant to say.

Amma just harrumphed. "It is not natural to place so much value on control."

"Perhaps. But I think it is natural and necessary to ask questions."

"Yes, questions are good. Knowledge is good," Amma said. "But it is peculiar to America, this idea that somehow you can make your way in life by yourself."

"But what is the alternative? Give up? Do exactly what you're told? Admit defeat before you even have a chance to begin? That's not what I was raised to believe."

She sat back and considered my words. Aha, I thought. I am finally making her understand. But I became conscious of noise from outside – a hawker sharpening knives and scissors rang a bell and announced his presence on the street in front of the house. Amma smiled when she heard him, self-assured once again, grounded by her reality. "OK. I am defeated. By your American arguments. But you will see one day. You will see what I mean when your daughter is born."

I shook my head firmly. "Uh-uh. Sorry Amma."

Her smile remained unbroken though, as if she knew something I didn't.

ᚨ

"Please, I cannot do this."

Luna and I were alone in a corner of the Girls' Common Room in the Arts Faculty.

"You're going to have to sooner or later. May as well be up front about it," I said. "Just tell your mother. Then you and Razzak won't need to sneak around anymore."

"You do not understand."

"I'll go with you. We'll make Amma understand together."

"No, Apa, she will be too much angry."

Luna had just asked me to hand-deliver a love letter to Razzak. I, of course, refused. My participation in such a foolish scheme would only further the deception and make it more difficult to disentangle the affair later. However, I saw a window of opportunity to meaningfully help Luna get her life back under control. She needed to tell her parents about Razzak.

"The answer is no. Sorry."

"But you are my friend."

I wavered, but only for an instant, then steeled as I thought of a solution. "Then get Ruby to deliver the letter. She's your friend, too. Besides, she said Razzak's place is right by her uncle's."

"She cannot help," Luna said. "If her baba, her bhai, anyone sees her passing letters to a Bihari boy, ahh –" She drew a breath. "People talk too much in Dhaka city. There will be trouble." I closed my eyes. She grasped my hand.

It was just a letter.

"I am trusting you," she continued.

"That means a lot, but –"

"You are the only one who can help me."

"Okay." I nodded. "Thik ache. But only one time. Then you're going to have to tell them."

"I will, I will. Oh, thank you, Apa."

Her delivery instructions were detailed and explicit. I was to go to Jahangir's Bakery, the place with the greasy windows she'd shown me on Elephant Road, at precisely 5:15 – right in the middle of my Bangla lesson with Amma, so I would have to excuse myself as best I could. When I got to Jahangir's, I was to order a cup of tea and a sweet, syrupy gulab jamun – we practiced the words together. And when the cola delivery van pulled up outside, I was to walk out of the bakery and leave an empty notebook on the table beside my tea cup. On the cover was a drawing of an iridescent blue dolphin leaping out of the water, silhouetted by a full moon. Inside the notebook would be the letter.

Razzak would take it from there.

"It is simple," Luna said. "And no one will suspect you of anything more than being forgetful."

"What if someone else picks it up?"

"Razzak will be there first," she said. "If he says he will be there, he will be there."

So I told Amma I needed to see a girl from my history class to lend her my notes. "It's urgent. She lost hers."

Amma was predictably reluctant. I would miss half my lesson. And I'd be wandering the streets by myself, a feat which she was not yet confident I would be able to master. Though it was true that I hadn't yet been out anywhere by myself – more by accident than design since everyone seemed happy to accompany me wherever I wanted to go – I thought her reaction typical Amma: over-protective and controlling.

But Amma also understood very well duty and responsibility. She wanted me to make new friends, too. Helping a classmate would be high on her list of priorities. She offered to send Shafiq to meet the girl.

"But I'll only be a few minutes. He's busy, and besides, too slow."

Amma's face opened and closed as she weighed the arguments. Then she sighed, defeated. "Go, then. But don't dawdle over tea and gossip, thik ache?"

In Jahangir's, I placed my order. Then it was as Luna predicted. Razzak entered the bakery with a friend. They did not look my way. The delivery van arrived. Razzak's friend went to the counter to place an order. No one noticed when I left. Or when the young Bihari man sidled up to the table I had just vacated, picked up the notebook I'd left and tucked it under his arm.

I was back with Amma in less than twenty minutes, though unable to focus on how "pora" as a verb meant either to study, to read, to wear, to be uncultivated, to be vacant, to be unpaid, to ooze, to burn, to attack, or to fall.

"How is anyone supposed to know which one it is?"

Amma sighed when faced again by my now rather predictable question.

I buried my face in my hands and wailed. "I'll never learn this language."

Luna glowed when I told her about the letter later that afternoon. "Did he give any letter for me?"

"No. Sorry."

"Then you must help again."

"No, Luna," I said. I had already fulfilled my part of the pact. Now it was her turn. To tell her parents.

"But it was easy. You said so yourself."

"No. I said one time only."

"Apa –"

"I don't like lying to your mother."

"Fine. Then I will take care of that. I will tell her – I will tell her you are going to see Afsana. With me and Ruby. Then you don't need to say a thing."

"But –"

"Not a thing."

And the next day, at the same time, I left Luna at a bookstall half-concealed by a pair of Radha-Krishnachura trees whose flowers had long since disappeared. I went back to the bakery to pick up the dolphin notebook. It was propped up behind a menu on the same small table. There was a thin, dirty envelope inside. I had only two sips of tea and a single bite of a biscuit. The delivery van pulled up and belched a plume of black smoke. While it coughed and idled, I stashed the notebook in my bag and left the bakery.

When she asked about a third letter, a week later, I said, "Definitely not."

"Apa –"

"I said once, and I did it twice. No more." She flopped down on my bed and buried her face in my pillow. I stood up and opened the door to my almirah, contemplating the contents. "You said you were going to tell your mother and father how you feel and you haven't." I turned. "You have to now. They're eventually going to support you, you know."

Even muffled by the pillow, I could tell Luna was exasperated. "You do not understand."

"I do understand. It's not easy. It never is. But who said it? Shakespeare? 'The course of true love never runs smooth'? Do you know that?"

"They will kill him," Luna said, lifting her head. "And then me."

"You're so dramatic, you and Ruby. Your mother with what – a gun? Kamala's boti? Come on." I pulled a long woven dupatta Luna had given me off a hanger and held it to my face. The smell was warm and woody, slightly musty, faintly soapy.

"I have already written it." She showed me the envelope

– drawn on the back, over the glue-stained seal, was a heart around two hands, their fingers entwined. The childish image jerked my heart. "Please."

But I held on, firm in my convictions. "No, Luna. And I'm very sorry. I've got to go. Amma's taking me to the tailor." I was being measured for two new sets of salwar kameez. Amma claimed I needed the new clothes for propriety's sake. I didn't argue, but I wanted them for entirely different reasons – it was time to retire my peasant skirts and big blouses. They were worn and faded from Kamala's vigourous washing, but most importantly, I wanted to wear what everyone else on campus wore.

"That's perfect!" Luna's face lit up. "Amma? Amma!" She ran from my room.

And when I finally found her and Amma in the drawing room, both faces fixed with radiant smiles, I realized I was sunk. "Luna will take you to the tailor, Robin dear. I have too much to do this afternoon. And now, this headache." She grimaced, then smiled proudly at her daughter. "It's only because I trust Faizul bhai perfectly, one hundred percent. He will not dare to misbehave with you girls. He is like a brother to this family. Now go."

By way of dismissal, she held hand to temple and turned away from the mid-day light that forced its way through the opening in the drapes.

❦

"Where were you all afternoon?" Hasan asked from the threshold of Luna's room. Luna and I were on her bed going through fabric samples hastily collected from Faizul the tailor who appeared slightly insulted when we refused both cups of cha, and to see the exclusive prints he'd set aside for Amma.

"I like the blue," I said. I lifted the frayed little square, pulled it between my fingers. I ignored Hasan.

But Luna wasn't able to brush him off so easily. "The tailor." Then, to me. "Georgette is pretty. But the lilac is better for you."

"Which tailor?" Hasan wasn't letting us off. "In Calcutta?"

"Amma's tailor," I jumped in to defend Luna. "It was Amma's idea. She sent us." But Hasan ignored me.

"You were gone more than two hours." He allowed a rebuking silence to grow. Our hair was still damp from the cloudburst that began just before we got back in the house. I had strands clinging to the nape of my neck. "Two-and-a-quarter hours to be exact."

"We stopped and had a cup of tea," I continued. That much was true. "With Ruby." That was not true. "At Jahangir's," I threw in for good measure, it also being true.

Luna's face fell. But it was too late.

"Jahangir's is the unsavoury meeting place of mastaans. It is not fit for girls unless they seek the cheap attention of criminals. Don't go there anymore."

"There's nothing wrong with Jahangir's," I protested. "Nothing wrong a little soap and water wouldn't fix anyway."

But he continued with his tirade. "And Ruby Islam is a silly, shameless girl. The way she smokes in public – like a man. It is a disgrace. You should spend time with your studies, not with your silly gossips and talks about clothes and film stars." Luna said nothing. "Now come. Amma is calling you for tea. Abba has been waiting."

We followed him into the drawing room. "He shouldn't tell you where you can and cannot go, or who your friends should be," I whispered. But Luna hushed me.

Shafiq, in his usual cloud of silence, was arranging the tea things on a table. I was surprised to see Hasan had a friend over, too. Not that he was anti-social – just the opposite – but he and his friends rarely spent time with the rest of the family, preferring their own company and what I imagined to be dull, dogmatic conversation. Anyway, a friend here, now, was good. Perhaps Hasan and his friend could withdraw into a corner to discuss the finer points of Bengali independence – and as a result, be less focused on Luna and me.

"Asalaam aliekum, chotto bon," the friend said when he was introduced. Little sister. "Kemon acho tumi?" How are you?

His name was Shaheed. I summoned up the Bangla words I knew to reply. "Bhalo achi. Ki khobor, boro bhai?" I'm fine. What's your news, big brother? I stammered, especially over calling him brother when we'd only just met, but I knew these were the right words.

Laughter burst from Shaheed's lips, and I would have been offended had it not been for the admiration which was as much in evidence as was his amusement. "Bhalo." He looked at Amma.

"Yes, she's a very fast learner," Amma said. She motioned to Shafiq and he placed the teapot next to her. "She has an ear for languages. Soon she will be giving speeches."

"Oh no, Amma, not me," I laughed. Shaheed watched me rather intently, but it was not unnerving in the least. "Ami korte pari na." I can't do it.

"Inshallah you will," Shaheed declared. God willing.

"Now please sit," Amma said. Tea was served.

Shaheed's presence changed everything. Light as a brook in spring, his chat flowed over and around the room. Difficult family topics were immersed in goodwill, a silent conspiracy to let them be invisible and for the moment, irrelevant. He complimented Amma on the tea, and Shafiq on something I missed, but I thought I saw the old man crack a smile. He talked cricket with Mr. Chowdhury, and told Luna about a film that was coming to Dhaka next month. He was Hasan's antithesis. I couldn't imagine on what their friendship was built.

But even babbling brooks eventually reach the plains, and when Shaheed ran out of steam, a long silence ensued. Perhaps I needed to fill it. Perhaps I was still angry with Hasan. Perhaps some part of me felt all Shaheed's benevolence needed a balance, or maybe it was as simple as I needed to impress him further. Whatever the case, I'd done some reading, and the political situation was no longer such a mystery. I couldn't resist showing off.

"I was just wondering," I said. Everyone sat up. Polite smiles flowered around the room, residue of all that affability. "When Sheikh Mujib says the six-point plan represents the demands of fifty-five million East Pakistanis of their right to live, do you think he meant everyone?"

"Aha. Someone has been studying, isn't it?" Mr. Chowdhury looked up from his cup, and settled his gaze on Amma.

"I just gave her a few things," Amma murmured. "Nothing much."

"Of course," Hasan answered my question. "He is not elitist."

"Then, does he include those members of the civil service and the armed forces and police who are here from West Pakistan?"

"If you read the Six Point Plan carefully, he says that all right-thinking patriotic elements of West Pakistan are also in agreement," Hasan said. "It is right there, on the first page. How could it be otherwise?"

"Robin, dear, take another biscuit," Amma said. "They're quite tasty."

I did. "Does he mean the Biharis, too?"

Luna blushed, a violent shade. Mr. Chowdhury's eyebrows scaled his forehead. The mood in the room changed.

"They are different," Hasan said.

"In what way?"

"They are not Bengali," he said. "However, in any case, they too, at least, those who are right-thinking and patriotic, if there are any such in this country, they would also be included by Bangabandhu."

"What I wonder then is who can really say what is 'right-thinking' and what is 'patriotic'? Surely that depends on your particular point of view."

"What is your point?" Hasan raised his voice. "Get to your point."

"There's no point. I'm just wondering, that's all."

"Well." Mr. Chowdhury forced a laugh. "Usually it is I with all the questions. But this afternoon, our exchange student beats even I for curiosity."

"Can I ask one more question?" His eyes glazed and he nodded apprehensively. "When Sheikh Mujib says there are agents of vested interests lying in ambush everywhere, who does he mean?"

"It's very complicated Robin," sighed Amma. "Perhaps you should not take it so literally."

"Does he mean the Biharis?" Luna's right eye twitched. "And if so, how are they ambushing the plan? The Biharis Amma and I saw last week were breaking bricks on the side of the road or fixing rickshaws in the dark." I had managed my visit to Mohammedpur by tagging along with Amma one day while she visited some relatives in a nearby neighbourhood. She had pointed out the quarter where many of the Biharis lived. "They didn't seem to have time for lunch let alone ambush."

"That is a most interesting question, isn't it?" Shaheed said.

"You show supreme ignorance." Hasan ignored his friend. "Plus unbelievable stupidity in reading comprehension."

"Hasan," Mr. Chowdhury warned.

"Is it wrong to ask questions? Or does asking questions make me a so-called vested interest?"

"No, no," Amma said, soothingly. "Everything is perfectly alright."

Luna rolled her eyes.

"I respect the frank ways of your people," Mr. Chowdhury said, following Amma's lead. "A healthy state can weather the trials of dissent, isn't it?"

"Then tell me this. Say someone wanted to go for full independence. Not autonomy, as is stated in the plan. Couldn't they also be considered an agent of vested interests lying in ambush?" I looked directly at Hasan so there could be no misunderstanding my meaning.

Bull's eye. His chair clattered to the floor as he threw himself to his feet.

"You are a stupid American girl," he shouted. "Go home before you shame your people any further. And before word of your ignorance spreads so far that I will no longer be able to protect you. I will no longer sit in this room with that infidel," he said to Mr. Chowdhury, and stormed off.

Mr. and Mrs. Chowdhury exchanged glances. Luna cradled her face in her hands. Shaheed, it appeared, was trying hard not to laugh.

Me, I was flabbergasted. Not at Hasan's violent reaction. Not at Shaheed's amusement. Not at Luna's embarrassment or her parents discomfort. What really caught me off guard was this: who on earth had asked Hasan to protect me?

This was a question for Beth.

❧

"Do you know Hasan? I mean, *know* him?"

It was another monsoon day in Dhaka, so we stayed off Beth's terrace. Her drawing room curtains were open to the weepy skies. The plants outside were jeweled with water drops.

"Since I've come to Dhaka. Since he was a boy. Is that what you mean?"

I spilled like an overflowing tank – everything poured out, from our first clash at my first dinner, to our walk down Elephant Road, and the latest incident. "You should hear the way he talks to Luna," I added. "Even his own mother. It's outrageous. He's as tyrannical as Yahya Khan!" I laughed at my own cleverness.

Beth's face remained still. A pointed finger traced the knots on the tatted antimacassar draped over the armrest of her chair. "There are many adjustments to make when you come to this country. It helps to remain open-minded."

"Well, of course. But Hasan would drive anyone crazy."

"It takes several years to figure out what's going on around you, several more years to understand it all and a lifetime to accept it. It's not easy to enter this society. Don't let your first impression be your only impression."

"But it's got nothing to do with me," I said. "He's the problem."

"Hasan is Hasan. And there are thousands more boys in Dhaka exactly like him. Loyal, smart, passionate. It takes time to see his good qualities."

Loyal? I wouldn't trust him with my wastepaper basket. Smart? I had seen no evidence of anything at work in his brain but the most knee-jerk reaction. Passionate? There I had to agree. Most of the time, the man verged on hysterical.

Beth continued. "It took years for us to appreciate one another. I support his commitment to his country. It's vital to instigating the change he believes is inevitable. But I have learned to get out of the way when I sense his fervor may be headed in my direction." She paused. "You would be wise to do the same."

"But this is all Hasan's fault. Why should I have to do anything?"

"Did you ever consider why he monitors what American newsmagazines have to say about East Pakistan so rigourously? Perhaps at some level he is interested in America. And, whether you like it or not, you are, to him, a first-hand experience of America. He's curious about you, too. And trying to come to terms with that."

"But he's already made up his mind about me. He thinks

I'm nothing more than a goonda at the beck and call of the west wing." I laughed. "The twisted thing is he also seems to think he's supposed to protect me. Can you imagine?"

Beth smiled mildly. "That's exactly what I'm talking about. There are many levels to Hasan."

"I don't need anyone to protect me." I spat the words out. "Especially not him."

"You may as well tell a tree not to have leaves and branches."

I waited until the rain had passed before I went home, unsatisfied with Beth's advice.

⚘

I didn't like my involvement in Luna's romantic correspondence, yet somehow I continued to be convinced to deliver and pick up letters on demand. I wanted to support her, especially once she agreed to raise the subject of her romantic relationship with her parents before the year's end. I suspected it was again an empty promise, the deadline a chance to buy time. Still, I made a decision to take her at her word, and tried to remain patient.

But I had another motive. Every letter that passed through my hands was a slap in Hasan's face, a rejection of every backward idea he stood for. If he had his way, he would have confined me to my room. Every letter was a reminder of my independence, a subversive act to undermine a bully.

The phone calls began after the monsoon was over, on a sultry day in early October, when I knew in Michigan, cold autumn winds from the Great Lakes were blowing leaves to the ground, and the inevitability of snow could be felt in the air.

"There is a message for you," Amma said when Luna and I returned home from campus that day. "From the embassy. A Mr. Razzak." I tried to hide my reddening face. "The number is there by the telephone. Is he new?"

Luna was standing slightly behind her mother, beyond Amma's peripheral vision, and good thing, too, for she was transparently guilty and desperate. She folded her hands, begging for my complicity.

"Yes," I finally said. "He's the new – education liaison." Luna's face blossomed into gratitude.

"Please give him my best regards then," Amma said. "I'm sure we will be hearing more from him."

"Oh, I doubt it."

Later in my room, I lost my temper. "You tell your boy-friend never to do this again."

"But Apa, there is a big problem."

"Yes, there is. You promised nearly two months ago that you were going to tell your parents. I've been very patient. If you don't tell them now, I will."

"No, listen to me. Razzak's being accused of collaborating with the army."

"But that's ridiculous."

"One worker in Jahangir's he has seen you and Razzak with letters every week. He telling Razzak you give money or I telling Awami League. Apa, you must help."

It was a predictable, yet totally unforeseen consequence. How could the three of us have been so blind? I'd witnessed the quiet, but unbroken growth of political tension since I had arrived. It had shot out roots everywhere. Everyone had become, in my opinion, paranoid and suspicious. Physically, as a stereotypical fair American, it was impossible for me to blend in with the crowd. And since the political ties between my country and West Pakistan were widely acknowledged and loathed, I was of course a potential target of that mistrust. However, I thought Razzak and I had been surreptitious enough, our movements unworthy of scrutiny.

I considered the remote possibility that I'd done something in Jahangir's to tip off the busybody. I sighed. Maybe the phone would be easier. With all the comings and goings of the family, there would times when Luna could actually speak to Razzak without anyone knowing. And I would no longer have to make excuses to disappear by myself.

"Will you promise, absolutely promise to tell your parents before the end of the year?"

"I will, Apa, believe me. As soon as the time is right."

I nodded, though my agreement still did not sit comfortably with what I knew to be the right course of action.

☙

Amma presented me with a saree in November for my first Bengali wedding. "Rose is perfect for your complexion," she said. She rolled the pink silk around my hips, necessarily, as I had no idea how to dress myself in it.

"Let me do the pleats," Luna begged. Amma indulged and handed her the fabric. Luna began to weave it in and around her fingers.

"That is too loose," Amma said. Luna adjusted. "Two more. No, one more."

"I can do it," Luna said.

"You are learning," Amma allowed. But she took the pleats, lined them up expertly, and tucked them into the waistband of my petticoat. "Does it feel tight?"

"A little."

"Then it will be just right." Amma arranged the pallav so it cascaded down my back. "Now you are ready. Take a look."

My hair had already been brushed and pinned up with sweet-smelling flowers. As usual, the ends were coming loose and curling like wood shavings in the humidity. Luna had done my make-up. "This the kohl," she had said, a tiny black brush poised just over my eyelid. I blinked. "Don't move." "I'm not," I had said. She rested the heel of her hand against my cheek as she drew a black line on my eyelid. Though I feared I might end up looking like a campy version of Ruby, I let Luna have her way.

Around my neck, Amma had closed the clasp on a thick gold chain inlaid with emeralds and blue sapphires. If they were artificial, they were convincing fakes. At least, I had been allowed to put on the matching earrings myself. Prepared for a transformation, I stood before the mirror. But the transformation was not what I expected. I hardly recognized my bizarre reflection. I looked like an Italian pastry, not a wedding guest.

"Adorable," Amma pronounced.

"You are ravishing," Luna said. "Like the bride."

Like a science experiment that should have been terminated.

"Perhaps it's too much," I said, not wanting to hurt their feelings.

"Nonsense," Amma said. "Come. We go."

Shafiq opened the front door to let us out. It blew ajar and nearly knocked him off his feet. A strong wind was coming up from the southeast. The trees sighed in gusts, the shrubs and flowers shivered. The atmosphere was thick with the beginnings of a big storm. We packed into the Citroën – Amma, Luna, Mr. Chowdhury, Hasan and me. On the roadside, palm trees swayed to the wind's force. Tin signs shuddered against the bolts that attached them to their iron frames.

"This does not bode well at all," Mr. Chowdhury said. "What must it be like on the coast?"

"Actually, Abba, the meteorologists have downgraded their alerts," Hasan said. "I heard it on the radio this afternoon."

"I hope the evening will not be spoilt," Amma said.

The reception was held in a large hall whose outside was draped with coloured lights and strings of pungent marigolds. A white tent extended onto the street in front of the hall and flapped in the wind that threatened to lift it from its bamboo supports. I felt a raindrop as we entered.

It was hot and humid, and packed with noise, perfume, sweaty smells and colour. Amma and Luna pulled me along, and introduced me to aunts, uncles, cousins, sisters, brothers – a kaleidoscope of family, many of whom wore the nowka pin, a tiny boat that symbolized support for Sheikh Mujib, on their lapels and blouses. Once greetings were spoken, we moved on – out of necessity. The flow of people was strong. It proved impossible to resist the current.

"Come. We view the bride," Luna said, and we joined a stream of people headed for a brightly lit corner.

Mira was perched on a dais bedecked with red and gold

fabric, her body even more elaborately dressed. Significantly younger than me, she trembled. It may have been the weight of all her gold jewelry, but more likely, it was the attention. Women, children, Luna and I – we all stared as though she was a mannequin in a shop window. Three attendants, also ornately dressed, stroked the bride's arms and shoulders, pushed strands of her hair into place, adjusted her red and gold saree, and touched up her make-up every time a camera came near.

"Salaam aliekum," I said when we were close enough. She had small shoulders, and a child's hands. An angry pimple, not quite veiled beneath face powder, adorned her left cheek. She was even younger than I had first thought. We both blushed. "Mubarak." Congratulations. But she lowered her eyes, as though she had sensed my shock. Luna murmured to her, something which I could not decipher. The crowd pushed us along.

Just then, a young man with a camera emerged. Luna pulled me close and posed. "Smile," she said. The flash burnt into my eyes.

There was no custom of gawking at the groom on a little platform. Unlike his new and very stationary wife, Qashem moved with a pack of young men. I couldn't see him until Luna pointed him out. Dressed in a very stylish suit, he had to be at least ten years older than Mira. I heard he was from a very respectable family, and lived now in Fresno, California. I found the relationship a curiosity, the logistics nearly impossible to understand.

"How did they meet?" I asked Luna.

"Who?"

"Mira – and Qashem."

"Apa, don't you know arranged marriage?"

Of course I did, but I thought it an outdated custom. I never imagined I would meet a modern couple going through the practice, especially if one of them already lived in the United States. Why wouldn't the groom have found his own bride? Why hadn't he already fallen in love with someone of his own choosing?

"Razzak and I will have love marriage," Luna whispered. "Like Americans." She squeezed my hand.

When the meal began, Luna, Amma and I sat with all the other women on one side of the hall, the men opposite. This was nothing new to me. Every function I had attended so far in Dhaka had had the same guest configuration. But it still irked me. I considered what might happen if I excused myself, stood up, crossed the floor and took a seat at one of the men's tables. I imagined with glee the heavy silence that would come crashing down on the guests. I pictured with delight Hasan's raging disapproval.

Halfway through my tantalizing daydream, a strong gust blew open a door. Leaves and dust swept into the hall. Conversation lulled and people looked up expectantly. The door was slammed shut, and I remained in my seat, exactly where I was supposed to be.

A waiter shoveled greasy pullao onto my plate. He was followed by another who put chicken curry rich with cardamom beside it. A third carried a platter with fish stuffed with chilis and onions. It was all rich and oily, and completely delicious. After I began to feel like a glutton, I shook my head to the offer of second and third helpings. But the waiters put serving after serving on my plate anyway. Every mouthful I ate was instantly replaced with another spoonful. It was useless to refuse.

Suddenly, Luna pushed her plate away and stood up. "We go to Abba's table now. Come," she said to me. Did she mean the men's side of the room? I was too stunned to move and besides, still chewing. "Come," Luna insisted, and pulled on my arm. Amma gave a brief nod without looking up from her plate.

I rose and followed Luna. No deafening silence followed our crossing. No one even looked at us. I was so confused about the mysterious rules of this society that seemed to shift on a whim.

At Mr. Chowdhury's table, I recognized Hasan, of course, as well as one of Luna's uncles, a man with a skillet-flat face, and Hasan's friend Shaheed who had his fingers resting on the side of his emptied plate. But the rest of the men around the table were strangers. Conversation stopped when we approached.

"Have you already finished your meal?" Mr. Chowdhury asked. He was impossibly built – a short man with a belly like a beach ball and legs like broomsticks. When he had entered the hall earlier, I had the feeling he would be toppled over by the wind. His face was round, like Luna's, his head mostly bald. His eyes, dark brown, were deep as a forest and set behind glasses so thick he seemed to be much further away than he really was.

"Yes, Abba," Luna said.

"Did you enjoy the meal, Robin?" A half-full plate rested before him.

"Too much." I patted my full stomach.

"Join us," Mr. Chowdhury said. "Please." He gestured

avuncularly to an empty chair. A couple of the men shifted, unprepared for our invasion of their territory. An awkwardness, impossible to ignore, took shape and landed on the table like a centrepiece. Shaheed smirked.

"I'm sorry. We're interrupting."

"Not at all." Shaheed gallantly signaled a waiter to bring us another chair. "Now sit. We were discussing international relations."

Luna and I had no choice. Mr. Chowdhury turned to one of the older men and asked a question in Bangla. I could only understand a word or two of his reply – he seemed to be chewing on his tongue while he spoke. Another man jumped in. Then another, and another, until it seemed like everyone was talking. Shaheed caught my eye and winked.

Finally, Luna's skillet-faced uncle raised his hand until a hush fell around the table. When he spoke, they listened. Then all eyes turned to me. Expectantly.

"Chacha is right," Luna said, breaking the silence. "For our guest, we will speaking the English."

"We will *speak* English," Hasan said. Luna glowered.

"Stop your bickering," Mr. Chowdhury warned. "Behave nicely." A long silence followed during which every man found something fascinating to look at – on the ceiling, their plates, at the place where the wall met the floor.

Bang. Hasan plunked down his water glass. "I have nothing to say in English."

Mr. Chowdhury grinned. "Well, that is a relief. My son with nothing to say for a change." Everyone laughed, except Hasan. "Please don't mind," Mr. Chowdhury said to me, affable as always, as though Hasan's words were no more than a mosquito bite. "Our language is a very sensitive topic. Especially lately. Sometimes we can only express what we really mean in our own language, isn't it?" I nodded. "We need to defend it from forces that would have it vanquished. Perhaps one day you will come to understand."

"I want to learn your language," I said. "Ami Bangla shikchi. That is why I am here."

"Yes, we need such all-out support now," Mr. Chowdhury said. "Not just from people like you. But from foreign governments. Britain, France, America..."

"The American government is nothing more than a puppet of the Mir Jafars," Hasan said. "We don't need such support."

"So you do have something to say. In English, my son?" Mr. Chowdhury said dryly.

"The American government is not Apa's fault," Luna said.

"In a democracy, all are accountable for their governments," Hasan said. "And yes I have plenty to say."

"Hasan!" admonished Mr. Chowdhury.

A waste of breath. Hasan leapt to his feet, Luna followed and the arguing began in earnest.

"Children!" Mr. Chowdhury raised his voice, increasingly aggrieved. The others smiled awkwardly, shook their heads or tried to stop the argument. Only Shaheed sat back and watched like it was a spirited moment in a long cricket match.

"She is a guest from abroad," Luna's uncle said in English. "You must behave properly."

"Bas! Bas! Enough!" Mr. Chowdhury was turning purple.

"Stop," I said when I could feel other eyes in the hall turn toward us. "Please."

They didn't.

"Please."

I wrapped on the surface of the table like a wizened congressman or a schoolhouse ma'am – *thunk thunk thunk* – until slowly, finally, silence fell over at our table, and then, one or two tables nearby. Luna, then Hasan sat. "You can speak whatever language you want. In fact, please speak Bangla. I can understand some. Besides, it's the only way I'll learn."

"I thought you Americans already knew everything," Hasan said.

Another sweeping statement. It was somebody's wedding – but how many more insults could I let pass? "What do you mean?"

"That's what you believe, isn't it?"

"You're wrong. Besides, that's not fair. You're not giving me a chance." I was so flustered now. I knew of no way to respond to his accusations. There were so many. He was like a hungry flea the way he jumped from one contention to another, never remaining on any long enough for me to be able to formulate and speak clearly my thoughts.

"What chance are you giving us? You think you have come from some supreme nation and we're all supposed to walk on eggshells to avoid insulting your delicate feelings."

"Hasan!" Mr. Chowdhury scolded again.

"What gives you that idea? You don't listen to a thing I say."

"When you say something worthy, then I'll listen."

"Bas!" Mr. Chowdhury spoke loudly.

"Your government is offering full cooperation to the West Pakistanis," Hasan continued. "Why? Self-interest. So the dictators of Islamabad will keep the red Russians out of this region."

"And what exactly have I done? Whatever it is, I apologize. And if it helps explain anything to anyone who might be tempted to believe the ridiculous propaganda you spout about me, not every American blindly supports the government. That's democracy. And there's nothing I can do about that."

I pulled all six metres of saree up off my chair and left the table.

❧

"You must not let him get to you like that," Shaheed said. We were in a corridor, leading to the kitchen. There was nowhere else to escape. Though waiters streamed up and down beside us like trout, this was the one place where we could be, in effect, alone. They were busy. No guest was likely to venture near the area where food was being prepared. "He is often too serious and at times a little quarrelsome."

I shook as my anger coursed down to the tips of my fingers. "At times? Everything he says is hateful. And wrong." I fought to prevent the rage spilling from my eyes.

"Please don't worry. No one believes what he says."

A waiter balancing four partially-filled jugs of water slipped by us, sideways. I gave in, and cried.

"Then why doesn't anyone say anything? Why don't you? He's your friend."

Shaheed took my hands and squeezed. I let my fingers go limp. I knew as well as he did that this physical contact between us was inappropriate. Yet he held tight. "All right. I shall. Now calm yourself." A shared breath later, he released my hands, for which I felt glad, knowing it would not be prudent to be seen in such a compromising position, but also disappointed because I hadn't yet figured out what the gesture meant, if anything. "Now don't let the evening be spoiled so soon. I'm sure you and Hasan have many more things to argue about tonight. Besides, the second and third course of our meal is coming up –" He laughed when he saw my face. "Fooled you."

I rolled my eyes, but smiled as I left him with the waiters and the overdone smells from the kitchen that reassured me the meal was indeed over, even if Hasan and I were nowhere near such a détente.

჻

The celebrations and arguments distracted us temporarily from the storm outside. It had intensified during our meal. When we finally went to leave, I opened the door into the wind, and the handle was torn from my fingers. Rain and hail blown horizontally pelted my face. My hair collapsed and I feared my saree in the style of a gothic romance would be ripped from my body.

Days later, when news of the full impact of the cyclone reached Dhaka, I found out this was not uncommon. The newspapers published pictures of naked women and children, wandering around a swampy moonscape, looking for their families, homes, livestock and belongings. Not even a shred of clothing to cover their bare flesh. The force of the wind literally ripped the clothes from their backs.

Imagine celebrating a wedding anniversary, as Mira and

Qashem would, on the same day as what one newspaper called "the worst disaster of the century." November 12, 1970. No one would ever forget it. Two hundred and fifty miles of coastline on the Bay of Bengal was devastated, a huge V chewed out of the side of the country. Homes, crops, cattle and poultry, everything blown or washed away. To where? It was impossible to say. Though I imagined this place, somewhere to the north, butted up against the Himalayas, where the wind and waves had died down, and a massive pile of wood and metal, clothes, shoes, steel pots, pans, broken dishes, bodies of chickens and cows and goats, family photos, jewellery, school projects and notebooks, dolls, diapers and every single edible thing in the country lay. Cemented together by that distinctive silt that was the soil of East Pakistan.

One million people died. Unofficial, but the Chowdhurys had more faith in that than the first official estimate of fifty dead.

Though I felt embarrassed and bruised by yet another argument with Hasan – it was the first in which we had such a large audience, and the first in which I had truly lost my temper – my feelings faded in the wake of the disaster. The Chowdhurys lost a window that night. Six panes shattered when a gust of wind snapped a large bough of a neem tree and tossed its bulk against the side of the house. I was awake, of course, listening to the storm and alternately fuming about Hasan and wondering about Shaheed. The house's foundation trembled with the impact.

"God has blessed us," Amma said as she oversaw Shafiq picking up the shards the next morning.

"Indeed," said Mr. Chowdhury.

The Chowdhurys suffered nothing compared to the rest of the city. Trees were uprooted. Sheets of corrugated iron were lifted off their shanties in the exposed areas. Billboards bowed to touch the ground, their iron support rails bent into arches so perfect, they would be the envy of any architect. The pathways between the homes in the slums became rivers that toted away shoes and pots, baskets and buckets. Anything not fastened down. Several generations worth of possessions.

When people finally emerged from their houses, they wandered the streets like ghosts and shook their heads. They marvelled over the tree, the shack, the pole, the wall, the sign. *Yes, it was there, I remember, don't you?*

When all the details emerged, Kamala cried and Shafiq took leave. Coastal Hatiya, their ancestral village, had been flattened by the tidal wave that followed the cyclone.

"We need him here," Amma said, "but what can I do?" I looked at spindly Shafiq. He would never survive the trip. Nonetheless, Amma gave him three hundred rupees, a kilo of rice and some dried fish. He rolled up his prayer mat, tucked it under his arm and left the next day on a launch.

Barisal, Patuakhali, Khulna. In some places, fewer than one in five people had survived. Places I had never heard of before, statistics that numbed the mind became part of my daily vocabulary. Burying the dead was an impossible task. There were so many bodies. They swelled up on the riverbanks and, in the hot sun, threatened to burst with disease. Cholera spread like fire in wood-shavings. No one could explain why it took more than four days for the armed forces to get out their shovels.

"Abba, Amma," Hasan roared into the house, returning from Friday prayers. "They knew. Those black bastards knew."

"Knew what?" Mr. Chowdhury pulled a newspaper from his face.

"Do not use such language in this house," Amma said.

"And they dare to question our piety. Who deserves to be called 'half Muslim' now?"

"Go on, go on." Mr. Chowdhury was impatient.

"For two whole days the meteorologists knew about the storm. The early warning system works fine. But they were too lazy to tell the people. Our imam has revealed all. Filthy swine. They are not fit to wipe dirt from my shoes."

According to Hasan's report, the public had been warned – once. Someone in charge then had assumed that adequate precautions would follow. Surely people had the sense to tie down their possessions, and move their families and livestock to higher ground. Regular radio programs resumed, uninterrupted. Whatever updates were necessary were contained in regularly scheduled weather reports.

It took the president six days to visit the disaster areas. Only then was the official death toll raised to 175,000. Only then was the notion of relief taken seriously. Only then was the international community asked for help.

But of course it was too late for West Pakistan's political forces. By then, all support had galvanized around Sheikh Mujib and the Awami League. Within hours, he spoke before a crowd of twenty thousand in a little town called Moulvi Bazaar. It was so quiet, you could hear a pin drop.

Finally, Hasan and I could agree on something. Victory at the elections, scheduled for a mere three weeks after the disaster, would most certainly go to Bangabandhu.

※

Luna picked a day in late November when she knew the Students Action Committee was having a meeting beneath the banyan tree on campus that Hasan would never miss. "I want to show Robin the Botanical Gardens Saturday morning," she told her mother.

Amma was troubled of course, and suggested another day, another time, when Hasan would be available to escort us, but Luna had prepared herself with excuses: a test she had to study for; an important but fictitious phone call I was expecting from the dean's office in East Lansing; my own twentieth birthday which was mere days away now; the weather forecast. She had prepared such a barrage of excuses, even Amma couldn't withstand it.

"Go then," she said. "My head is aching too much to fight with you any longer." She placed her hand on her temple and closed her eyes. "But stay on the pathways and don't waste your paisa on the mehendi-wallahs." All it took was ten minutes and a couple of coins, and you could have a dark woman or a man with missing teeth paint the palms of your hands or the soles of your feet with henna. Luna was a fan of the lavish designs, but the one time I had it applied, flowers and vines drawn up to my fingertips, it tickled as it dried. I involuntarily curled my fingers – an instant of forgetfulness – and the pattern blurred.

The garden was overgrown and damp. As we set foot in it, I could almost feel my hair curling from the humidity. Brick pathways snaked around specimens of trees, hand-painted tin signboards hammered crookedly at their roots, identifying their local and Latin names. Sundari, sal, kathal, magnolia, bel – I could now read the Bangla script. The sunny areas were brimming with rows of flowers, new buds and blossoms nurtured by thousands of gallons of monsoon moisture, and the soil of entire mountainsides washed down from the Himalayas to the delta of East Pakistan. The scent of roses, jasmine, and marigolds was layered with the aroma of fried pakoras and singharas from the street stalls at the garden's gate, and the dank odours of human waste from the nearby Buriganga River. The fertility felt oppressive.

Luna paid no attention to any of it. Single-mindedly, she led me deeper and deeper into the garden. We passed children who ran up and down the pathways, and called to their parents when the man selling chewing gum or hard candies in crisp, cellophane wrappers appeared. Groups of college-aged girls hovered aimlessly and furtively watched the groups of college-aged boys who were, in turn, watching them. Couples, heads bowed together, were the least active. They sat on benches or beneath trees, laying claim to whatever quiet, shady corner of the garden they could.

We found Razzak in a clearing, thick with bamboo, arching branches knit together in dusty, dried knots. He sat on a shawl spread on the earth littered with dry leaves and curved slabs of bark. Though we'd been creeping around the city together, our lives inextricably linked by the secret we shared, this was my first official meeting with him. Face to face with him, finally, I found him assessing me with the same curiosity I had about him.

"Did you have any problem coming here today?" he asked. His eyes were webbed with red as though he hadn't slept.

"No," Luna said. "Thik ache."

"Just Amma," I laughed. But Luna, finger to her lips, hushed me. Amma – and Mr. Chowdhury, Hasan, Razzak's father – these people had no place with us in the garden.

"Apa, this the bamboo. Bash bagan we say," Luna mumbled and self-consciously sat on the edge of Razzak's shawl. She turned her face toward him, her eyes lowered, and smiled. The pretense of my botany lesson evaporated, and was replaced with romantic tension.

I stood nervously not knowing where to sit. But when I saw Razzak stir to shift and offer me his place on the shawl, I quickly lowered myself onto the earth and leaves and crossed my legs. Facing them.

"No, no," he said and rose.

"Please, stay where you are. Sit down." Razzak hovered. "I insist." And I must have spoken decisively enough, as he did as I asked.

I had a lot of things I wanted to ask him, but I hardly knew where to begin. Everything I had learned about him so far suddenly seemed tangled, his background impenetrable.

"You like it here?" Razzak asked finally, breaking our silence.

"Sure. There's a lot to like and Luna's been great."

"I agree with you on the second point." He smiled slyly. Luna blushed and fussed, but still did not meet his eye. "But I am not so sure about the first."

"What do you mean?"

"This place is a hell." An ant, its rear jacked up into the air as if its waist had been cinched too tightly, crawled onto the shawl. He flicked it away.

"But it's your home."

Razzak's parents had come to East Pakistan more than twenty years ago, fleeing parched land and religious hostility following partition – just as Afsana had described. They did not know what lay in wait for them across the border, but the uncertainty was preferable to waiting for famine or communal rioting to notice them. Razzak's mother was almost eight months pregnant with him when they began their migration. She gave birth early, in a village just inside the border of East Pakistan. Two women she barely knew called the village birth attendant who had a cast eye and bony fingers as twisted as the trunk of a banyan tree. Together they helped her push, cut the cord, wash and wrap Razzak, and deliver into her arms a child blessed with their new nationality.

His father could not wait until the two were strong enough to travel. He kept going. In Dhaka, he located the Bihari community and nudged his way into a slum. When Razzak and his mother arrived a few weeks later, stronger, thanks to the hospitality of the two village women, there was a tattered hut for them to call home.

Razzak's father accepted what work he could find, but most often, it was temporary and the kind of work no one else wanted to do. Razzak's sisters were conceived and born, one after the other, and the family moved into a larger hut. Eventually, in the same way he nudged the family into the slum, Razzak's father nudged his way into a typist's job in the government. The fact he could fix a typewriter – not to mention read and write Urdu placed him above the Bengali candidates.

"My parents suffered too much for me and my sisters. When Abba was able to join government service, they believed the suffering was over. But his good fortune was the beginning of my family's true sorrow in this land."

Seven years ago, when coming home from work, Razzak's father was stopped by five men. They pushed him down, kicked him, accused him of taking a good job away from a Bengali, and left him lying in a patch of urine-soaked weeds growing at the base of a brick wall. He could barely sit up, let alone work. But when his department threatened to find someone new to fill his place, he rushed back to the office. As a result, his body never healed properly and his back and arms still gave him much pain. But he could never take the time off to have them fixed. He would have lost his job.

Last week, a neighbourhood mastaan had demanded money from Razzak's father. If he didn't pay, the thug threatened to fabricate reports of spying which he would convey to both the army and the Awami League. His father had managed to avoid the man ever since, but had not yet decided what to do.

"Will you vote next week?" I asked. The long-awaited elections were six days away. He shrugged. "What do you think of the independence movement?" I continued.

"Robin-Apa, even if I had an opinion, I would not tell you. Everyone is a security threat to my family. But just so you understand my point of view: independence movements are for people who have good jobs and nice houses and always enough food on the table. So are elections. The rest of us are too busy just trying to survive."

It was impossible for me to equate Razzak and his family with the picture of Bihari villains painted by Hasan, Ruby and their ilk. Was I missing something? The disparity in the stories was nearly unfathomable. Was Razzak lying?

No one could have invented such detail. I looked at Razzak and wondered, though my doubt, however slight it might be, felt disloyal to Luna.

Luna stretched out her legs and shifted, and I saw Razzak reach for her fingers. She swatted his hand, and turned her shoulder away, but her smile said she was pleased he had tried. They sat, joined by the shawl and protected by the bamboo, lovers with one foot in this world, and the other in a world of their own. I looked away. It was all I could do to offer a few moments of precious privacy.

Even the azan seemed to respect their space. Though I knew there were two mosques not far away, the sound of the noon-time call to prayer barely reached us.

When we became thirsty, Luna gave some coins to Razzak to fetch us drinks. While he was away, she showed me the tiny lajja-patta plants whose delicate fringe of leaves folds up when touched.

"How does it work?" I asked.

She shrugged. I brushed another to see it happen again. Then, I remained still, waiting until the pale, closed up plant unfurled itself once more. It took much longer to open than it had to close.

Luna gently stroked a patch of lajja-patta and as the leaves lay down she said, "Thank you, Apa, for giving me the most perfect day of my life."

Razzak returned with three sodas, flimsy straws bubbling up from the narrow necks of bottles. We drank. The whisper from deep within the bamboo grove was the only conversation. We respected the silence – we recognized one another's mute spaces. Razzak, an exile in this country, me a foreigner, and Luna, a woman incapable of publicly declaring the love that shaped her life. We basked in this familiarity, while leaves rustled around us. It seemed impossible that we had known one another for only a few months. For the first time since I had entered East Pakistan, I discovered a corner where I belonged.

Then down the path. "Holy shit," I said. "Shafiq."

Luna jerked away from Razzak, while he pushed himself off the ground like a sprinter. He ducked behind the bamboo. "Koi?"

I pointed. I didn't even know he was back from the village.

She smoothed her fingers over her clothes, her lips and cheeks. She arranged her dupatta like a schoolgirl's, so it concealed her chest. "Taratari," she whispered to Razzak. "Jao." Quickly. Go.

Razzak crawled on his belly to the other side of the grove, and when a group of school girls in uniform, white ribbons like stiff-winged insects in their hair, darted across the path in front of Shafiq, he rose and nonchalantly walked away.

Rickety old Shafiq strode through the trees in a way that made me marvel. His chappals flopped as though they might slide off his feet. His spindly legs buckled, but did not let him down.

"Asho," he cried. "Tomar ma hospital giyeche." Your mother has gone to the hospital.

Amma.

Luna leapt up.

"Asho, asho," Shafiq urged.

"Where is the car?" Luna cried. "Come on." She pulled my arm so hard, my sleeve tore at the shoulder seam.

And Shafiq scooped up the shawl we'd been sitting on. The shawl that belonged to Razzak.

Amma sat in bed, her face as grey as the over-laundered and worn-out sheet wrapped around her hips and legs. She was wired to a monitor that flickered in time to her heartbeat. A bandage was looped under her chin and tied on top of her head. It gave her a comical look, like a magician's rabbit with a cartoon toothache.

"Thik ache, thik ache," she said as we burst into the room. "All this fuss for a clumsy old woman. There's no need." She struggled to get out of bed.

"Amma, calm yourself," Hasan ordered. "Sit." He pushed her back onto the bed, with more force than necessary. Even at a moment like this he could not be gentle. She raised a hand to the back of her neck and squinted in pain, but said nothing.

"Amma, what happened?" Luna cried. "Where's Abba?"

"He's coming," Hasan said. "He was in Tongi."

Amma had passed out in the long hallway that led from the front of the house to the bedrooms at the back. Kamala found her right away, called Hasan, who called an ambulance which took her to Holy Family Hospital. Doctors took care of the rest – high blood pressure and a nasty knock to her head. No serious damage, they said, other than the bump.

"But your pressure," Hasan said. "That is no joke."

Amma brushed away his words. "Rubbish. Perhaps I did not eat enough breakfast."

"You didn't take your medication, did you?" Hasan said.

"Don't be foolish." She patted her belly. "An old woman's empty stomach is all."

"We were so worried," I said finally. "Amma, you have to take care of yourself."

She was sent home before nightfall with two more prescriptions and instructions to rest in bed for ten days.

Mr. Chowdhury finally arrived an hour later. "That daft messenger became lost – he is a stupid – and then no one would allow him entry into the meeting. The fools at the door did not understand the urgency of his message. I went straight to the hospital as soon as I knew, isn't it? But they told me you had been discharged."

"What was the outcome of the assembly, Abba?" Hasan said.

"Unfortunately, I do not know, as I had to leave."

"But in general. What was the mood of the delegates?"

"Not good," he said, shaking his head. "Not good at all." Amma's chest began to rise and fall. She wheezed like a concertina. "But this is no time for idle chatter. We must do the needful, isn't it? Go. Your mother and I have matters to discuss." Luna, Hasan and I dragged ourselves away from her side. Like zombies we slid down the hall to our respective rooms.

Luna closed her door, leaving Hasan and me alone. I was about to enter my room. "You can do what you want with your private affairs. But leave her out of it."

"Are you talking to me?" I asked. But there was no one else in sight, and the answer to my question was obvious.

"Trying to stop you is like standing up to an armored tank. But you leave her be."

I felt caught although it was not possible that he knew our whole outing was a set-up and that Razzak had been there.

"What are you talking about?" I feigned what innocence I could summon.

"Don't pretend. She is a respectable girl from a respectable family. You will not get away with it."

I considered briefly that Shafiq could have told him something. But no. It was far more likely than Hasan was fishing for information and hoping I'd stumble over some detail that would allow him to figure everything out.

"Get away with what?" My innocence this time sounded forced.

"Amma will be informed."

"Amma's sick." And with that, I decided I would no longer play this game. "Butt out. It's not your business."

"And what makes you think it is yours?" he asked. "Before you introduce any more modern ideas to my sister just ask yourself: why am I doing this? What will happen to her when I leave for my so-called free country and she must stay behind here and feel the consequences of her secrets? Ask yourself if you are acting in her best interests."

He spun around, his outrageous questions pulled away in a wake of air. The door to his room slammed.

I entered my room and closed the door behind me. Of course I had Luna's best interests in mind. Why else would I have been going to such lengths – risking Amma's disapproval and possibly jeopardizing my home stay? I agreed with one thing he said: it was detrimental to keep her relationship a secret from her family. Eventually, there would be consequences. Likely after I had left the country. Hasan had a point. But hadn't I been the one encouraging Luna to open up and tell the truth?

Amma recovered. However, her bed rest consisted of

ten hours, not days. Next morning, I overheard her on the phone with Beth, downplaying the whole event. "Just an empty stomach, that's all," she said. "But perhaps I will take the medicine. Doctor's orders."

She went marketing Monday morning, visited her sister's for lunch, and by the following day, except for the now uncovered and fading bruise on her head, she was the same old Amma. She tottered home in the evening with a new picture for the sitting room. She had Shafiq hammer a nail in the wall using a heavy iron tava from the kitchen, and hang the shrink-wrapped photograph of a tiny chalet in the Swiss Alps. The mountains were unnaturally green, the sky a disturbingly vivid blue, but you could only see them under a certain light and from a certain angle, confined as they were to their cellophane wrapping. "So beautiful," she sighed, smoothing a wrinkle in one corner with her thumb. "It will do me good to see this peaceful corner of the earth every day."

The only difference in the house following Amma's collapse was that Kamala now had three bottles of pills cinched in the bag around her neck. She'd shake once, twice, three times, and palm the pills over to Amma, then push a glass of water into her other hand.

❦

There was another change in the house, though far more subtle and therefore, impossible to ask Amma about. There were more closed doors than ever before, more quiet voices, more somber faces around the dining table and the tea trolley. Amma and Mr. Chowdhury, Hasan and a squadron of relatives came and went – I was not included in their discussions. In fact, when I appeared, silence fell, then harmless topics of conversation were raised – weather, cricket, the rising price of essentials – mundane matters that had never concerned me before. I put it down to the election, which was now just a couple of days away.

Even Shafiq and Kamala were more grim than usual. They went about their duties with funeral parlor solemnity. The kitchen door was pushed shut whenever I passed. Their voices were muffled and indistinguishable through the wood, though once I heard Kamala cackle.

Another piece of business in the house remained strangely unfinished. Razzak's shawl disappeared. Luna and I weighed the possibilities.

"Maybe Shafiq kept it," I offered.

"No. That not his way."

"But what would he do with it?" She did not answer. "Anyway, what does a shawl prove?"

"I think Shafiq telling something."

"But how would Shafiq know? He's too blind to have seen anything, and besides, he's too cowardly."

But I was not convinced. In that house, nothing disappeared. Not with Amma around. Certainly not with Hasan. That was a house in which gossip traveled so fast, people knew your business even before you did. And no one hesitated to solicit public opinions on even the most private matters.

But Luna and I could not locate the incriminating garment. We had to brace ourselves and wait for its reappearance.

❧

My twentieth birthday went nearly unnoticed in the
intrigue and pandemonium. Amma made sure there was
a cake – pink, ornate, insubstantial – and painfully sweet,
as she herself would like. But when Mr. Chowdhury was
absent from dinner and Hasan left the table before dessert
was served, she apologetically told me that birthdays were
not a big deal in Bengali culture, and I should not take it
personally. I was not used to being so cavalier about birthdays. But Amma and Luna made a point of staying at the
table with me until I'd finished my piece of cake and for
that I was grateful.

Three days later, we learned the results of the election:
Sheikh Mujib and the Awami League won, and the People's
Party of West Pakistan came a close, but undeniably second
place. Still, the martial law administrator, Yahya Khan
refused to call a parliament, refused to resign his presidency.
The two leaders toured parts of the country from where they
received support, loudly declaring their victories, each de-
nouncing the other for lack of cooperation.

"Bhutto is desperate. He is a lame duck," Hasan declared
at tea time, "and he knows it."

"Unfortunately, I suspect he wields more power than we
acknowledge," Mr. Chowdhury said, and emptied his cup.
"Now come." The two of them were headed for the mosque,
hungry for new rumours to fuel their discussions.

Politically, the country was in upheaval. Though some
political prisoners were released and Bhutto announced
support for maximum provincial control in a new constitution, these were seen by most people in East Pakistan as
empty gestures. The prices of rice, oil, dal and vegetables
shot through the roof. People postponed their plans for

holidays, weddings, moving and other major changes until there was clear indication of what would happen in the coming days.

The political situation distracted everyone, including me, from Christmas. Though aware of its approach, I had none of the cues I'd get back home – no shopping malls, no tinsel and lights along The Gut, no advertisements, no frantic people scouring the shelves of Knapp's, or Jacobson's if they were flush enough, for festive purchases. No snow. In Dhaka, the sun was much lower in the sky and it was cool during the day – I carried a shawl. It was cold and foggy some nights, and I snuggled up underneath the mothball-smelling, cotton-filled kantha, that mysteriously appeared on my bed one evening. No doubt it was Shafiq's doing, though I wondered how he lifted and folded the bulky quilt without tumbling backwards.

So I allowed the arrival of Christmas to become absorbed into the background of my life. I thought little about it until my father phoned from Lansing. It was Christmas morning for me, Christmas Eve for him.

"Busy these days?" I asked.

"The girls' hockey team's doing well. We might make the finals this year." He taught physical education, and coached most of the school's teams in the area tournaments.

Hockey seemed so far away. "That's good."

"Roo, I'm sending a gift," he said abruptly. "Some money."

"Oh Dad, you don't have to. It's not like Christmas means anything here. We can celebrate when I get back."

"It's for your ticket home – plus a little extra. Think of it as a Christmas and graduation gift combined. Roo, I want you to see a little of the country. Maybe go to India for a week or two."

"But I have classes."

"When you get a break then. No point missing the opportunity. Who knows when you'll get back to that part of the world?"

There was a wheeze on the line, followed by a high-pitched squeal, and I was connected to another conversation entirely. Two men shouted over one another in a language I could not identify.

"Dad?" Then, a pop, and my father was back on the line.

"Are you there, Roo?" His voice was more distant.

"I can hear you."

"Good. The bank said someone will call."

"Merry Christmas, Dad. Thanks."

But the line faded. "Can you hear me? It's only fifteen hundred –"

"I can hear you." One thousand five hundred? Where on earth did he get that kind of money? "Dad – " I started my protest, but there was a burst of static. Before I could tell him such excess was not necessary, before he heard me say thank you, the line went dead. No amount of effort on my part could rouse the operator to put a call back through to him.

We gathered around Beth's table for Christmas dinner – her family, the Chowdhurys, and me. Beth's two boys were dressed in little velvet vests and miniature bow-ties, one in red, the other in green. Her husband cut the turkey, though from the way he held the knife, like a hacksaw, I could see this was a task with which he was not familiar.

"Where did you find turkey?" I asked Beth.

"Wild," she said. "You can get anything here, if you know where to look or who to ask, isn't that right Salma? White or dark?"

We were quietly eating – it felt awkward to be back to knives and forks – when Beth turned to Mr. Chowdhury. "So Yahya Khan is coming to Dhaka next week."

"He dare not show his face here," Hasan said.

"Tch tch," Mr. Chowdhury said. "And why not? We are not yet barbarians, though they may be." He turned to Beth. "It is true there is talk of such a visit. There is need for high level political meetings right now, isn't it?"

"Where is Bhutto then? Why is he not coming?" Beth asked. "As leader of the new official opposition, surely his presence is demanded."

"He will not accept the opposition mantle, you know," Mr. Chowdhury said. "This is between Yahya Khan and our future president, Bangabandhu."

"But Bhutto must be made to cooperate. His alliance must be secured, whatever the cost," Hasan said. "Just yesterday, Noor Alam Siddiky told us…"

"Noor Alam Siddiky is a boy trying on men's shoes and stumbling with each and every step. His father should have given him a good thrashing years ago. These student leaders are spreading harmful gossips. You should not pay heed to such speculation. It will only serve to draw us into battle."

"Your papa is right, dear," Amma said. "Bangabandhu has instructed us to remain non-violent."

"But such a course is no longer possible. Our people have no choice but to fight back," Hasan cried.

Nervous glances were exchanged around the table.

There was still a great deal of concern about the state of Amma's blood pressure, and topics of dissension were definitely out of bounds until her condition improved.

"But it will be the non-cooperation movement that will win in the end," she persisted.

Hasan was right about one thing: Bhutto, despite clearly coming second place in the election, refused to cooperate with the democratic process, and things were heading nowhere without some sort of alliance with him, no matter how tenuous or brief. But Bhutto refused all overtures. He was as stubborn as Hasan when it came down to it. Convincing either of them of anything would take extraordinary measures. But war? I didn't believe it. Contemporary world affairs and recent history were behind me.

"I agree with Amma. Non-cooperation is definitely the way to go. Look at history. Gandhi proved it and the rest of the world is following," I said.

"We have tried Gandhi's way for nearly twenty-five years now," Hasan said, "and if you were following *our* history, you would see just how little progress we have made with it."

Beth's husband chuckled. "You know the definition of politics, do you Robin?" I shook my head. "It's two people in a room."

"Now, hush, you two," Amma cut in. "Please don't get started. Not today."

But I wasn't finished. "You have to give it time," I said to Hasan. "It takes years to build a conflict, and an equal number of years to defuse it. Anyway, in practical terms, peace is also the most productive. You catch more flies with honey than you do with vinegar."

"At a time like this, you talk of vinegar and – flies?"

"Hush," Amma repeated. "This is a celebration. And a time of peace."

"Yes," Beth said. "Let us remember why we are here."

Considering the occasion and Amma's blood pressure, I held my tongue. So did everyone else.

But the silence lived only a brief life. "Well, you had better enjoy it," Hasan said. "From what I am hearing, the time of peace will soon be over."

Beth's husband raised his water glass then, and proposed a toast to peace. Our glasses rose and came together obediently, bringing immediately to mind the image of drawn swords colliding in union before the big battle rather than the usual images I associated with the season.

❧

In mid-January, the weather turned, and at midday, I felt a hint of the heat that I remembered from my arrival seven months ago. Though it felt good, I remembered the way it seared my skin just before the monsoon. I packed away my shawl and when, one night, I folded the kantha and pulled it to the foot of the bed, it disappeared just as mysteriously as it had appeared a few weeks ago.

Shafiq, who no doubt was responsible for the removal of the bedding, was not so fortunate. A nasty cold settled into him just after Christmas. While the rest of us were shedding our woolens, he wrapped his head in a shawl, his body in a couple of thick sweaters, and coughed and horked his way through the day. The extra layers made him waddle like a penguin, though his body was far too emaciated to really bring to mind one of those rotund creatures.

My Bangla took a sudden turn for the better, and I discovered I could understand more conversation and actually participate – not as intelligently as I wanted, but it was an improvement. I signed up for a course in modern Bengali lit. When I entered the classroom, I was surprised to see Shaheed among the students. Legs askew, his kurta bunched up at his waist, he slouched behind a little desk.

I reddened. Though I had seen him several times since the wedding, it was always in the presence of several of the Chowdhurys. Not that I would have wanted to be alone with him either. I needed to first understand the meaning of our moment outside the kitchen at the wedding, and it was hardly something I could ask him about.

The shape of his hands had remained with me and yet, I still did not quite know what to make of our moment in the kitchen corridor. I would sometimes lie in bed at night with all the lights off, raise my hands and curl them into the shape they were in when Shaheed had held them. By the insubstantial light from the night sky, I found that if I stared at my hands long enough, I could almost see his hands cradling mine again. The image seemed perfect, and as much as I tried to convince myself that such a notion was silly and naïve, I kept arriving back at the same place. Yet I remained uncomfortable when it came to naming it.

He'd been friendly enough since then and we exchanged the usual winks and wry glances mostly having to do with the Chowdhury family's various dramas. But I'd detected nothing different in his manner with me, leading me to suppose I was forcing significance onto a singular event that really amounted to nothing more than affection between friends. Perhaps it was our cultural differences that blinded my ability to understand.

"Chotto bon," he cried. He sat up, pursed his lips and laid a hand on his heart – a wicked imitation of Mr. Chowdhury greeting a relative to whom he felt just slightly inferior. Shaheed's trademark grin slashed across his face. He knew I knew.

It would be good to share a class.

The professor entered. She was tall and angled, physically Amma's opposite, with dark skin and a droopy bun on the back of her head. Her saree was plain cotton with minimal trim. Simple sandals shuffled across the floor. People sat, papers stopped rustling.

She wrote on the board with chalk that seemed to disintegrate with each stroke – Prof. Selina Akhtar. "Welcome," she said. "Take your reading list." She nodded at a boy, who leapt up and began distributing the papers she handed him. I glanced at it – Tagore and Nazrul, of course. I knew them already. But Sunil Gangopadhyay, Syed Waliullah, Akhtaruzzaman Elias? Intellectual hunger welled up in me. This was the course I'd been waiting for.

Professor Akhtar began lecturing right away in a voice thick as melted chocolate. She spoke slowly and clearly, and even though it was all Bangla, I understood.

We were to read ten novels in her course. With a nod to me and a student from Czechoslovakia, she offered the option of reading English translations – though three of the books were available only in Bangla. I was still struggling over the script, sometimes arcane, for there seemed to be no end to the ways the consonants could be jammed together to make sounds unheard of in English. But I vowed to try, certain the books would make clear the things about Bengali culture that had been puzzling me, things I could never ask Amma, even if I knew she were able to explain them. I wanted to understand the coarse thread that wove the divergent levels of society together; I wanted explanations for unwritten and unspoken rules; and desperately I needed to know the true meaning of respectable and what it meant not to be born so. I sensed there were layers and contradictions, though mostly I just found them incomprehensible and, as a result, frustrating. I knew there had to exist concrete answers and I hoped these writers would provide them.

Protest poetry by Sufia Kamal, Shamsur Rahman and Sukanto Bhottacharya were also on the syllabus. I thought it an admirable way to affect change, certainly preferable to the violence espoused by Hasan and his type, more of which seemed to be appearing every day.

As the liberation movement flourished, and advocated more aggressive tactics, Hasan ate and breathed it like a small boy collecting hockey or baseball cards. He let his hair grow even longer, as long as Amma would permit, in imitation of his heroes. A beard grew in patches on his cheeks, jaw and neck. He spoke of Mao, Marx, the people, and the revolution. The tiny, outdated nowka pin which began to sprout rust never left his lapel. His urgent pleas to Amma to allow him to join the movement were rebuffed. "It is the wrong course of action, your Abba and I agree. Besides, you have responsibilities to your studies."

"But Amma – studies cease to be relevant in the face of such intolerable oppression as our nation is experiencing."

"Studies are always relevant. Studies are your future. Violence is not."

"All the boys are joining. Some girls, too."

"And since when do we take a course of action because others have chosen it?" Mr. Chowdhury asked. Amma nodded vigourously.

I thought skeptically about this question, in light of all the things Amma had told me I must do – and not do – in order that others not get the wrong impression. Was there a subtlety that I was missing, that allowed double standards to sit so easily on their shoulders? For the moment, though, I saw no reason to point out their inconsistency lest it interrupt the castigation of Hasan.

"You will do as your mother says. Studies first. Politics only when they are satisfactorily completed."

"You should look to Mahatma Gandhi for guidance," I offered.

Hasan bristled. "Guidance? What guidance has he to offer? The man's deteriorating mental health was well-known, as even a junior student of world affairs could tell you."

"He practiced what he preached. Civil disobedience is the only way to deal with intolerable violence. He knew what it meant to turn the other cheek because he did so often himself."

"When the most pivotal moment of his life occurred, he was a coward. The fool sat idly by while Pakistan was hammered together from pieces that any child would tell you do not fit."

"What was he supposed to do? Get a rifle and shoot the dissenters? Is that what bravery means? They'd just have gotten some bigger rifles and shot back. That's all violence can do – make more violence. And in the end, is that justifiable? Where does it stop?"

"It is good you mention the end. Because it will come for Bengalis. For our language and culture, if we do not fight back."

He left the room, drawing the argument to a close – for now. I didn't think Gandhi deserved all the blame for the creation of a divided Pakistan, but for certain, especially with people like Hasan, the two halves would never see eye to eye.

꽃

It took six weeks before I found out that all the closed doors and silences in the Chowdhury home had nothing to do with fallout from the election or the by now impending confrontation of east and west. I was sure Amma had not meant to tell me. She interrupted a lesson on the different words Muslims, Hindus and Christians use to describe their family relations. Fingers yet again pressed to her temple, she slid into her familiar refrain in English. "You cannot possibly understand what a burden it is to raise a daughter."

"Sorry Amma, I know I've asked you before but I still don't understand. Why would it be any different from raising a son? Why wouldn't it depend on the child?" I knew these were among the questions about society that Amma found the most difficult to answer and though I didn't expect any answer today either, I couldn't let her comment pass.

She sighed deeply. "Though I explain everything, you still do not understand our culture. Luna must be protected."

"From what exactly?" I considered that I had again

missed something, and that perhaps Luna was in danger related to the unrest.

Amma pressed her lips together. "It is time," she said finally, "for Luna to marry. Mr. Chowdhury is looking for a suitable boy and if the families agree, we will have the wedding before grishokal."

Wedding? A suitable boy? Her words whirled like a storm. Grishokal, grishokal, it was a season, but which one, when, I couldn't remember. "You mean arrange a marriage for Luna?"

"But of course." Amma frowned. "What else would I have meant?"

Then I remembered. Grisho was the hot season. It began in three months. I was struck dumb. Luna would have an arranged marriage in less than three months.

Of course I knew about arranged marriage. It happened all the time, and had even happened to California Qashem. I must have been naïve to think it would not happen to Luna. As eventually it would happen to Hasan. And Shaheed, too.

I had just never imagined an arranged marriage happening to anyone I knew. I couldn't imagine myself married to someone I didn't even know, let alone love.

"We have been too distracted of late – elections, the cyclone. We have not been doing our duty to our daughter," Amma continued.

I needed to help Luna. Though I knew I could never sway Amma from the idea of an arranged marriage, perhaps I could try to delay the proceedings – at least until she found the courage to introduce Razzak to her family.

"But what about her studies? You always tell Hasan his studies are important."

She dismissed my words with the wave of a hand.

There was one more chance to help Luna though it carried some risk. "Perhaps she knows someone she'd like to marry," I ventured.

Amma laughed. "Oh, Robin, you have very American ideas. A love match is not possible and besides, where would she meet anyone – suitable? And it precisely because I am her mother that I need to take this decision. The more I think about it, the more I am convinced. Luna must be married before summer."

⋇

Then Shaheed disappeared.

His parents called early one Friday morning when he failed to show up for breakfast. They became even more frantic when they discovered he had not spent the night at the Chowdhurys. It was early February, and the days were growing longer and warmer and the flamboyant spring blossoms danced on trees that lined the paths on campus.

"We will find him," Mr. Chowdhury said. "I will make inquiries, isn't it?"

"Abba, you must pull out all stops," Hasan said.

"His poor mother," Amma declared with hand-wringing. "Inshallah, another tragedy shall not befall his family." Though his mother had remarried long ago, his father by birth was a national hero who had died in the 1952 language movement. Shortly after Shaheed told me about his father over tea and biscuits, I began to repeatedly spot his father's scratchy, indistinct photo in the newspapers.

I, too, felt worried, but refused to give in to panic.

Though it was not like him to stay away all night without telling his family, it was possible. More than likely, I surmised, he'd been visiting another friend's home and when he finally decided to leave, it was quite late, and so he'd decided to stay. Then, not atypically, the phone lines were down when he tried to call home, and were probably still down. It wasn't hard to find a plausible and comforting explanation. He would turn up shortly.

"Don't worry, Amma. They'll find him at someone else's place. And if not, he'll be back after Jumma prayer."

They all looked irritated. Mr. Chowdhury blinked as though facing a sandstorm.

Hasan seethed. "Don't you understand? He's been taken into custody."

"Shaheed? What for?" I almost laughed.

"You are a stupid." Hasan stormed from the room.

Shaheed was not found at anyone else's house, was not back after the prayer as I had predicted, did not get home for supper, nor for breakfast the next day. In fact, he was gone three whole days and nights. After the second night, I had to admit my version of things was wrong. I had to consider the possibility that Hasan was right about the custody.

I then began to think the worst – everyone had heard the stories about boys being taken into custody and never being seen again. Though my anxiety and distress were strong, they were lost in the Chowdhury home as Mr. Chowdhury and Hasan came and went, struggling to locate him, while Amma and Luna cried or wailed with each bit of news they discovered.

Finally, his mother called to report his reappearance. Amma and Luna cried, but Mr. Chowdhury and Hasan skulked off behind the study door. Low voices could be heard through the lock and the cracks. "I knew they'd find him," I said though by that time no one else was in the room.

As soon as I could be alone with her, I asked Amma, "So what happened?"

"He has returned, thank God. God, in His graciousness, has seen fit to return a son," she said piously. "This is the only important fact of the matter. The rest we need not mention – ever."

I didn't see Shaheed again until the following week, on campus, outside the TSC. Students lazed on the steps to take in as much pleasant weather as possible before the heat enveloped us. But when Shaheed surfaced, boys and girls sprung to their feet and jostled for a look at the celebrity. He was mobbed.

Between the bodies, I tried to locate his face. I expected a bruise, a broken nose, a missing tooth. Or perhaps something less physical – the kind of wound that remains trapped inside, a darkness that slips out through the eyes. But no. No broken bones, no apparent injury. When I finally caught Shaheed's eye, I flashed him a peace sign. But he held my gaze without expression, and then turned away. At that moment, I felt the ground slip out from under my feet, and I had to sit back down on the steps. The notebook I'd been holding fell too. It was open. Pages and pages of things I'd written scattered. Inside me, light had turned to dark, up to down. I felt more alone than I had ever felt in my life – as though everything I'd ever understood came up short when laid up against some great measuring stick I hadn't even known existed.

.

It took days before I could see him alone. We went for tea at the canteen. He hunched over the table, and with a crooked finger, spun his worn glass in slow circles, as though winding it up.

"I still don't know what happened to you," I began, not wanting to ask directly.

He looked sad as a clown.

"Was it bad? I mean, of course it was –" I cut myself off before I said anything else asinine. Three students walked behind his chair and whispered all the way to the other side of the room.

Still, I wanted to know and I couldn't keep quiet. "And why you of all people? OK, your father's a martyr, but you're not your father. That much is obvious. I don't get it."

But more than wanting to know why and how, I wanted back the old Shaheed. I wanted him to wink and tell me everything was fine. I wanted his experience in custody to be erased at least for this moment so we could be as we once were. I needed the chasm of language and history and culture to stop widening and reverse its direction.

I reached across the table in an effort to retrieve his old self, and cupped his hands which cupped his tea. I thought how he had held my hands at the wedding, and so I adjusted my hands to assume that same shape. There arose from that gesture something meaningful and gentle I wanted to say, but not knowing what it was, or how to form the words, I instead found myself falling back on ideas. "Custody – what a ridiculous idea. The violence perpetrated by institutions in authority in the name of politics is reprehensible. Everyone must commit to peace through negotiation."

He sighed, deeply and painfully, so wearily I thought

I might cry. I held on across the divide, though I felt him slipping further away. "I envy you your commitment to your beliefs," he finally said. "You make it sound so simple." He looked up, his face naked and aged. I withdrew my hands.

"You are right about another point as well. I am certainly not my father. If there was ever any doubt, now I know. I don't have it in me."

৵

Rafiqul Alam was completing a Ph.D. in chemical engineering in New York City. During reading week, he would be in Dhaka to view prospective brides, pre-selected by his family. He was, according to his family's report, tall, fair-skinned, intelligent, gentle, athletic, family-oriented, literate, God-fearing and anxious to marry. The photos showed a serious but stunningly handsome man. He could have been a Greek god.

Like the obedient daughter she was, Luna looked at the pictures and said nothing, reluctant to be the cause of any more of Amma's fainting spells. Inside, I willed her to speak up and say something but my message was lost and she remained silent.

"His father's business is reputedly worth several crore," Mr. Chowdhury said. "Very respectable."

"But America," Amma moaned. "When will I see my daughter?"

"He will join the family business here in Dhaka. An office in Motijheel has already been designated in anticipation of his return. I expect this will be their home base, but that they will retain some presence in America. Perhaps a small flat in Manhattan?"

Their home base. *They* will retain. Had Mr. Chowdhury already made up his mind? Did he have no interest in his daughter's feelings?

"Luna? Would you like to see the new World Trade Centre?" Amma grinned like a scarecrow and spoke as though coaxing a toddler to down a forkful of liver and spinach.

Luna again said nothing.

"He is a son of this soil, through and through," Mr. Chowdhury said. "Of course, if Luna doesn't like him –" But the way he said it made it clear: this was a suitable match and Luna had better like him.

Even I had to admit Rafiqul Alam appeared to have everything and Luna would have a hard time finding fault. When we were finally alone, she buried her face in her pillow.

"Maybe it's just a flattering photo," I offered. "Perhaps he's not as tall as they say. Maybe he's not very nice. When you meet him –"

"I will not meet him," Luna said, her voice muffled. "I will not."

But she did. Rafiqul Alam and his parents appeared for tea that Friday afternoon. The photo was, indeed, not accurate. Rafiqul Alam was even more gorgeous in person. It was almost unnatural. He spoke English beautifully – with a perfect British accent, better suited for the other side of the ocean, yes, but lending him a sophisticated and intelligent air. He carried himself like royalty, but there was nothing snobbish about him. He was *so* nice. He listened attentively while the parents exchanged pleasantries, spoke jovially with Hasan about cricket, politely inquired about my impressions of East Pakistan, and offered other opinions only when asked.

He was not the demon I had been expecting. I had been prepared to dislike him, and to spend hours later with Luna dissecting his many flaws. But Mr. Chowdhury had located not only what he thought was a suitable son-in-law but someone who was just a really pleasant person. Even from this one brief meeting, I could see Luna and Rafiqul together. Maybe not married, but dating. Maybe one day falling in love and getting married – but of their own accord, not because of some antiquated tradition that oppressed women's rights. But such imaginings felt disloyal to Luna. The fact was she *had* met someone somewhere else and *had* fallen in love with him and *did* want to marry him of her own accord. Surely this was more important than having one's parents find a successful match.

Rafiqul Alam smiled generously at Luna from time to time, though she refused to look at him.

"Luna?" Amma prompted when it became obvious and uncomfortable. "Tell this pleasant young man what you were saying about New York City."

For the first time since the Alam family arrived, all eyes turned to Luna. It was as though they were finally getting down to business. Luna, however, would not speak.

Amma laughed nervously. "These prospective brides! So bashful! But a little modesty goes a long way in a young girl, don't you think?" she said to Mrs. Alam, while I bristled into my tea. "Luna was just saying how much she would like to visit the new World Trade Centre."

"Oh." Rafiqul smiled. "But it's just opened – and not

really very interesting inside – far more impressive from the outside. Nevertheless, there are many more beautiful places in the city."

"Excuse me," Luna said. She rose and left the room, leaving behind stunned silence.

Amma waited a discreet ten minutes. If this was a washroom break, Luna had to be finished. Then Amma went to fetch her.

It became increasingly uncomfortable in the room as we all awaited their return. The Alams were shifting nervously in their seats, and just when I thought for certain they would leave, Luna and Amma reappeared. Luna's eyes were red, the flesh around them swollen and moist.

After a decent interval, the Alams took their leave. "Thank you for the lovely tea," Mrs. Alam murmured.

Rafiqul graciously thanked Amma, then carried his majestic body out of the house without looking at Luna. The Chowdhurys never heard from them again. Afterward, I felt a little badly for Amma who was embarrassed by the whole episode, though she would never let on, and for Mr. Chowdhury, too, who had, I thought, found a reasonable match which, I assumed, took considerable thought and care. But I didn't feel badly enough to change my mind about Luna's future.

"You have to help," Luna said. "My heart will break." Her hand stroked Razzak's shawl, which rested beside her on the bed. Though we halfway expected the incriminating evidence to reappear, we didn't count on Amma's strategy.

As soon as the Alams left, Amma staged a mother-daughter showdown behind the bedroom door. She quietly blind-sided Luna with the shawl.

Now I understood why Amma kept the incompetent but inordinately loyal Shafiq in their home.

"Then make it clear what you want."

"I can't. I can't. They will never allow it. They will rather kill me."

I was fed up and tired. Tired of the creeping around, and having to always watch my back. I was tired of Luna's constant melodrama, and how every little event in her progression toward marriage assumed some gargantuan proportion when all she had to do was tell her parents. I confess I also felt slightly sorry for poor, rejected Rafiqul, though I was certain he would land on his feet. Maybe I was wasting my time butting up against a tradition that, I had to admit, I found incomprehensible. Perhaps Luna should just listen to her parents and marry the next boy they found for her and save everyone a lot of grief.

"If you won't tell them how you feel, then only one thing is possible," I said more harshly than I intended. "You will marry someone else."

Luna's tears began anew. "But I cannot. I would rather die. You are the only one who understands me."

Contrite, I toyed with the fringe on the shawl and thought about the idyllic afternoon in the Botanical Garden we had shared, when our world was entirely different. Why should she have to live her entire life like this? It seemed so unfair.

"Tell me Apa, what can I do?" She wiped her face with her dupatta, a broad stroke from chin to forehead. Her nose was runny, but even still, she was beautiful. "What would you do?"

I answered honestly and spontaneously. "I would run away."

"Run away?"

"Sure. If I really loved him, and I felt there was no other option. But hey, that's me. I still think you should give your parents a chance."

She looked doubtful.

"It's not such a big deal as you think. And even if they do get upset, they'll come around."

Luna thought for a moment, her eyes searching the corners of the ceiling for answers.

I sensed advantage. "Trust me. I know exactly what they're like."

Luna was her father's favourite and could do no wrong in his eyes. As for Mrs. Chowdhury, she'd do whatever her husband said. So I knew it was just a matter of time before they'd come to accept their daughter's choice of husband.

Luna bit her lip and looked worried. Then a smile bloomed on her face. "You are right, Apa. I will do it. I will run away with Razzak. I don't need Amma or Abba or Hasan if I can have Razzak."

"No, no, no," I said. "That's not what I meant. Just because I would do something doesn't mean you should – not while there are other options –" But then I heard myself. The hypocrisy I was spouting. If it was good enough for me, why wouldn't it be good enough for her?

"And you will help us," she continued.

"No – how?"

"You give me money."

Fifteen crisp hundred dollar bills, handed to me through a barred wicket by a bank teller with oiled hair, sour breath and fingers covered with gemmed rings, were stashed beneath the mattress in my room. I didn't want to give them away. I'd already begun planning a train trip to Calcutta, Benares and Bombay at the end of my stay; from there, I'd fly home. But I thought about all Luna had given me. Her friendship, her sisterhood, sharing her friends, her clothes. My ally against Hasan. Was this friendship not worth several times fifteen hundred dollars? And the idea of my friend ending up in an arranged marriage, even to a man as perfect as Rafiqul Alam, made me sick. I had no doubt Luna and Razzak were right for each other. And if no one else would intervene to make things right, then it would be up to me. It took me less than a minute to put aside my doubts and decide. I knew what the noble course of action was, what was required of me.

"Oh Apa, you are saving my life. Thank you." She scooped up my hand and kissed it. I shivered.

※

A boy in a green kurta distributed notices on campus. Like a Spartan quarterback in the Rose Bowl, he shouldered his way through the crowd until he blocked my path. "Take it, American girrrl." He growled out that "rrr" like an angry mantra, then disappeared in a flutter of cotton. I couldn't stop to see what he'd given me. The flow of students was too thick and persistent, and I had no choice but to allow myself to be moved along with it. It was like the weather. I didn't like it, but if I wanted to get to class, what else could I do?

I was finally able to slip out of the crowd's current and shelter beside a water tank near my next class. In the shadow, I smoothed the thin, yellow notice. In the centre was a grainy black and white photo of a dead man. Cloudy eyes, chest bare and smooth like a child's. His slit-open windpipe poked out of his gaping throat. He looked like butchered poultry. A blotch beneath the slash was either ink or blood.

I looked up. Had anyone else received a notice? Had anyone seen me? I spotted Ruby in the throng. "Ruby!" I waved the notice to draw her attention. "Ruby!" I called louder. But she was swallowed up in the chaotic tide, though I suspected there were other reasons she didn't hear me. She never seemed to spend time with Luna anymore whenever I was around.

The rest of the notice was covered with blurry, smudged script. I could make out and understand only one word. Kukur. Dog.

I showed Amma during our lesson that afternoon. "Where did you get this?"

"University. What does it say?"

She sighed. "It is troubling news. From Khulna. It says this farmer – a local politician – was found last week beside his paddy. He was killed after speaking in support of independence at a meeting in his village. Who gave you this?"

I told her. Also how he had growled.

"Robin, dear, you must be more careful."

I laughed. Me, even more careful? Under Amma's thumb, not to mention Hasan's vigilant eye, I could be no less careful unless I shackled myself to the bedpost. In any case, I had no idea what I could possibly do to prevent someone handing me a notice. "But Amma – it's not personal or anything."

She gave me another bewildered Amma look. "You do not understand."

"Amma – the guy was looking for attention, that's all. He was probably pagol." I tapped my finger on my temple.

She ran the heel of her hand down the spine of the book in front of us and appeared to be contemplating what to say next. "Just heed my warning, if you please. And beware. Now – shall we begin your lesson?"

"Wait. Please explain it."

She examined me. Though neither of us moved, it was, for an instant, as though we were magnets, our identical poles meeting, then pushing us apart. I felt, rather than saw the physical differences in our skin, eyes and hair. "It's just that these days people know Americans are supporting the government of West Pakistan. You are giving guns to protect your regional interests."

I looked again at the farmer's windpipe. "But no one associates me with decisions made in Washington."

Her voice lowered. "They say the guns will be used – against the Bengalis – not the communists." She paused. "And then who will protect us? When attacks like this occur in our motherland, where is the American government with its guns and bombs?"

"Amma, I'm fine. Everyone is friendly and really nice." I decided not to mention the apparent cooling of my friendship with Shaheed, or Ruby's turned shoulder. "Thik ache. We're all going to be okay."

"I worry that our world is changing. You may not be safe here any longer."

The birds chattered outside, a rickshaw bell rang in the distance, an ice cream wallah called down the street, and Kamala or Shafiq rattled aluminum pots in the kitchen. I couldn't imagine feeling further from danger. So the country was going through a troubled period which would be worked out in time. It was safe here, as safe as anywhere. "You shouldn't worry about me. I'm not worried." I offered a confident smile to sweep aside Amma's concern.

"Your Embassy called this morning," Amma said. "The security chief asked my husband whether it would be more prudent if you went to stay with an American family in Gulshan."

I was stunned. "But that's ridiculous."

"Initially, we thought so, too. Now I wonder. This notice is disturbing. Perhaps the Embassy is right and we can no longer protect you." There was that absurd notion again. This country was filled with people who wanted to protect me and yet, what protection did I need? "I will show this notice to my husband and we will inform you of our decision in the morning."

"But I don't want to go. Please, Amma – "

Amma wheezed a dramatic sigh. The subject was closed. She pointed to the text. "A Day in the Life of a Farmer. This is a useful lesson."

"They're overreacting."

"Krishok. This means farmer."

I sighed now. "I know, Amma. You already told me."

꙰

Mr. Chowdhury announced his decision over breakfast.

Luna cried, Hasan looked smug, while Amma tut-tutted and declared it was the only sensible course of action.

I argued. "But I've got a major essay due for my Bengali lit class, and then there will be exams. I need to concentrate on my studies or I might lose my year. Besides, the Embassy is known to err on the side of caution."

Mr. Chowdhury was adamant. "This is for the best. You can finish your studies in Gulshan as well as you can here. Please attempt to understand our position, too."

"I do understand," I said, "it's just that I'm perfectly safe right now. And I'd rather stay here."

"You will visit us, Robin dear. Our home is your home," Amma declared.

Then I had a flash. "Could we ask Beth? Whatever she says, I will do. I promise." Though a gamble, I was fairly certain Beth, whose views were measured without being extreme, would understand right away and do what I was unable to do – convince them to let me stay.

The Chowdhurys glanced at each other. Mr. Chowdhury barely inclined his head – Amma understood he had given his consent.

That afternoon, Beth came for tea. I didn't have a chance to speak before Amma squirreled her away in the drawing room. The door closed with a great flourish. After half an hour, I was invited to join them. I could read nothing from their faces.

"You are brave, Robin," Beth said. "You know the foreign missions have begun the repatriation of children and dependents?"

"Brave?" I snorted and rolled my eyes. "There's nothing to be afraid of."

"Perhaps. But you understand the position you are putting the Chowdhurys in?" Beth continued. "If anything happens –"

"But it won't."

"Pardon me?" Beth's eyebrows shot up.

"Nothing's going to happen. Everyone's exaggerating the danger. You know it."

"How could I know what even the country's leaders do not?"

I blushed. "What I mean is that it isn't so bad that I should have to leave. Not yet, anyway. Let me stay – for now. And then, when you think it's become too dangerous, I promise I'll go. I won't argue."

Beth and Amma exchanged a glance. Then Amma sighed. "All right. You may stay for now. But you must make adequate preparations in case it becomes necessary to leave the country quickly."

I leapt up and hugged her. "Anything, Amma, anything. Thank you."

Though I longed for her approval, Beth would not meet my eye. It made me suspect her advice had not swayed Amma, but rather Amma had come to her own conclusion. Whatever the case, I would have a few more days or weeks – perhaps even months – with the Chowdhurys, depending on how the political situation unfolded.

Besides keeping a suitcase packed, I had to make arrangements to fly home. On Friday, after mosque, Mr. Chowdhury and Hasan took me to the airport to get an official chit. The national airline, anxious to have the exodus appear calm and orderly, was assigning numbers to people who, in case of serious violence, would have to depart.

Passengers would be called according to their assigned place in the queue. We joined a throng of people jostling to reach a small desk.

A woman in front of us, very pregnant, fell down. A young man wearing an obscene opal ring stepped over her to take her place in line. With one hand, Hasan helped the woman up, while with the other, he grabbed the young man's shirt. Mr. Chowdhury tugged Hasan's arm. "Aste, aste," he cautioned. Slowly, slowly. But Hasan shrugged his father's hand away. Others jumped into the fray, and one shoved the ringed man, who stumbled and bumped up against someone else. When two armed soldiers appeared, Hasan and the crowd simmered down. Confrontation was then limited to hostile looks.

We passed the rest of the time waiting and listening to the roar of jets as three planes took off, one after the other. I wondered who was in them, where they were going.

Then a plane landed. If it was so dangerous, who on earth would be coming to the country now? A troubled look passed over Mr. Chowdhury's face, and he gave a significant glance to Hasan, but his son was looking off in the direction of the runway.

Finally I reached the desk. A harried woman in an airline uniform wrote down my name and gave me a chit. Number two hundred and three. She told me to watch the newspapers, and keep in touch with the airline and my embassy. When my departure date was determined, they would tell me. On that date, I would have to come to the airport with my luggage and cash for my ticket.

"Come," said Hasan. He cleared a path through the crowd.

We drove back to Dhanmondi in silence. The cars lined up to get to the airport far outnumbered those cruising out the gates.

⁂

In the midst of this change, Shafiq and Kamala fell into the background of my life. I knew they were there, for my bed was religiously made, my bathroom consistently cleaned, hot food always on the table. But I paid little attention to them. I was fully engrossed in Luna's situation. We schemed to avoid the next prospective groom. I covered for her, made excuses to Amma and Hasan when she and Razzak had arranged a rendezvous.

"I needing him like desert needing the water," she declared one night. It was disgraceful that they had been kept apart.

I was curious about their plans. "Where will you go?"

She frowned. "Razzak say I must tell no one." She looked down. "I sorry." I squeezed her hand. I understood.

I was so completely involved in their situation that Shafiq's announcement that he wanted to leave immediately for his village took me by surprise. The anti-Pakistani demonstrations were growing in his district, and he wanted to help. Amma was reluctant because she needed him in the kitchen. But as with all troubling decisions, no matter how trifling, she deferred until she could take matters to her husband.

"That man a protester?" Mr. Chowdhury said, disbelieving. "Well, good for him. The autonomy movement knows no bounds. I give my blessing."

So Amma again handed over three hundred rupees and provisions, and released Shafiq from his duty. Once more, he tucked his prayer mat under his arm and left the next morning.

Hasan was green with envy, I could tell. For what he desperately needed and would never get – Amma's permission to join the independence movement – an ordinary house servant was easily granted.

꙳

Then Amma announced the arrival of the next prospective groom. Mohammed Akhtaruzzaman was a thirty-two-year-old businessman living in Calcutta. His pedigree was distinguished, his prospects excellent. He was already a junior vice-president in his uncle's jute export company. "Very respectable, Luna," said Mr. Chowdhury. "He is known to your cousin in Jessore." Mohammed Akhtaruzzaman would be in Dhaka at the end of the month on business, and would like to view potential brides.

"Razzak and me leaving," Luna said when we were alone.

"Don't you think you should wait?" Now that I had permission to stay, I did not want Luna to go so soon.

"For what? For more of Abba's pressures and Hasan's criticisms? For Amma to cry like the broken water pipe again? No."

She and Razzak had a plan. They would leave the day I did. That part of the arrangement pleased me. I would have as much time with Luna as was possible. But there was sound strategy behind the decision as well. Amid the confusion and emotion that was certain to erupt that day, their absence would take time to percolate through the family's consciousness. And I would not be left in the uncomfortable position of having to account for her. I would be on a plane.

That left one huge problem. The money. I hadn't yet had the courage to tell her I now needed it – or, at least, most of it – to buy my own ticket. And there was no way I could ask my father for even more money. In the denial part of my brain, I kept thinking something would happen to resolve the issue before it came to a head. Now I had no choice but to confess.

Luna thought a moment. "You give me money. You tell Amma Shafiq taking your money."

"No!" I was horrified. "That's a lie."

"Apa, why not?" She spoke quickly, her words jumbled, as thoughts and feelings cascaded over one another. "Shafiq gone now. He is too much old. Probably he will not come back. He is getting another job. Maybe he staying in village now. No more working. Maybe he breathing his last. No one is knowing."

"But it's wrong. Besides, what good would it do? I still need to pay for my ticket."

"Apa, everyone feeling so sorry and worried. Abba give you money. I know it."

I was startled. I never expected Luna to be capable of such calculating deceit. Was Razzak behind this? No way. He could not possibly know about the money problem.

"But what if your parents call the police?" I said, thinking of another argument, though I was still most concerned about implicating rickety old Shafiq. "What happens if they want to interrogate me?"

"You don't tell until last minute. There will be much confusion, they won't knowing. Apa, they never will call police. Abba thinking Shafiq is take money for autonomy movement in his district. Maybe he think this not so bad. And Abba not like these police from the west wing. Amma agree, because they will take Kamala into custody, maybe beat her. There will be no police."

Luna's plan made sense. She knew her parents well, and their reactions were as clear to her as the palms of her own hands. Slowly, my reluctance diminished. By the time I handed over the fifteen hundred dollars, I was certain I was doing the right thing, proud of my part serving justice. Any suffering that Shafiq or the Chowdhurys would experience as a result of our plan was, I supposed then, a necessary sacrifice, and they would eventually get over it.

※

My number was called, and once Beth heard the news, she said, "Now is the right time." "But –" I said. But nothing – I had promised. My flight would depart March 25, just before midnight. I didn't have to be on it. I could move to Gulshan instead, then queue up and get another number, wait a while longer. But the streets of Dhaka were tense and Beth sensed this opportunity might not come again soon. I argued, but didn't put up much resistance. I knew Luna was now waiting for me to leave, so she could escape. Amma remembered my promise to heed Beth. "You are good to your word," she said. In the face of Amma's admiration, my strength wavered. But I pushed the uncertainty aside, and by the time I had finished packing, I once more felt noble about my sacrifice.

I remained a little nervous about the ticket and money. It was a lot of cash for anyone to have to come up with at the last moment. But even if Mr. Chowdhury could not, what was the worst that would happen? I would get a few extra days in East Pakistan until I got another chit and my father wired more money, which of course I would pay back once I found a job. In the meantime, I could withstand the queries about Luna's absence.

As March 25 grew nearer, rumours of an impending military crack-down spread up and down the street, magnified with each retelling. For three weeks, Hasan kept hearing of platoons of Pakistani troops secretly being flown into Dhaka. Word was the martial law administration would attack once they were in place. Mr. Chowdhury dismissed these reports. "Not while talks are continuing," he said, referring to the troubled but ongoing negotiations among Sheikh Mujib, Yahya Khan and Zia Ali Bhutto. Then he chuckled. "There are too many young men with overactive imaginations on our side, I fear." But Amma was nervous. To me she murmured, "You are getting out just in time."

Behind closed doors, Luna and I rehearsed our drama in whispers. She asked all the questions we thought might be possible. I practiced my answers until they sounded natural. Still, I was terrified Shafiq would reappear at the last minute and foil the plan. Or that I would collapse under pressure and be incapable of carrying out my role.

Two days before I was supposed to leave, Sheikh Mujib called for a national Resistance Day. Hasan left after breakfast and joined a crowd outside Mujib's house. After Bangabandhu spoke, Hasan attached himself to a group of demonstrators marching along Topkhana Road, throughout

Purana Paltan, and Ramna Park. He came home mid-afternoon with Shaheed, both of them dusty, hungry and flushed with excitement.

"Bangabandhu raised the flag of the independent Bangla Desh at his own house this morning," Hasan declared. "Surely the tide is turning."

"You boys must remain disciplined," Mr. Chowdhury warned. "Never forget that our chief strongly condemns all acts of violence and attempts to sabotage the movement through instigation of communal riots. Otherwise, what little progress has been achieved in the talks thus far will have been for naught." Though I concurred with his sentiments, I said nothing, so worried was I about my pending performance upon which Luna's future would depend.

"Take lunch," Amma said to Hasan and Shaheed. "I have mutton and roti."

After lunch, during which Hasan spoke passionately about the demonstration, Shaheed, in a gesture reminiscent of his old manner – perhaps now that I was about to depart, he felt duty-bound to perform some final act of friendship – offered to take me to Ramna Park to see the site where the masses had gathered so peacefully. Amma examined Shaheed as though assessing the odds of his becoming kidnap material again and then shook her head.

"It is too much tense today. You should instead take rest at home."

But Mr. Chowdhury surprised everyone by intervening. "On the eve of her departure, our American exchange student may like to have the opportunity to view this place which will no doubt go down in our history as a vital birthplace of autonomy. And when you are back in

America, you must tell your people. Go," he told us, "but remain cautious."

We careened down the streets toward Ramna Park on a rickshaw. Buoyed perhaps by the morning demonstration, something of Shaheed's old self emerged. He laughed and told the rickshawallah jokes many of which I understood until he reached the punch line. The two of them laughed again and again while I sat grasping at puns that seemed to fly about and then evaporate before I had the chance to take them in my hands long enough to make sense of them. Still, their laughter made me laugh and I was happy to witness Shaheed's joy that afternoon.

I could not still a suspicion that Shaheed was only putting on this façade of happiness out of a sense of duty toward me. However, I felt so relieved and happy he was back, and that we were alone once more that I decided to ignore my doubt.

When a moment of silence fell upon us, or Shaheed was between jokes, I was reminded that I still didn't know what to make of us as a couple. We'd never explored beyond our tentative hand-holding experiences, never discussed his recent retreat from our friendship. But as my departure loomed, every emotion felt disproportionately weighted, and frankly, I was confused and petrified. Did I really want to know exactly what I meant to Shaheed? I mentally ran from one extreme to the other and back again. He's my soul mate. No, a friend. Soul mate. Friend. I couldn't bear the thought of either one because even then, on the back of a rickshaw bouncing to Ramna Park, I could see how either answer would colour my time in East Pakistan and ripple through the rest of my life.

He paid the rickshawallah generously, and we walked through a gate and set out along a paved pathway. Shaheed showed me where the people had stood and chanted. The grass was flattened and strewn with rubbish. He pointed out the stage where Bangabandhu had stood only hours ago. It was being slowly dismantled.

We continued further down the path and wove around the stagnant fountain. Through some unspoken agreement, we found ourselves a private corner. A thick shrub rife with small white pin-wheeled flowers shielded us from much of the rest of the park, and certainly from other park visitors. We sat on untrampled grass, still moist from the gardeners' early morning watering. I crossed my legs while he folded his and hugged them against his body, his fingers intertwined.

"So now that you have seen this place," he said lightly, "what do you think of our Bangla Desh?"

"You're still East Pakistan as far as I know," I said, smiling and hoping not to change the mood.

"You can sit here – where the people have spoken just moments ago – and deny us the right to name our motherland?"

I laughed. "Mothers name their children – not the other way round. In any case, you can call it the moon for all I care. I will still remember it forever."

"For you, Robin Rowe, the moon it is then. One small step of the tongue, one giant leap of your imagination is all it will take." Ah, here was the irreverence I had been missing these past few weeks.

Birds called from the trees and in the distance, a tinny bell of an itinerant mistri was rung over and over again. True, the people had spoken – loudly, historically – but in proper Bengali fashion, it was now time to get on with the business of life.

I waited until I summoned and felt the force of my courage. "Shaheed, I've been wondering about something – and I might never get the chance to ask you again. You've been avoiding me. Why?"

He shifted. His eyes narrowed. I saw him contemplate a raft of responses, dismissing each one as unsatisfactory. How to answer the unanswerable. He squeezed and twisted his twined fingers.

"These days are troubling," he finally offered. "I'm sorry."

I nodded. "That doesn't really answer my question."

His face wrinkled as though he was in pain. "I don't know how to begin to explain it. I'm sorry." When he saw my face, he added, "I'm sure I must disappoint you."

It did disappoint me not to know what had happened between us and not to know how to discuss it and work it out. But it wasn't him. He didn't disappoint me at all. I thought of all the moments with the Chowdhurys when I needed an ally in the room, and there he was. When I needed a joke or a pat on the back, it was Shaheed who delivered it. When I needed some help with Bengali lit homework, he was always available and happy to help. True, I felt sad about the time we had lost. But it wasn't that *he* was a disappointment. Never.

"Oh no," was all I could manage. "That's not it at all. I'm so – pleased we met," I murmured, knowing 'pleased' was perhaps the most inadequate word I'd ever used in my life.

We drew closer. We kissed. So awkward and tender, frightened and desperate to feel his skin and hair, his blood and bones – the hollows, the shadows, the places he reserved for himself – it was hardly the best-executed kiss of my life, but it was certainly the most memorable. When we stopped, we hung our heads together, our cheeks, jaws, temples touching, our breaths seeking common ground, a harmony.

Outside the tiny circle we two formed, life revolved, huge and messy, on the brink of war – and irrelevant. A door closed – boro-bhai and chotto-bon shut out there where they belonged. Ours was not the great and tragic passion of Luna and Razzak, but I loved the feeling of believing that for once, I knew what was truly important, and I was exactly where I was supposed to be – right in the middle of it.

Finally, we pulled away, sat back, apart once more. My eyes focused on one small bird that skirted the sky just above us, but no other part of me was anywhere but in our small corner, letting the moment settle. Back home, in Lansing, it would not have ended so suddenly. We would have kissed again, touched, and while making love, I may have accessed the secret places of his body I sought. But here, in a park, in this culture, it was like we had already slept together, had grappled and twined until we both came – so bold was a public kiss. Free love be damned.

"I will remember always your commitment," Shaheed said finally. "People think I must have it – because of my father – but I don't. I cannot muster what you and Hasan and Ruby seem to have so easily."

I had nothing to say then. Of all things to be remembered by – not my lips, not my hands, not my eyes, not even my honest and loyal character – but my so-called *commitment*. To be lumped together with Hasan and Ruby – that was not how I wanted Shaheed to see me. At that moment, it seemed the least attractive and most problematic aspect of my personality because at the very bottom of my heart I understood that that was exactly what Shaheed could not articulate earlier. My commitment had kept us apart all those weeks.

"Come. I'll take you home. Amma must be wondering whether I have kidnapped you," Shaheed said.

He offered a hand, and I took it. But as soon as I was standing, he let go.

The shape of your hands around mine, I wanted to say. That's what I will remember about you. But the appropriate moment was already gone.

꙳

The afternoon of my departure, the first step of our plan was taken. Luna told Amma she wanted to dash over to see Afsana's mother, who had unexpectedly and conveniently taken sick. Amma was reluctant. Mr. Chowdhury had received a phone call with troubling news – political talks had broken off, and Yahya Khan had flown out of Dhaka. The cantonment was unnaturally hushed, and the streets tense and hectic as people scurried to buy up batteries, soap, rice and kerosene.

"I back before dark," Luna said. "I promise." By rickshaw, Afsana's home was less than fifteen minutes away.

Hasan eyed his sister suspiciously. "You should remain here. This is serious. Besides, these are your final hours with your friend."

After months of scolding and scheming to keep me away from his sister, now Hasan was concerned that we spend time together? He didn't seem the least bit aware of his hypocrisy. But I saw through him. He'd exploit any situation he could in order to criticize his sister. I had to help Luna.

"If you're going, perhaps you could take a gift," I said. "I have a little something for Afsana's mother." There was no such present. But I suspected Amma would see Luna's visit in a new light once she heard the word 'gift.' "It's small – really nothing much –" I looked at Amma, my face half-apologetic, half-pleading while I tried to assess our chances.

Amma beamed. Even in the face of potential incursion, she had time for social niceties and anything related to duty. "You girls are so considerate. But please Luna, do not ignore the time." She turned to me. "She is so forgetful."

Hasan harrumphed.

I followed Luna to the gate. Her eyes, cheeks and hair were electric. Every pore in her body had absorbed and could no longer contain knowledge of the adventure she was beginning. But only she, Razzak and I really knew of the passage on which she was embarking. I was fiercely proud of my role helping this young woman to liberate herself.

Traffic was heavier than normal, and in the distance, along the main road which we could just see, pedestrians streamed. It was just as Mr. Chowdhury had heard. We had to wait some time for a rickshaw. I thought about when I would see Luna again. I thought about the uncertainty facing us both.

A rickshaw finally pulled over. Its brakes squealed.

Unfortunately, Luna and I hadn't properly considered our farewell. Now that it was before us, I longed to hold her close and cry. But I couldn't. We had to look like friends who would see one another in an hour or two. We had to make it casual.

"Don't forget to write," I said as though I was speaking to a mere acquaintance. I was fairly certain the rickshawallah would not understand English, but he would understand if I betrayed too much emotion.

"Of course not," she said. She climbed on board. She did not smile. I remember that. I also remember the little bulge of fabric where she'd knotted up the money and tucked it underneath the waistband of her shalwar.

"I will miss you." I looked up when a doyell, a kind of magpie, flitted through the scope of my vision. The sun, approaching the horizon, was a fire ball, much like the sun depicted on the new, illicit flag of independent Bangla Desh, which Amma had placed in the drawer underneath the good silver.

"Of course," Luna said.

"Dekka hobe." See you later.

"Dekka hobe."

"Be careful."

The rickshawallah was scraping dirt from under his fingernails with a bent scrap of wire. "Jao," Luna cried. "What are you waiting for?" She winked at me, and the rickshawallah grunted as he threw the wire to the ground and pushed off. Her rickshaw rolled down the street to the main road. I looked away before I could see which way it turned.

༈

"Money cannot disappear, isn't it?" Mr. Chowdhury said. "It defies the laws of physics."

Amma wrung her hands over and over, like they were wet dishrags that refused to dry. "Are you certain it is not amongst your papers?"

"I looked everywhere," I said. "But I know exactly where I left it – in an envelope under my mattress."

The silence was complete. The only person with business underneath my mattress – because he made my bed – had gone to his village.

It unfolded as Luna had predicted. Kamala was questioned. Of course she was incredulous. Of course she knew nothing. Behind closed doors, Amma and Mr. Chowdhury decided calling the police was in no one's best interests. Only one thing did not come to pass as we expected. Mr. Chowdhury did not have the money to buy me a ticket.

Amma called Beth.

❦

Amma packed the box on the dining room table while I watched. She chose from among papers, reel-to-reel tapes, and several records. Everything scattered as though collected in a hurry.

Inside it was dark. The power was out, and our only light came from a single, smoky candle.

We whispered, in deference to the blackness, and to the blasts of gunfire that had just begun. The otherwise quiet night was split open by the noise.

"Where is that silly girl? She knows she must say goodbye before you leave," Amma said.

"It's okay. Tell her I'll write soon – inshallah," I said. God willing. The candle sputtered, faded, then leapt to life once again. "It's better that Luna stays put now, don't you think?" I spoke to a small shadow cast on the table by a teacup and saucer, beside Amma's open medicine bottle. I couldn't meet Amma's eye. Fortunately, she paid no attention.

"Hasan!" But her son was already in the room, in a chair near the curtained window, for once quiet. We hadn't noticed. "Please help your mother. I can't think."

More gun shots. These were closer.

Amma grabbed the phone and punched in numbers again. We already knew it was not working. "What's wrong with this thing?" She began to cry. "It's too dangerous. Why didn't she have the sense to stay home?"

"Luna will be in big trouble, with only herself to blame," Hasan said. "My sister is a stubborn and senseless girl."

"Leave her alone, for god's sake." Like the gunfire, my voice cracked open the hushed night. Thank god she had freed herself of any further censure from him. In the meantime, I would defend her. "You don't know anything about her."

Still, it was dangerous to speak like that, to draw attention to oneself, one's family, one's home. Soldiers and spies could be anywhere, including the patch of sidewalk in front of the Chowdhury's home.

"Amma, forgive me," I whispered immediately. "It's just that he's so hard on her. She's very intelligent and he should mind his own –"

"Robin, dear, we don't have time. You have to get to the airport." She told Hasan to arrange a rickshaw. It was too dangerous to take the car out. At least in a rickshaw, we'd be quiet. We could keep to the alleys of Kalabagan, the narrow lanes through Monipuri Para, hide in the shadows, if necessary.

"You don't mind about the box then?" she said.

"No. Thik ache. It's all right. I want to help. Sahajjo debo." Stronger than my anti-war sentiments and my distaste for war propaganda was my desire to help Amma one last time. Certainly it was risky to carry these things to the airport tonight, but less risky than if the marauding military found them in the Chowdhury's home. My guilt also made me compliant.

"Then take this." She took the flag from her silver drawer and placed it in the bottom of the box.

"And this, please. 'Joi Bangla,'" she read from the sleeve. A recording of a song for the independence movement. "Shahnaz Begum has such a pretty voice." She put the disc in the box.

More gunfire in the distance.

"That sounds like it is coming from the direction of the airport. We have to hurry. Where are your bags?"

Kamala had brought them to the door.

Hasan reappeared. "Transport is here."

"Good," Amma said. "Not too soon. Take this, too." She placed a book in the box. "*When Bhashani was in Europe*. Pity for Mohammed Elias. Such a brilliant writer should never be banned. What else?"

"Give her the seventh March speech," Hasan said. "It's a precious part of our history."

She put a reel-to-reel tape in the box.

"And these, please Robin." She picked up a sticker that said: Each Bengali alphabet represents the life of one of us. Amma had shown me that during one of our sessions. Then, a poster that said: Finish them. The scowling caricature of martial law administrator Yahya Khan was gruesome.

Finally, with fingers that didn't seem to want to let go, she slipped in a poster of Sheikh Mujib. I'd seen this one, his chubby cheeks, thick-rimmed glasses, and seemingly benevolent face plastered to utility poles and brick walls all over Dhanmondi. Torn down, every single one, the very next day.

She topped these contents with three red balloons, printed with the flag.

She closed the box and tied it with a piece of jute twine. "One day you will return these to us," she said. "You are true to your promises." She pulled me close and kissed me as she had when I had arrived and we were all innocent. She pulled a dark scarf over my hair and tucked in the ends around my collar. "Keep your head covered."

"Come," Hasan said. "It's late."

We stepped outside. Amma trailed. I pulled myself up on the bicycle rickshaw which already held my suitcase. I draped my legs over its bulk, and cushioned the box at my side.

We heard an explosion, but it sounded like it was coming from the other side of New Market.

Hasan pulled the rickshaw cover over our heads and locked it into place. "Jao," he said to the rickshawallah. Pushing with all his weight, the driver got the bicycle rolling. He flung himself onto the seat. We pulled out through the gate and onto the road.

"Khoda hafez," I called to Amma.

God go with you.

"Shhh," Hasan said. "Quiet."

And in the distance, Amma's thin voice. "Khoda hafez."

Gunfire. We turned down the street in its direction.

- 133 -

Something whistled in the darkness overhead then exploded in the distance. The earth shuddered. But I barely felt it, overcome as I was with fear for myself, worry for Luna and Razzak, longing for Shaheed, and guilt for lying to Amma. In a lowered voice, Hasan spoke to the rickshawallah, who stopped pedaling and squeezed the brake levers. A squeal slashed through the night.

"Choop!" Hasan said.

The rickshawallah released the brake and jerked the handlebars to the side. We careened through the iron gates of a school, open only because the chain and lock were broken. I thought we would tip over, but the bumpy ground slowed us and we regained balance. We crossed the empty playground, a cracked concrete surface. Rusty posts stood where nets would be tied once more, but not until play became possible again. The idea of children smacking volleyballs or swatting badminton birds here seemed absurd that night. We then bumped over a hard, clay surface, scattered with weeds, grey under the dim lights. The rickshaw rattled like machine gun fire. I looked around, certain we would be detected now, but the place was deserted. We passed through a second gate and were back on the street. There was another whistle and a blast, these even more distant. I thought of Luna and shivered.

"You're cold?" Hasan whispered.

"No."

But he put his arm across the back of the rickshaw anyway.

If it had been anyone else, it would have been touching. And though some part of me would have liked that night to have given in to that feeling, to have surrendered to someone else willing to take charge for a change, I had to remind myself that this was Hasan and therefore, there was an underlying motive. Before I figured it out, I pulled away. But there was nowhere to go. With the box squeezed between us, I could not shift my body away from his.

I looked at Hasan, his beard, sideburns – they needed a trim – long hair, the narrow gleam of his glasses as they reflected what little light existed that night. He was alert like a wild animal. He watched the street ahead, the houses and gardens to the side, scouting for movement. Though he was not my first choice of escorts, his vigilance instilled great confidence in me. Nothing would escape his notice, and he would make sure we had the best chance of arriving at the airport safely.

We followed the deserted lanes through a block of government staff quarters. The guards, afraid, or perhaps recruited to the army, had abandoned their posts. All the windows were dark.

We moved along lanes and alleys, staying parallel to Green Road. The blasts and shots continued, sometimes behind us, other times, apparently, ahead. Perhaps it was just the acoustics – sound bouncing off the brick and concrete of the city. But I was not anxious to find out how close we actually were to the fighting.

Hasan muttered something to the rickshawallah. The rickshawallah replied over his shoulder, his voice so low I could not make out what he said. Hasan said something else. The rickshawallah shook his head. What were they talking about? As their discussion heated up, it dawned on me. If we were to get to the airport, we would have to cross the intersection at Farmgate. Open, exposed, six roads met, and there was no way around it.

"We have to go back," I said.

"It's not safe to go back."

"We won't get across."

"We will – inshallah."

God willing, God willing. What madness. I had no faith in God at that moment. I had no faith in anything except my feet and a vague sense of how to get back to Amma's. I rose, grabbed the side of the rickshaw and went to jump off.

Hasan seized my arm. "Are you crazy?" My head scarf fell, was pulled under the wheels into the dust and was gone. My hair flew out around us, a corona in the dark night.

"Are you?" As if to prove my point, guns went off, one, two in succession, five, six. Then we lost count. They were ahead of us. I shrank down in my seat and pulled my hair back.

The rickshaw slowed, then stopped in the shadows. The Farmgate intersection lay before us. We looked up the street. A rail car had been dragged across the road. Otherwise, nothing was amiss. No one moved. Perhaps there were others like us, lurking in the shadows, but I saw no sign. We sat beneath the canopy of a small tree with saucer-shaped leaves. The ripe scent from its boughs seemed out of place.

Hasan and the rickshawallah conferred. Though there was no one in sight, once we made the decision to cross, we would become visible and vulnerable. If we made it, we would be camouflaged by a park until we entered Monipuri Para. We were perhaps twenty seconds away from protection. We listened to the blasts and shots, and waited, though for what, who knew?

The rickshawallah climbed off and wrung his hands. He paced a small circle, then squatted on his haunches. He was silent, but waved his hands back and forth, in debate with himself. Finally, Hasan stepped down too, and walked a few metres up the sidewalk. He moved at the edge of the shadows, where he would be noticeable only if someone was looking carefully. I stayed in my seat, though I still wanted to run back to Amma.

Eventually, Hasan finished his scouting. He returned and stood beside the rickshawallah. His voice was quiet but commanding – he told the rickshawallah in no uncertain terms to get back in his seat and pedal. The rickshawallah stood and shook his head. Hasan raised his voice and waggled his finger. The rickshawallah clasped his hands together. "Saheb, saheb," he repeated, until Hasan sliced his hand through the air between them. "Bas!" Hasan cried. Then, to me, "Let's go."

Hasan grabbed the handlebars with those bear paw hands and pushed. I was thrust back in my seat by the force. He threw his leg over the rickshaw driver's seat and pumped the pedals.

"What are you doing?" I shriek-whispered. Hasan cycled for all he was worth. I clutched at the seat, then the box, as it began to slide. "Stop. You're going to get us killed."

The rickshawallah, reluctant to let his sole means of livelihood disappear at the hands of a madman, ran behind. I felt a jerk. It was the rickshawallah pushing. He hid in our shadow as he helped us along. The twenty seconds to cross the intersection at Farmgate felt like twenty minutes, and yet, once we stopped beneath a tree on the other side, I wondered if our passage had ever happened.

Hasan panted. The rickshawallah, too. Both their faces were drenched in sweat.

We waited for someone to call out, to come running down any of the roads. But there was no one. Nothing. Just silence.

I shook, my hands fluttering from the box to my hair to the rickshaw seat. Hasan's smile was grim, but he was relieved.

Then the rickshawallah pointed. Down. My heart sank. The chain had snapped.

"But he can fix it, can't he?" I said. I looked at the rickshawallah's hands. "They can fix everything. On the side of the road, everyday – "

"Not without tools."

"Fuck." I stomped my foot on the tin footrest of the rickshaw.

"Shh!" Hasan said. He spoke to the rickshawallah, then turned back to me. "He has a cousin near the rail station at Tejgaon who can help."

I calculated. "That's a good thirty minutes by the time he gets over there and back. If he runs. And if he doesn't get caught. What are we going to do?"

But what could we do? We pulled the rickshaw into the park and concealed it behind a shrub. While the rickshawallah went off to find his cousin, Hasan and I crouched in the shadows.

"You should go home," I said finally. "Go back to Amma."

"Don't be ridiculous."

"The rickshawallah knows the way. We don't need your help."

"He's a coward. You cannot depend on him."

"Then I'll walk the rest of the way. It's not so far."

"You have luggage." We both knew the walk would be impossible, even in daylight, even without a war going on around us. "You're not going alone. It's out of the question."

Even then, in the most desperate of circumstances, I let his words, his tone under my skin like a burr, let them aggravate my insides, until I could no more bear the irritation without bursting.

"Stop telling me what to do."

"You require protection."

"I don't want your protection."

"That's enough. Soldiers will hear you. And then you will have much more to worry about than your luggage."

Gunfire. Then gunfire returned. I shuddered. Here I was, senselessly drawn into argument with Hasan once again. Where was Luna? I prayed she had already left the city. That she and Razzak were on their way to Aricha or Mymensingh, anywhere closer to India. I thought of the cantonment which lay just beyond the airport. The unspoken deeds which had been done there to Shaheed. What might happen there, if rumour could be believed, to Luna.

I thought hard about Amma, too, at home, both her children out on a night like this. I tried to send her a mental message to tell her not to worry. It would all work out in the end. We would all be okay. Eventually I convinced myself, and I calmed down enough to hold my tongue.

The explosions, shots and whistles continued. They seemed to be coming from all around now. We lacked only the pretty coloured lights in the sky, blossoming before our eyes, to differentiate our circumstances from Spartan Stadium on July fourth.

Hasan and I sat in the dark, alarmed by the noises around us, frightened because we could not see, did not know what was happening. When I let the sting of his words fade, I realized it was the first time we had ever shared something. The first time we had ever met on common ground. Brought together by fear. The irony did not escape me, but I rejected the softening I felt for something stronger. The urge to speak welled up. I struggled to keep my tone of voice casual.

"I want to ask you something. What exactly is it you dislike about me so much?"

He rolled his eyes and turned his face away. But he said nothing. I took this as encouragement.

"Do you find me outspoken? Forward?" I leaned in, and when he still did not answer, I gave up all pretense of neutrality. "By the way, I use these terms for your convenience only. Others would say instead I have self-respect and dignity, and I speak honestly."

"What are you talking about?"

"Perhaps it's simpler. Biological. Is it because I am female that you dislike me? Because I don't sit home and obey Hasan's petty rules of engagement?" I could feel his breathing change. "Just tell me what it is. Then I can go home in peace and forget about you."

Finally speaking the words was a relief. I sat up, invigorated by my sense of injustice. With no Amma or Abba to defuse the situation, Hasan had to respond. I was ready for battle. I waited. And I refused to look away. However, it surprised me that he was not affronted as I had expected. In fact, he seemed – puzzled.

"You will go home," he said finally. "And it will be in peace. You are lucky." He picked up a dry leaf and slowly crushed it in his palm.

An explosion. Shattered glass. A man screamed, "Rehana, Rehana," over and over again, until the woman's name degenerated into a wail, a screech dragged over my flesh like a jagged blade. Hasan twitched and made as if to rise, then hesitated, and again, I thought he would get up, run and help. But he hesitated once more and at last, the cries faded away. We sat in silence for a few moments.

"Your father will be waiting for you," Hasan continued. "Your home, too. Your classmates. Everything exactly as you left it – when? Only nine months ago?"

Detecting a slur, I replied huffily. "Well, some people like it that way. There's nothing wrong with enjoying a world you can depend on. You might not like it –"

But he did not wait for me to finish. "Do you know what this street will look like in nine months? This country?" The dust of the crushed leaf fell through his fingers and was lost on the ground. "Do you think you will be able to recognize it if you ever come back?"

Guilt rose inside me, like a bubble rising through oil – slow, viscous – but I pushed it down. It was thick, yes, but it wouldn't protect me against Hasan. "But you want to fight. You said it a million times."

"I would do anything for this land. I will never forsake it." His tone was strangely calm.

"You don't have to go to war to achieve your goals."

"Sometimes, drastic measures are called for."

"And so – you'll stop nowhere?"

"And you? You'll just give up?"

"I have convictions, too, you know." I said it but it felt like a lie. I knew the words for the things I thought important. But I felt washed with doubt about my own ability to act on them.

He looked at me then, for the first time. Right at me. His eyes were dark and clear. I pulled back, disarmed. It was like a beam of light had been directed right into my core, into the shadowy place where my duality, my ambiguous feelings, my contradictions were concealed. I felt reduced – able to sense, yes, but lacking both maturity and the ability to understand something big, important and vital. Hasan broke off the stare. But it was I who had backed down.

"Shaheed is joining the movement."

His news was another bomb dropped. "He can't. He doesn't believe."

Hasan laughed. "He told me this afternoon. He says it is all due to you. You have taught him the value of commitment."

I was certain he was lying. Tossing this tidbit my way to see how I would respond. Perhaps he knew something about our kiss, and was baiting me to reveal more about our relationship. A moment ago, I had felt stripped before his gaze, unsure of myself; but this revelation and the manner in which it was delivered reminded me once more exactly who he was and would always be. He'd say anything – even something to damage his best friend's reputation – just to continue his insane attacks.

"Shaheed believes in peaceful negotiation and passive resistance. You're so cowardly, you're using him to put me in my place – but it's not going to work."

"Your self-appointed place is of no interest. Like the

traitorous country that sent you here, you are abandoning us."

From down the road, footsteps faded into our hearing range, though we could see no one. Then the rickshawallah appeared, the chain a perfect circle again. While I continued to feel the nasty sting of his words, Hasan helped slot the chain over the gears, and turn the pedal until it slipped into place. "Cholo," he said as he climbed on board.

The rickshawallah pushed us down a path in the park. We entered a deserted Monipuri Para, followed its lanes, then crossed another major road where we saw soldiers huddled in the distance, too busy with something to even hear or turn their heads to our rattling rickshaw. And then we reached our destination.

The gate to the airport was a contrast to the rest of the city. Thick with people, luggage and vehicles, noise and confusion battered us. I could hardly see the terminal. Clearly, I was not the only one hoping to get out tonight. The rickshawallah tried, but guard after guard stopped us from entering. They yelled. Grabbed his handlebars and steered us away. Finally, one approached, brandishing a nail to puncture the tire if we proceeded. We backed off.

My suitcase was heavy, the box awkward. Hasan found a hungry-looking man and slipped him a brimming handful of coins to carry my luggage into the building. From the look on the man's face, I knew the payment was more than he expected, even in a time of war.

So this was it. My good-bye to my Dhaka. There was no time for apologies, no time for promises, last minute confessions. Still smarting, I held out my hand. Hasan shook it as though we had just met.

"Dhonnobad," I said. "To your family. I enjoyed my stay." It sounded cold, and was not what I meant, not at all, but I couldn't really find the words I wanted in that crush.

"I hope your journey is pleasant," he returned, and pulled his hand away. I felt cheated. All his passion, his anger, had been reduced to polite words, the kind offered to strangers. I wanted more – one last joust perhaps to prove to myself that I was right about him. "Go. Your coolie is waiting." And indeed, the thin man had lifted my suitcase on his head. He balanced it with one hand, while with the other, he propped Amma's box against a bony, lungi-clad hip. He appeared to be jumping from one foot to the other, but it was just the effort of trying to steady my things against the jostling of the endless stream of people.

When I turned back, Hasan was already on the rickshaw. The rickshawallah rang his bell, adding to the confusion, and pushed into the throng. I watched him manoeuvre the tightest circle I had ever seen one of those ungainly machines make. It curled around like smoke.

And they headed off. The rickshaw hood rose above the swarm. And on the back, in faded crimson letters, a single word eaten away by the hungry crowd: Surinder.

2001

"Thank you, Falguni," I say. Dutifully, she has led me back to the Sheraton Hotel. Now, hands neatly folded, dupatta draped evenly over her shoulders, she stands at the bathroom door beside a small plastic stool and waits for instructions. It depresses me to see her behaving so obediently, just as Luna did. Has nothing for young women changed in thirty years?

She lingers, and though we both pretend otherwise, watches my hands, which, I notice for the first time, shake. I presume she sees the tremors as a sign of my guilt, so I entwine my fingers until there is no room in my palms for shame. I hold fast until they are red and still.

"No need to wait around. You can go." She redirects her gaze to a corner of my room, where flaky paint reveals pockmarks of mildew. "Falguni – go." The words come out harsher than intended, but then again, maybe firmness is necessary with girls like her.

Falguni looks at me as though leaving has not occurred to her. I get the feeling she and I are performing together using different scripts. But she finally slips away, into the hushed corridor, and when she does, the click of the door latch is clear, final, and a deliverance.

Alone again. At last.

I must have been crazy to think I could come back to Dhaka. Hasan's raging face resurfaces in my mind. I hear his voice, then the sound of the shouting audience, incomprehensible words beating at auditorium walls. And me, in the spotlight, a spindly insect with hinged legs pinned to a silk background. Only I consciously chose my torment when I accepted the invitation to come back.

I turn on the television. I watch news in Bangla. A moment later, I change to a music show. Tinny instruments, a misdirected spotlight, a singer who clutches hands to chest and warbles in a falsetto that could curdle milk. I turn it off.

I lie on the bed. The lumpy pillow smells of mould. I throw it across the room. The stool falls with a muffled and dissatisfying thud.

I wonder if the Bangla-American Women's Friendship Society will ask for its money back. I'm sure the organizers never expected controversy. A presentation on my once outspoken and misinterpreted views of student political movements – such a singular and minor work, hardly worth anyone's attention, certainly not trouble of this sort. Should I have warned them? About what? That I helped a young woman in love find happiness? Of this, I am guilty. Of collaborating with the enemy, I am not.

My stomach grumbles. I should go for lunch – oily parathas. Maybe some mustardy ilish mach, if it's on the menu, bitter, salty karela and whatever saag is in season. But leaving this room has no appeal. The three days before I return home, to Canada, stretch out interminably. Relief is possible if I change my flight. But I lack the energy to pick up the phone and deal with anyone who could make the arrangements. My stomach grumbles again.

Then I remember the box. When I'd arrived, I'd put it in the closet until I had time to deal with it. Now I have plenty of time.

The box should have been returned years ago, once the war was over. That would have saved me all this grief today. But it wasn't. The excuses swirl around my head – the war and the resulting lack of communication between me and the Chowdhurys. Then it was my self-exile from my country of birth. Then it was the patina that coloured my life once my child was born and made it difficult to look anywhere for years but at the baby in my arms. And it is true: a task delayed will diminish in urgency as it is replaced by new demands, though that says nothing of that first task's importance. I never forgot my obligation. I just pushed it into a corner where I didn't have to think much about it.

When I found out I'd be making this trip, I mustered up the courage and wrote to Amma, my second letter to her in thirty years. I told her I was finally coming back with the box, and would bring it to her. I mailed the letter, having no idea what would happen to it. There'd never been word from her or Luna or anyone else since I'd left. The one letter I'd sent – after several agonizing months of waiting for them to contact me – had gone unanswered. I had no idea whether they'd received that letter, or whether they'd just decided not to reply. Just as I had no idea whether the letter announcing my return had reached its address.

But what will happen now when I show up with the box? Hasan will have told everyone that I'm back – Amma, Mr. Chowdhury, Luna, Razzak, maybe even Shaheed. He'll have instructed Shafiq not to open the door when I knock – no, that would be impossible. If that rickety man is still alive, surely he's retired. He'd be living comfortably with one of his nephews back in the village. Hasan will have told Shafiq's replacement: she's a collaborator. Don't let her in.

But I have done nothing of such magnitude, and Amma is no fool. She will realize Hasan's accusations are just that, and welcome me again into her home. Besides, she wants the box back. I promised her, and how can I leave Dhaka again without fulfilling the obligation which has hung over my head for the last thirty years?

I dismiss shame and guilt, and decide to go to Amma's. In the lobby, Falguni rises with a warm smile. It's been an hour since I sent her away.

"Mrs. Robin, you want go out?" She reaches for the box. I pull it away.

"Yes, I do – no, no – Falguni, why are you still here?"

"This my duty. You give me box."

I hold fast. She assumes the stance of a football player about to snatch the ball from an opponent. "It's alright. Please go now. I can take care of myself."

"But I am junior protocol officer, Bangla-American Women's Friendship Society. I take care of you." She reaches again for the box.

"I don't need anyone to take care of me, thank you."

Her eyes grow big and wounded, but I walk away with my box.

Three glass doors lead back into the heat. One by one, I push against them. None opens. Where is the doorman? I try again. But I can't get out of this eyesore of a hotel.

"What you want?" Falguni asks. "I help." She pulls the handle and the door wheezes open.

I give up and hand her the box. "A taxi. I need a taxi."

The driver leans on his horn and squeezes into a tangle of traffic. He skirts around a rickshaw laden with burlap sacks, then narrowly avoids scraping the side of a multi-coloured lorry carrying potatoes.

Whack. Someone slaps the back of the car and I jump. But it's nothing. The driver honks his horn again. The roads are much more crowded than I remember, with cars, trucks, buses and motorized rickshaws, still called baby taxis, though now they seem to be everywhere, trailing noxious black fumes. The garishly coloured bicycle rickshaws weave throughout the fabric of traffic as they always did. Cows, goats, pedestrians, beggars, and hawkers with their goods spilling onto the streets, continue their fight for space.

"This the jadugarh," Falguni points to a broad-faced building looming behind a brick wall. "National museum. I take you tomorrow."

"Please. No need to go out of your way."

But she dismisses my words with a wave that looks too senior for her years. The junior protocol officer is practicing for bigger things.

We stop for no reason I can detect. Move ahead a few feet. Stop again. We crawl through a crowded roundabout. I look for landmarks, which should be easy to spot at this speed. But the entire city is under construction. Rickety scaffolding fronts every building. Iron bars and stacks of red bricks are heaped on the roadsides, and seem to go on forever. Workers with baskets and tools crawl over them. I wonder if the Chowdhury home exists anymore.

One thing becomes clear, however, as we creep along: the Bangladeshis won the language war. There's no Urdu, and very few signs in English. A green sign points the way to the airport and the prime minister's office. I see Coca-Cola. Pepsi-Cola. Some wars never end. A billboard for a brand of prophylactics called King Congdom hangs threateningly over a bus stand. Otherwise everything's in Bangla.

"This the New Elephant Road. You buy jamdani saree? New shoes? I take you."

I sit up. A small woman with a long braid and a woven shoulder bag crosses the street. I am about to call out. But she turns and pulls the end of her long dupatta off the dusty road, and I realize it isn't her. Of course, it would be impossible. Like me, Luna would be grey and haggard now, her simple beauty faded.

And then, I twist my neck to see again the corner we rush by – a familiar face, I was not mistaken. A poster of Sheikh Mujib, the Chowdhurys' adored Bangabandhu, hangs crooked from a utility pole, the same picture from thirty years ago. I'm confused by this flashback, glance at the driver, who surely must be Mr. Chowdhury, then to Falguni who, for an instant, I am also certain will have transformed into Luna or Amma.

"He the father of our nation," Falguni says. "His daughter is our leader now."

"Really?" It should have smoothed with her explanation,

but instead time warps into even loopier shapes and I am left more confused than ever.

Finally, we ease down a street lined with trees whose leaves resemble hearts, feathers and bayonets. The driver, who has resumed his rightful identity, slows.

"Here," Falguni points.

We're in front of an old white bungalow that I've never seen before in my life. I look around the street. I don't recognize anything.

"This is not it," I say.

Falguni and the taxi driver begin to argue. I wonder if the Chowdhury's house and entire neighbourhood were destroyed in the war. What about the Chowdhurys? No. I just saw Hasan a few hours ago. I refuse to believe everyone else is dead.

Finally Falguni turns to me. "Apa? You saying Road 14. Taxiwallah want to know: new or old?"

I shake my head. "What do you mean?"

They confer once more. At the end, Falguni says, "He think you meaning new Road 14. Now we go old Road 14 and see."

The taxi driver turns the car around and heads back from where we came.

"The addresses changed?" I ask.

"Only some," Falguni says. "Sometimes we using old numbers, too."

So the Chowdhurys couldn't have received my letter. But what about the one I wrote soon after I'd gone home?

"When did they change the addresses?"

Falguni shrugs. "Few years back."

I shudder now. Perhaps they did receive my first letter. But then, why didn't they write back to me?

The taxi turns onto a much quieter street. And I recognize this one right away.

It *is* still standing. And still mildew-spattered. The brick boundary wall is twice as high as it used to be though. And from the little I can see, something is missing. A flower bed? A big tree? And yet, it is exactly as I remember: pale yellow, lumbering at the back of an impressively smooth lawn, surrounded by greenery. When Falguni and I step out of the cab, three green parrots squawk from a neighbour's papaya tree whose trunk is laden with tiny fruit that resemble light bulbs.

Otherwise, everything is hushed.

A shrunken man, wobbly on his feet, opens the door to our knock. For an instant, I think it is Shafiq, and again, time mysteriously freezes thirty years back. Then I recognize the eyes. Rheumy now, but familiar. This is most definitely Luna's beloved Abba.

"Salaam aliekum," I say.

He sighs weightily, and runs the back of his hand across his mouth and chin. "Yes." His eyes close. "Hasan warned us, isn't it?"

He opens his eyes, glances at Falguni, then stares beyond. I am tempted to turn around to see what he is looking at. But his eyes are vacant. He is not looking at anything. I see now where Hasan learned this technique.

"Did you get my letter?" I ask. But he does not even blink.

I hold out the box. "I wanted to return this to Amma – Mrs. Chowdhury."

His eyes dart to the box, then back to the beyond.

"It's hers."

The box is heavy but I continue to offer it.

"Is Amma home? I'd like to see her." My arms begin to ache, but I will not pull the box back. "Where's Luna?"

In the hush of their garden, the tension which has taken root since I arrived suddenly flowers. "You shouldn't have come," Mr. Chowdhury finally says.

Even Falguni, obtuse as she is, understands this. "Baba," she begins, then a deluge of Bangla gushes forth. Like the Buriganga when it breaks its banks in the late summer monsoon, her words flow on and on. Mr. Chowdhury lets her talk. Finally, she seems spent. She sputters out.

Mr. Chowdhury ignores the speech. He inhales deeply and coughs. "Please. Don't disturb us again." He steps back into the house.

I shift the box under one arm, grasp the frame with my other hand before the door closes. "Can I see Luna? Amma? Will she at least come to the door?"

He shakes his head. "She is bed-ridden. It is her wish that you leave us alone. Good day."

I am forced to pull my hand away as he closes the door. Falguni and I face grainy wood. The box pokes into my hip bone.

Before I get into the taxi, I glance at the windows. Where is Luna's wave calling me back?

"We go to hotel now?" Falguni says.

"No. Sidheshwari."

I hadn't communicated with Beth since I left, though she'd be the only one who'd have listened. Whether or not she agreed with what I had done, she would ask questions, measure her words, speak carefully. I should have sought her understanding right away, but it felt pointless during those early months when I first got back to Lansing. She seemed so otherworldly. It would be like trying to contact Pluto.

About a year after I'd arrived home, when the war was over and I thought some semblance of normal life must have resumed in Dhaka, and I still hadn't heard from the Chowdhurys, I resolved to write her. I went to the plaza to buy envelopes. But the sight of a sack of dog food being loaded onto the roof of a station wagon stopped me in my tracks. Such an ordinary act seemed a symbol of the great divide that separated my life in Lansing from the world I'd left behind in Dhaka. There was no way of reconciling the two, no matter how many letters I wrote. I left without buying anything.

Besides, the money issue hung heavy and I wanted to wait until I had enough to pay Beth back, having no idea that over the course of my adult life, my financial situation would never improve. While I mulled over my words and counted pennies, I let things drift. And drift some more, until any contact seemed shameful and unnecessary.

A thin girl answers Beth's door and although I remember well the corridors and doorways that lead there, she shows Falguni and I onto the terrace.

The city has mushroomed up around Beth. Where there was once a striking panorama of neighbour's rooftops, now apartment buildings that climb five and six stories overhead box us in and cast deep shadows over the terrace. Beth has attempted to keep the garden. Pots, lined up in rows angled to catch the slivers of sunlight, contain the marigolds, asters, dahlias and gladioli I remember, though they are pale and stringy from lack of sun. There is one red bougainvillea, thick and florid at the top, the only plant which seems to be winning the battle for light.

I put the box on a cane settee. The old swing, Luna's preferred spot, is gone. Falguni stands and waits for me to choose a seat but I can't. I long for the swing.

A grubby child grasps iron bars that cover a window in one of the new buildings. From her perch overlooking the terrace, she clocks our movements. I catch her eye, and expect her to look away. But her gaze is steady, disarming.

A rattle announces Beth's arrival. She holds herself up with steel crutches. Shocked, already raw from the day's events, I forget etiquette.

"My god. What happened to you?"

Her frown mirrors mine, then settles, smoldering on her face. "Well. I didn't expect I'd see you again." She must be more than sixty, an age that once seemed ancient, yet now is right around the corner.

She hobbles over and sits beside the box.

"What happened to you?" I ask again.

"Car accident." A crutch slides to ground and rattles on the concrete. "A long time ago. What is it you want?"

"I'm in town for a few days," I begin. "– this is Falguni." I don't know what else to say. Her abruptness distresses me.

"I from Bangla-American Women's Friendship Society. I am junior protocol officer."

Beth acknowledges her with a small smile, which disappears when she turns to me. "I'm surprised you have the nerve to show up."

The child at the window presses her face against the bars. One eyelid is pulled down, revealing anemic pale flesh inside.

"I tried to see Amma," I say. "But Mr. Chowdhury wouldn't let me."

"Do you blame him?"

- 155 -

I don't remember hearing Beth speak like this. She's become hard and unyielding over the years, maybe because of her accident.

"I don't *blame* him. I just don't understand him," I say. It wouldn't bother *me* to see Amma bedridden. I shrug. "I wish Hasan would stop interfering. I don't know why I thought he'd be any different. But then again, I always was a slow learner." I laugh.

No one joins in. We sit and stare at the surrounding concrete.

Beth breaks the silence. "Not a day goes by that Salma doesn't pray for Luna's return."

"Return?"

"She's never come back. Didn't you know?"

"But where is she?"

It is Beth's turn to shrug.

"That's awful. She's alive, isn't she? I mean, she probably just decided not to –"

"There was a war, you remember," Beth says, her voice dry as an old stripped bone.

Now I have to sit. I don't even bother to brush the dust off the tattered cane chair, though I avoid the rusty nail, its head thick with corrosion, protruding from the broken arm. "I can't believe it," I say. Falguni remains standing, looking slightly subservient. "Is that why Hasan is so angry?"

"Perhaps," Beth says. "Though it could be the beating he received the night he took you to the airport. He never recovered in time to join the freedom fighters."

"Beating?"

"You don't remember? All young men were potential targets. When the army picked him up that night – Salma was just happy he came back. He was missing for two weeks."

"Two weeks? What happened?"

"It took the doctor three months to get the wounds on his back to close and to stop the infection from spreading. He's lucky he didn't lose a limb. Or worse. Although being alive is in some ways far more painful for some boys like him."

Where is the air? I can't breathe. "But I didn't know."

"No. Of course you didn't."

I choke. But she's not being fair. She's forgetting, too. "They were going to marry her off." Beth shakes her head as though I have said something preposterous. "She was in love with someone else."

"Did you live here with your eyes shut? That's what people do. They marry. Arranged marriages." I wish she'd shout. The evenness of her voice is chilling.

"What about the others? Shaheed?" Beth's face fills. "Did he join the movement or not?"

"He did."

"Then?" I shake my head.

"No one knows how many people died in the war, but most of us believe three million. He was one."

Shaheed dead. I can't think about it. He should have lived and married and had children and made them all laugh and feel loved, days brimming with joy. Why did he think he had to go to war? He had nothing to prove, not to me, not to anyone who measured him only against his father. My hands feel cold and exposed. I fold them tightly, squeezing out the vulnerable places between my fingers. My eyes fill.

Somebody must have made it through unscathed. My sanity depends on it. "Ruby?"

Beth laughs bitterly. "She's a war hero. She was shot in the face in combat. She's completely disfigured and earns a living speaking to students about the Liberation War." Beth turns to Falguni. "You must know about Ruby Islam."

Awestruck, Falguni sighs. "She give her future for her country."

"She was so beautiful," I say.

"Everyone was touched by the war. It was unavoidable," Beth says. Falguni nods her head.

Silence wraps around us, interrupted only by noises from the street below. Traffic. Children. The distinctive crack of a cricket bat from some dusty patch of earth the teams were lucky to discover in this dense concrete maze.

One more time, I grasp for happy, or at least neutral news. "What about Kamala and Shafiq? Surely the military had no interest in old people like them."

Beth leans forward. Her eyes, sharp and narrow, glitter like the inside of a marble. I think she will hiss. "After you accused him of a crime he didn't commit, Shafiq couldn't face his family or the Chowdhurys. They found his body hanging from a mango tree in his village.

"As for Kamala...obviously you've never had a suicide in your family."

Everything stops. I want to vomit. Tear out my hair. Shriek and cry. I need to run away. Turn back the clock. Disappear. But my body allows no recourse. My brain sends signals which become lost in the web of my nerves. My muscles cannot respond. I am forced to bear witness to Beth's revelations in their entirety.

"Maybe now you understand Salma's reception." Beth supports herself on the shaky arm of her chair, and reaches for her crutch. Falguni, whom I'd nearly forgotten about, picks it up and hands it to her. "Thank you."

What now? What can I say? How did the good act I undertook to save Luna twist into this nightmare? Sorry seems pathetic and almost laughable. I have no idea where to begin.

We sit there. Sit and sit and sit. How much time passes, I cannot say. Beth finally interrupts, no apology in her voice. "I'm rather busy – "

This nudges me out of my fog. "Before I go, I want to pay you back." A slight gesture, and I still have no idea where I will come up with such money, but it must be done. "Can I give you a cheque?" I fumble for my purse.

"Forget it."

"No. Please."

"I said forget it." The words snap from her lips.

But I cannot leave without undertaking one act of atonement, however small. "I can help Amma and Mr. Chowdhury. I can pay for a good private detective who will find Luna."

"You should discuss this with them."

"But they won't see me. Maybe you could mention it."

"I won't do anything to open old wounds, Robin."

"Then tell me. What can I do? Perhaps Kamala?"

She shakes her head. "You have done enough already."

As Falguni and I leave the terrace, I take one last look. The child with her face pressed against the bars is gone. In her place, a thin curtain fades in a shard of hot sun.

On the way back to the hotel, I watch chaos unfurl outside the taxi window and try to come to terms with the fact Luna is gone. She can't be dead. Can't. She had a plan. Money. Razzak. She was too smart. If she's not returned to the Chowdhury home, surely it was a conscious decision.

An oncoming rickshaw squeezes by the taxi. Our driver swerves, but it's so close, we collectively inhale and wait for the scrape. When it doesn't come, the rickshawallah's mouth contorts into cruel laughter. He glances into the back seat to see if he's irked anyone important, and it is this calculated callousness that most upsets me.

҂

No evidence exists in the lobby of the Sheraton Hotel of the war waged on its front steps thirty years ago. It is hard to imagine that people quivered in fear, cowered beneath restaurant tables, desks and beds while mortars exploded on the street. It is impossible to imagine the screams. These manicured grounds had a trench dug through them, right next to where the swimming pool glistens today. Once, a bomb took out the glass front and the concierge's desk. Today, it is a sedate hotel, just going about its five-star business.

I send Falguni home in the taxi, and take the elevator back to my floor. Push the box to the back of the closet.

It was the Intercontinental Hotel during the war.

Back in Lansing, miraculously safe, I had watched television and tried to imagine what floor the camera was on when it filmed tanks rolling down the street. Through which window did they photograph the crows and vultures? Following the massacre the night I left – dubbed Operation

Search Light by the army – the streetlights, lampposts and trees were heavy with scavengers. All that death to consume.

I spent hours following the news. Mortar fire, strafing, tracer bullets – I came to understand a host of words I never imagined would be part of my vocabulary – when all I really longed for was to hear the names, see the faces, read the stories of the people I knew.

And I waited for a letter from Luna.

The conflict escalated. Slaughter, meetings, more slaughter, more meetings. The monsoon began. And ended. Eid arrived, and passed. Entire villages walked to India, only to find their existence threatened by another enemy: cholera. The Indian government appealed for international assistance. It came. Slowly. George Harrison gave a concert to raise funds.

I watched. And still I waited for word from Luna.

"A bit of fresh air once in awhile would go a long way with you, Roo," my father said. He was a strong believer in physical activity to cure a multitude of ailments. But I was not to be torn from my place in front of the television.

Images burned into my mind: a young man carrying the corpse of his emaciated wife to the border, unwilling to let go of her body or the hope that she might be saved.

A refugee girl and her mother squatting in a concrete culvert, one of countless arches occupied by families who'd fled for their lives. A straw broom lay before them, a harrowing symbol of the woman's futile attempt to restore order to their lives.

Fatted politicians, safe in their offices, behind teak desks, meeting, meeting, meeting. Saying they were aware of the urgency. But stalemated by nothing more than their stubbornness and need to save face.

But no mention of Luna. Or Razzak. Or any of the Chowdhurys. I thought about writing Amma, but decided it would be unwise until I heard from Luna.

I waited for the bulky Sunday newspapers from New York and Washington, though reading them was no easier than watching TV. A Bengali doctor reported taking blood from young rebels to supply to injured Pakistani soldiers. He cried to the reporter that he had been forced to drain the blood of one freedom fighter, until all that was left was a corpse.

Then, one day, finally, a name I recognized. Professor Selina Akhtar had been found dead in Rayer Bazaar. Naked, strangled, alongside other intellectuals and Bengali nationalists, her cotton saree was wrapped around and around and around her neck. It was the only time during the war I ever saw in the news the name of someone I knew.

Still, I kept hoping, and reading about the atrocities. An orphanage in Lalmatia was shelled. An anonymous source in the army claimed it was no accident. The soldier candidly explained how rebels were hiding out in the orphanages, and even if they weren't, eliminating Bengali children would help control overpopulation in East Pakistan.

A woman who spoke on the condition that she remain anonymous, told of a week's worth of sexual enslavement at the military cantonment. She serviced sixty-two soldiers. She remembered because it was the same number as the age of her father when he died. She was released on a deserted street in the middle of the night and warned: don't think of telling anyone, as if you would be believed anyway, you are noshto now. Spoiled. Rubbish.

A Bihari man threw a torch onto a thatch-roofed house in a village where a widow, her mother-in-law and five children were sleeping.

And a freedom fighter, for no apparent reason, shot a young, naked boy running down the street in the back. The war had ended twenty-four hours earlier. It was one week before Christmas 1971.

With still no letter from Luna and no mention of the Chowdhurys and their friends, I had substituted. The boy who had his blood drained became Shaheed. The sex slave became Luna or, almost unthinkable, Amma. The torched family, Kamala's. The gun-mad freedom fighter, driven insane by the violence that battered him day in and out for nine months, Hasan.

I remember how unbearable it was not to know what had really happened, and to be unable to find out.

Outside the hotel window, darkness begins to settle over the city. Here and there, streetlights and signs are turned on. A big blue bus rumbles around a corner, despite a traffic cop's frantic waving. The beggars thin out, children leaving first, then the women, finally the men.

And it is only then, when I decide to turn on the lights in my room, that I remember what was missing from the Chowdhury's lawn.

A guava tree. It was small but sturdy, planted in the centre of the front lawn. In the months I was there, Amma tied chunks of brick to jute rope and suspended them from its branches to train them to grow down and apart. From the moment the blossoms appeared, she tied a net around its top to ensure the fruit would be saved from the birds. Her efforts were rewarded. "Look Robin," Amma said. "Not a branch out of place, every fruit perfect." She ran her hands lightly over the leaves.

There was no sign of the tree now. In its place was nothing.

❧

The ferry I take back home to Saltspring Island is not crowded, but as usual, the trip's most garrulous passenger finds me on deck. I spot her immediately out of the corner of my eye, her radar working overtime, and successfully locating the one place she is least wanted. She wears binoculars and one of those jackets which withstands cyclones, hurricanes, typhoons, monsoons and cataclysmic flooding. "Splendid day," she says. "Makes one glad to be alive, don't you think?" I'd roll my eyes if they weren't paining so much.

I have a nasty flu. Aches began just as I was leaving the hotel. Fever rose in me at the airport. Over the Pacific, I believed I was watching myself in a movie. Then, as we disembarked in Vancouver, I spotted Hasan among the passengers: Hasan with a family. Hasan with his arm around a woman, ushering two small boys along the gangway. Hasan pulling suitcases off the luggage carousel. But each time I was about to call his name, he lifted his head or a hand, half-turned his shoulder, and I understood these were fever-induced hallucinations.

"It's gorgeous. Take a look if you like." The tourist proffers her binoculars.

"No." I head for the upper deck.

During the flight home, I reflected upon what I had discovered in Dhaka. I thought about it as we bumped along the jet stream. I turned Beth's revelations over and over again in my mind, trying to scare up new angles and fresh light. My rising fever bore down on my imaginings until they assumed grotesque shapes. When they became too monstrous to stomach, I would go to the claustrophobic washroom and splash water on my face.

On the upper deck of the ferry, seagulls dip along-side and cavort in the wind. Their beady eyes follow the movement of sandwiches and chips from hand to mouth. The tourists laugh like children at their antics. But next to tourists, gulls are the most irritating creatures, so perhaps they deserve one another.

If only Amma had received my letter. If only I'd been able to see her alone before Hasan told her I was back. We would have talked. I would have pointed out how Hasan had started everything with the nasty way he treated Luna, and ultimately his actions had harmed us all. Though he is her son, Amma recognizes his shortcomings. She would have understood my position, and everything would have been smoothed over between me and the Chowdhurys. Maybe we would even find Luna together.

I imagine Amma's embrace – softer now, but the strength that made her the hub of the wheel around which her family revolved would still be evident in her squeeze. "You have returned, just as you promised," she would mur-mur into my skin. "It is God's will." She would give me three brushy kisses and I would be enfolded once more in the scent of her talcum powder.

I leave the deck and enter the cabin. I find a seat, close my eyes and lean my head against the cool window. Passengers come and go, but no one else disturbs me for the rest of the trip, leaving me instead to my nightmares. They multiply and cluster like lenses on the surface of a fly's eye.

By the time the ferry reaches Long Harbour, I surrender to the fever. I will not make it home unassisted. Moreover, I don't care. I carry my bag and the Chowdhury's box toward the taxi stand anyway, and open the tinted glass door on the only car that is ever parked there. Len Harrington Jr., a young, foul-faced man with three days of stubble on his chin slumps over the wheel as though dead. Other than the name, he bears no resemblance to his father who, sadly, for those of us who depend on a taxi to get around the island, retired last year.

Len Jr. jerks awake, peers over the rims of his mirrored sunglasses as though I have just committed a criminal act. His look is so familiar, my own flesh and blood Surinder having mastered and made much use of the same expression of indignation. "Sorry," I say in a tone that makes it clear I'm not, and climb in. I sink into those pine-scented vinyl seats until I believe I will never reach bottom.

He sighs, and makes a huge fuss as he climbs out of the cab. I hear fumbling outside. The trunk opens, something thumps, thumps again, then the trunk closes. He climbs back into the cab and snaps his seatbelt closed.

"Extra twoonie for handling luggage," he says testily. But he could have left it there for all I care.

I know well the hill we climb out of Long Harbour; it leads to the seclusion I cherish. Too many hours have been spent in the company of others this past week. I long to be swallowed in the solitude of my home, my old stone schoolhouse. It's a miracle on this wooded isle.

"Turn here," I say, though I think Len Jr. knows. He grunts. Thank god he's not prone to chattiness.

We pull into a long dirt lane, behind one of the farmhouses near St. Mary Lake. The cab goes over a rut and my head opens like a crater. My eyeballs are pulled into the back of my head, the muscles taut. I close my lids and pray for the end of this trip.

And then we stop.

Len Jr. whistles. "Will you look at that."

I open my eyes to see what has uprooted an entire sentence from his mouth. It's my home. The roof has collapsed.

It must be fever. I'm hallucinating again. But as soon as my feet touch the ground, I know I'm not imagining this wreckage. The wet smell of ruin that hangs over my house proves its existence. Like a sleepwalker, I tread through damp grass. All the windows on this side are broken. Late afternoon sun glares off a splinter of glass barely attached to the frame. At the back, a section of the roof remains aloft, though it seems suspended by nothing. A single shingle, hanging by a nail, is stirred by a small breeze, then falls. I finish my circle at the front door.

What happened? Sure, the roof leaked when rain was heavy – but a couple of dabs of tar would have fixed that. I look to the trees which sheltered me. Perhaps a fallen branch? But they appear intact. An earthquake? A wrecking crew? A meteor? My explanations become absurd as I struggle to make sense.

I find my key, turn it in the lock, but the door will not open. I rattle the knob, push on it, and when the door doesn't give, I ram my shoulder against the wood.

Whump. And again. *Whump.*

"Wait," Len Jr. calls through his window. "Be careful."
My house groans. I step back. "Lady, you need help."
I laugh hysterically at his colossal understatement.

⁊⁊

When I saw the stone schoolhouse for the first time six
years ago, the collapse of the roof – the whole house in fact
– seemed imminent. Everything was run down, broken,
stained, corroded and dirty. Cobwebs festooned the ceiling
and corners. Squirrels, field mice, wasps and who knows
what other forms of life nested in every possible cranny.
A couple of windows were boarded up, most of the rest
cracked. The tin chimney for the pot-bellied stove was rusted through, and the toilet, scaly and discoloured, would
tolerate nothing being flushed, which made me wonder
how all those students and their teacher managed to get
through the day.

Outside was a tangle of blackberry canes, salal, stunted
cedar, fruit trees too old to bear anything other than scabs
of lichen, and grass, clover, vetch and buttercups, layer
upon layer choking itself to death. In the centre of the yard,
partly hidden beneath a snare of ivy, sat a charred, jagged
tree stump – struck by lightning long ago was my guess.
The only part of the property intact was the stone of the
walls.

As soon as I touched the stone, I knew I had found a
safe haven. A spot to rest. Away from the world.

I bought it.

It wasn't until I moved in and cleaned it up that I saw it
wasn't as bad as I had thought. Those broken windows, tall

and narrow, faced directly east and west, and welcomed the sun every day it chose to appear and bade it good-night as it set off in the direction of Vesuvius. In one of the western windows, a large Garry oak budded in early spring, was home to dozens of songbirds through the summer, and for two glorious weeks, flocks of frantic hummingbirds, dive-bombed for the caterpillars that plummeted from the boughs on fine threads like tiny arthropod paratroopers. When the birds departed, the leaves turned brown and dropped. I loved to watch the light and shadows on its scrappy boughs change with the seasons.

I'd never seen a ceiling like the one in my schoolhouse. Higher than a church's, it climbed acutely to a dark distant v. From there, everything fell into the heavy walls. I couldn't understand what held it aloft. I looked for solid cross-beams, support posts, interior walls that could bear the weight, but there were none. I supposed the technique used was from another era, a long-forgotten skill swallowed in the homogenization of the home construction industry.

I felt awed by the space that towered above me, but by no means small, lost or unworthy. The stones outside were never far from my consciousness. When I was alone in that house for the first time, I felt comforted in a way that I hadn't since I'd lost Graham four years earlier.

❧

Graham and I lived in East Vancouver in a bungalow built during the war; small, grey and boxy, stuccoed in and out like a bad case of acne. The neighbourhood was full of the same type of house. But it was all we could afford. Like any family just starting out, we made use of thrift shop furniture, public transit, and do-it-yourself everything. But I didn't mind. With Graham, everything was a novelty. Even refinishing the hardwood floors ourselves was exciting. When we were through, the least accessible corners of the floor glistened as though wet.

Surinder, barely four years old when we bought the house, joined our industriousness. A portent of her future self-sufficiency and ability to master everything effortlessly, she learned the contents of the toolbox and proved herself quite capable of fetching tools on command.

I canned and froze my way through the summer months. Our neighbour's damson tree gave a bountiful crop one year and when they offered us the works, saying they were sick of them anyway, I didn't hesitate. Graham and I were in that tree the same afternoon, perched on the mossy branches like two looting crows into somebody's picnic lunch. We dropped the fruit into Surinder's outstretched hands. I lined up the jars on a basement shelf, a handsome row.

I sewed all Surinder's clothes, mended everything, even leotards and underwear.

This was how we lived for years: me, Graham, Surinder. I hardly thought of Dad anymore, Dhaka and the Chowdhurys were fading memories upon which I had nearly given up, and I never missed home.

Graham worked summers as a casual landscape gardener – a day or two in North Van, another in Point Grey. It was the best he could do. Under-educated on paper and slightly tainted by politics, Graham was no different than other draft dodgers – good, steady work was hard to come by for them. He kept crazy long hours when a new garden was going in, then sat idle for days waiting for the next call. But after three or four years, and the government's official nod to draft dodgers, he was able to set up his own business. We scrimped some more and bought a used, but serviceable pick-up. Tools. "Cast your eyes on a masterpiece," he said the day the truck came back with his company name painted on the side: *Graham Livingstone Urban Jungles*.

On his own, Graham worked longer hours, all twelve months of the year. There was enough winter gardening in Vancouver to keep the money coming in, though he'd leave home later in the morning and return before dark. But summers, we'd hardly see him.

It was early September, well before the rains. Surinder was at school that afternoon. I was home, probably making or fixing something. Then the hospital called.

Graham died around about the time my cab crossed Main Street. Heart attack.

They were taking machines off his battered body when I arrived. His skin was pasty, except for a huge bruise on his face. His head was cut open on one side, and swollen. He was small on that hospital bed, as though he had sunk into not just the mattress, but himself.

An anemic nurse with white hair pulled an IV out of his wrist. I cried to see that arm I knew so well punctured and blue.

"These things happen," the doctor said, "though we don't know why so many more young men are experiencing them these days."

Was this consolation? To be honest, I barely took in what he said.

And then I remembered: I needed to call Surinder. She picked up the phone after the first ring.

Seventeen is young to lose your father. And thirty-nine is young to be a widow.

❦

I dragged myself around the house for weeks. I would have been happy to go with Graham, to choose death, in spite of Surinder. She'd already proven she could take care of herself. Self-confident, proficient, resourceful – she didn't really need me. She'd make a great orphan, though god help me if she ever found out I said so.

Graham had been trimming a laurel hedge high as a house, cutting off summer's least hardy growth, shaping the edges for winter. When his heart stopped, he fell from his ladder. No one noticed. Until the family came home to find the parked truck, the tumbled ladder and a half-dead gardener on their lawn. I suppose he had broken bones, too, but no one had told me that and I didn't want to know.

Among the shadowy yews and the pink rhodos of Dunbar, I lost everything.

I sought revenge in our garden. Pulled up the perennials he most loved: purple snapdragons and the apricot foxglove. Mounds of pink Japanese anemones. They were still in bloom.

I didn't want anything to grow around me.

❦

The tattered schoolhouse offered reprieve from grief. The floor was rough, but I knew where its soft spots lay. I replaced the broken windows myself with glass from Mouat's in Ganges, and duct-taped plastic sheets over them in winter to keep the draft out, the silver tape crisscrossed like thick spider webs. As for the toilet, we reached an uneasy peace. A 100-foot-long power snake with three alarmingly pronged blades that looked like they should be in the hands of Neptune or Lord Shiva guaranteed our harmony.

I slept in a corner, in Surinder's old bed. I ate at the small table she and I shared with Graham half a lifetime ago. I read and lounged and napped on an old sofa dumped on the property (I beat the dust out of it and covered it with a purple crocheted throw from my friend Fee). I had a fridge from the second-hand store and a propane double burner I chanced across among someone's trash the day I moved. My only connection to the bigger world outside was through a portable radio that ran on batteries, which, at night, if I held the antenna, could pick up campus radio from Anchorage.

But no more. All has been buried in the stone graveyard.

Everything I need to work is rubble, too – my books, my textbooks and the table where I tutor the kids from the high school. I help them with their conjugations, their articles and prepositions, their pronunciation, dentals and reflexes, rolling their rrrs, chewing their shchs and breathing their way (or not) through nasal vowels – in French, Spanish and German. I don't know what I'm going to do when the first one comes back for her tutoring in a couple of days.

I won't even be able to find a pen in this catastrophe.

Six hours after discovering my collapsed roof, I awake to a tap on another door. "Fancy a toddy? Or a cup of tea?" My friend Fee's voice is muffled, like a faulty phone connection.

"Go away! I'm asleep!"

She mutters something halfway between a foreign language and a curse. But I get my wish. Her feet patter down the hall.

Her house was the only place I could think of to go. She took one look at me on the doorstep and pulled me inside. "No," I said when she showed me to the guest room. It's directly over her cold cellar, and I was suddenly, deliriously terrified a spindly potato eye or colourless carrot top would push through the floorboards and choke me.

I don't recall exactly how she cajoled me into this bed. But here I am, jet-lagged, hungry, and sickened. My fever has gone down, but this is no improvement. At least, under the influence of a hundred and one degrees, I could pretend my life was nothing more than a bad dream.

It's ten o'clock at night. Now that Fee's knock has brought me back to consciousness, I am not the least bit tired. I consider getting up and having the tea. But then I will have to talk to Fee and maybe Mac if he's here, and even Jason, too, if he's up, and I'm not ready for explanations. How can I explain what I hardly understand myself? I try to chase the images of corpses and scars, wreckage and dust from my head, but they seem burned into my brain. I scuttle down under the duvet, and will sleep to take their place.

And it does, eventually, though I do not know how or at what time. I dream I fall from a ladder whose top rung is indiscernible in the clouds. I tumble so slowly, I can count the rungs on my way down. But then I realize it is not me falling. It's Graham. Everything accelerates. I want to scream but my lungs are empty and I cannot inhale. My mind says stop, but my mouth forgets how to form the words. Just as he is about to hit the earth, I realize there was no mistake. It is me falling. And I wake up.

It's dark outside. I have no idea what time it is. When my breathing slows, I become conscious of my pounding head. Ravenous, I creep to the kitchen.

I easily find bread and butter. I can't locate the bread knife though, so after one attempt to cut the loaf with a table knife, I settle for tearing it apart. I spread butter thick as icing, because I crave the grease and salt. Such habits always disgusted Surinder who, once she was old enough to both identify and correct her mother's many flaws, told me I would end up a poster child for obesity or in the hospital getting my arteries roto-rooted.

An irritating girl. Mouthy. And beautiful. Also sharp as a tack. She is a rare combination of qualities, and I have often wondered how I could have had anything to do with her creation.

I finish my bread, and the hunger is gone. But eating has had no effect on my head. Though it's still impossibly dark, the birds will stir shortly, and I want to be home when they do.

The floor rushes up to meet me when I try to stand. A pair of hands on my shoulders guides me firmly back down.

"Now, now. Just where do you think you're off to?" Fee.

"Home."

"In the middle of the godforsaken night?"

"The sparrows beg to differ. As do I."

She sighs. "You're not fit to walk out this front door, the shape you're in, let alone face the mess that's waiting for you, but if you're hell bent on going, lord knows it won't be me stopping you." She removes her hands.

Unsure what to do now I'm unfettered, I fall back in the chair.

"That's better. Can I get you that tea now?"

I nod.

Fee quietly busies herself with the sink, the kettle, the teapot. She darts from here to there, like the tiny bush-tits that come to the Garry oaks around my house every summer. Her stubby fingers are busy with soothing little movements.

"Feel any better?"

"Except for my head."

"Sorry about your place," she says. "Len's boy told me."

I manage half a shrug.

"So how was the trip?"

"Horrific." I don't even need to consider the appropriateness of the word.

"That good?"

"No, worse. I never should have gone. It was the biggest mistake of my life."

"Oh. Did you mean from conception onward? Or just birth?" I normally share her sense of humour. But in the dark, everything is warped. All that's happened in the past few days merges into a confusing, black void that threatens to swallow the little left of me. I do something I have not done in years, and never before Fee. I cry.

"Ooh. Sorry." She hands me a mug and sits down. I am

grateful she's not patting my shoulder or holding my hand. "Do you want to talk about it?"

It takes me a minute to recover. When I do, I lift the cup to my lips and blow across the hot tea. The surface flutters. "Did you ever do something that you were convinced was absolutely right, only to find out years later that things didn't turn out the way you planned?"

"Hmm." She studies my face. "What kind of something might that be?"

"I helped this girl I knew," I say. "Hell, she wasn't a girl. She was nineteen. And she was in love. I was sure it was the right thing to do."

Fee listens for details which I do not give. They seem too complicated. Finally she speaks. "And what happened to her?"

"I don't know. She's missing. She might be dead."

I feel rather than see Fee measuring me against this new information. I do not have the courage to look her in the eye right now.

"You just found out?" she finally says.

I nod. "After I left, I had no contact with anyone. It was – impossible," I say, not wanting to explain all the reasons now, all the reasons that seem pathetic and unworthy.

A moth rests on her kitchen window, its wings partly translucent. I'm afraid to look at Fee, afraid I may see in her eyes the same judgment the Chowdhurys have bestowed upon me.

"I offered to help, but the family won't let me. They won't have anything to do with me, for god's sake." I know this sounds petulant, but it's all because of the threat of a new flow of tears. "And now my goddamn roof's collapsed

and all I have left is a fucking pile of rubble and a headache."
I push my mug away.

"Well, that pushes things over the edge, doesn't it? That headache, I mean." Fee rises. "Can I get you breakfast?"

I glower. "I'm not hungry."

A frying pan clatters on the stovetop and she opens the fridge. "Once Jason's packed off to school, I'll walk you home. How would you like your eggs?"

"Fee – "

"And we'll clear up the mess. Toast?"

"You don't have to do this."

She cracks an egg on the edge of the counter. "I know."

⁂

Even in the hopeful light of morning, my schoolhouse looks bad. Though we agree it might be unwise, Fee and I chip broken glass out of a window and carefully climb through. Slants of sunlight illuminate the full extent of the damage. The floor is punched out in places. Stones are set in the holes like diamonds on a ring. Fallen beams sprawl like a wooden ribcage. Shards of glass glitter beneath each window. The sofa hides under a heap of debris that looks like it will collapse any moment. The table is splintered like firewood. The stove's tin chimney pokes out of a mound of waste like a periscope. Everything's soaked with rainwater.

The kitchen shelves have fallen. Food is everywhere, as though a bitter and disturbed intruder has scattered it in revenge for some ignominious and unresolved act committed against him in childhood. Even jars of beets Fee and I pickled – when? Last fall? Garbage. Red vinegar stains what's

- 178 -

left of the floors. The puddles are at once unsettling and beautiful.

"A mess indeed," Fee says.

I look into the bathroom. The huge mirror I never removed is now on the floor, and as I expected, most of the wall has followed it. The tub is filled with stone, wood and plaster-dust. The toilet's cracked open. A jagged wedge of porcelain lies beside it like a meat-eating dinosaur's tooth. Water drips from an unseen source.

I look around for something intact.

"You might think about calling someone," Fee says finally.

"But I can't afford anyone." I have no insurance. I couldn't afford that either.

There's my radio. Its plastic shell is cracked but it might be salvageable. I prod it with my toe. Static comes from it, then fades and dies. I kick it.

"Careful," Fee says.

The radio skids to a stop against a heap of shirts, skirts, jeans, and underwear. The wet, dirty fabric is tangled with scraps of building material. It's impossible to tell any of it apart. Almost certainly, there's nothing to salvage here. Almost certainly, all I have left is what I took to Bangladesh – one suitcase and the Chowdhury's box.

I can't make up my mind whether to cry or laugh. "Let's get out of here."

Back at her house, Fee scans the phone book. "Will you look at this? Three pages!" There's a cluster of new contractors in the phone directory. But when we review the listings, we find Ed Malone is still the only one who actually lives on the island. I know him to see him, and by reputation. He's supposedly a bit of a drinker, not the only one this island has spawned or attracted incidentally. But Fee and Mac hired him a decade ago to build the spare room on the back of their house which I now occupy.

"He's a good man," she says. "Stayed off the bottle while he was working. I heard it said he dried out since."

Before lunch, Ed and I meet at the schoolhouse. He has a funny, lopsided gait, and I wonder if he's drunk.

"You got a situation on your hands, for sure," Ed says, his voice clear. His breath seems free of alcohol. He lifts his cap and brushes a thinning thatch of yellow-grey hair off his forehead. As he replaces the cap, I see the sweaty band inside attesting to years of work that no washing machine could ever erase now.

When he moves again, I wonder if one of his legs is shorter than the other. Then, I get a whiff of something. Stale alcohol? Mouthwash? I'm not sure. I look for other signs of drunkenness, but see none.

"You know what Frank Lloyd Wright used to say about roofs? If it don't leak, how would you know it's a roof?" When he sees the look on my face, a chuckle dies on his lips, a short, merciful death. "Or something like that –" he murmurs.

Skip the levity Mr. Malone. Let's get this over with.

"So what do I do now?"

"Well, your roof's just the beginning. Look at the walls." A few stones have tumbled from along the upper edge of the roof and left behind concrete hollows like fossils. "And we might need to repair the foundation. I can't see any cracks, but I'd need to get right down into it to say for certain. Then you've got the inside – the floors, the windows. The bathroom from what I can see. Never mind your furniture." He tallies up my damage on calloused, dirty fingers.

"I can go over everything and give you an estimate – maybe tomorrow. But yeah, I'd say this qualifies as a pretty big job."

Though numb after Ed's assessment and exhausted from jetlag, I force myself to stay awake for dinner. Jason, Fee's insect-shaped ten-year-old, pulls his chair so close to the table, his thin chest is sandwiched between the chair back and the table edge, and his gangly elbows have nowhere to go but alongside his cutlery. Fee must have told him not to talk about Bangladesh or my house because the subjects are mercifully absent – as is all chatter. None of us knows what to say.

Fee's made spaghetti and meatballs. Dinner is hot and tasty. I'm as grateful for it, as I am for the silence, broken only by the tinny sounds of utensils colliding with crockery. I concentrate on my plate and its contents, but it's hard not to notice what's happening beside me.

Jason twirls his pasta around and around and around again. Then, when it appears the fork may bend from the weight, he jams a massive blob of dinner into his mouth. He chews. Bits of spaghetti, like beheaded worms, swim between teeth and tongue. My reverie shatters; I am sorely reminded of Hasan.

"Jason, love, do close your mouth. No one here needs a lesson on the digestive system."

He closes his mouth, continues to chew and winds his fork up for a second time.

Fee sighs. "May as well shout into the wind as try to teach you to eat like other than a shoat in a sty. I've news.

Your father called. He'll be back from Kitimat next week. Maybe Wednesday."

"Yeah," cheers Jason, and the worms re-appear. He fills his face again, then abandons his fork and with fingertips, picks vegetables out of the tomato sauce. Unexpectedly dainty, unmistakably like Amma.

"I thought you liked green peppers," Fee says.

Mac's return means I'll have to clear out of the guest room, the space he occupies when he's in town – and has occupied ever since he and Fee called it quits. Though I cannot understand how they manage this ménage, it seems to work as well as any other arrangement between ex-couples.

"I'm sure I'll be back home before then," I say, though the notion is so improbable as to be laughable.

"Don't be ridiculous. The welcome mat is out as long as you need it. You're no more trouble than a bad rash."

"I do have other options," I sniff. But she knows the only other option I have – Surinder – is out of the question. If I show up on her doorstep in Toronto, she'll make Mr. Chowdhury's greeting look like the Welcome Wagon.

"Anyway, it's just for a few days. Mac's contract's been extended again. Eat the mushrooms at least, for heaven's sake, Jason. He thinks they'll be working on that marina clear through September."

"Why can't I get a boat, Mom?" Jason says.

"You've got a boat, and I'll be happy to pump it up for you one of these days."

"That's not a real boat. It's a dinghy. And I hate mushrooms." He grimaces as he puts a tiny piece of mushroom in his mouth. "Can I go up north with Dad?"

"Well, you've already mastered the necessary table

manners. If you don't mind sleeping in a bunkhouse that smells like a cowshed, I suppose it could work. Can I fetch anyone more water?" She heads for the kitchen sink.

The tap runs. "He'll miss Hayley's convocation." Their eldest was finishing up at Simon Fraser. "He missed her high school grad, too." She refills her glass and mine. "These are important."

I missed Surinder's convocation. I wasn't even invited.

This meal suddenly seems cumbersome and unmanageable. Like peering into a kaleidoscope expecting pretty colours and designs, and ending up instead with countless selective reflections of the parts of the past that most hurt and shame. It matters not that we are politely avoiding certain topics of conversation. Uninvited dinner guests, they occupy space.

"Can I have some water, too?" Jason extends his glass back over his shoulder. When he still can't reach Fee's outstretched hand, he leans back in his chair, reaching even further. Then he loses his balance. Jason, chair and glass clatter to the kitchen floor.

"Mom!"

"For the love of Jesus!"

And for the first time since I've come back, I begin to laugh. It staggers out of my mouth, a hibernating bear emerging from a cave, thin, hungry and not really sure it is supposed to be there. I'm surprised to hear the unfamiliar sound. It falls flat when I become conscious of it. Creeps back into the darkness from whence it came.

※

Ed Malone hands me a paper adorned with black finger-prints and waits, crookedly, on Fee's front porch while I look it over. I have problems finding the final tally.

"I know a little about your situation – and I've done the best I can with the figures." I see the bottom line: $35,750. "And there may be contingencies –" He lifts the palm of his dirty hand, a question mark that hangs over my bank balance like a sword. "I won't know for sure about the foundation until we've dug around a little more. You want to go over it?"

"Can't you build a whole house for thirty-five thousand dollars?"

"That's an option, I suppose. But then the old building would need to be razed and disposal's no joke these days." He scratches his stubbly cheek. The skin beneath looks dry and soft.

I make a sound somewhere between a laugh and a cough. "But I don't have this kind of money."

"I'm sorry. Everyone I do an estimate for says the same thing. In your case, I actually believe it."

I think for a moment. "What can you do for – say, ten grand?"

He gives me a look. "I take installments. Let me know. I'm kinda booked the whole summer, but given the circum-stances, I could work on my schedule."

But neither his schedule nor installments matter. I do not have the money and there is no way I can get it, short of robbing a bank or winning a lottery. The only one who could help me won't even speak to me. How can I ask Surinder for one dollar, let alone thirty-five thousand? It'd be easier for my daughter to vote for the Communist

Party, certify the union at her law firm or ladle gravy at a soup-kitchen for drunken men and prostitutes. She has made it perfectly clear – there is no room in her life for a common thief like me.

※

The watch, well used, though hardly of heirloom vintage, had belonged to Graham. It was found on the lawn of the home where he had tumbled from the ladder, and delivered to me at the hospital. I had bought it and a card from the racks at London Drugs when such spending was a newly ac-quired extravagance. I wrapped it and wrote in the card: hap-py father's day to the world's best daddy. In the shaky script of a five-year-old, Surinder had signed her own name, and when Graham saw it, he squeezed her until she squirmed.

In the hours I spent alone, in our bedroom or aimlessly wandering the streets of our neighbourhood, I tried to understand his death. Nothing helped. The watch came closest though. The strap held the shape of his wrist. It smelled of his soap, sweat and his work with earth and plants. And be-cause he wore it when he died, the exact moment of his fall permanently set on its now-cracked face – 4:18 – I imagined a small piece of him being caught on the buckle, on the stem, on the second hand. It offered neither solace nor an explanation; still, I vowed to keep it forever.

During the funeral service, I played with it, turning it over in my fingers. When I felt a howl build at my core, I ran my fingertip along the cracked crystal. As long as I could do that without cutting myself, I was charmed. I would not make a spectacle of myself. That's how I got through the droning sermon – one stroke of a finger along cracked glass at a time.

Surinder, sitting beside me, must have seen, but she said nothing. It wasn't until she was moving out of the house, three years later, that she asked for the watch.

"Please Mom." She'd taken a suite in an old house on West Eleventh with two girls also heading for law school. Though the move reduced her commute to a single, seven-minute bus ride, instead of the forty-five-minute, two-bus trip she took from our home, I knew she was moving because she was ashamed of our working class, east side address.

"Let me think about it." I knew better than to refuse outright. She'd nag and badger, think of arguments and counter-arguments. She was already perfecting her court-room technique. But I wasn't going to let that watch go.

"Have you had a chance to think about the watch?" she asked weeks later, when I'd invited her over for some home cooking. I'd prepared a big Sunday dinner: roast, gravy, vegetables, the whole works. We'd eat in the dining room instead of the kitchen. Such culinary feats are not normally within my repertoire, but I wanted to do something motherly for my only child whose presence under my roof I was sorely missing. I fantasized introducing a regular Sunday dinner and talk into our schedules – much the same way my father had done with me – and saw this meal as the beginning of a tradition. I thought I'd lose my sanity when it came to the gravy, but miraculously, it turned out rich and velvety.

"I don't eat meat," Surinder sniffed.

"What are you talking about? Since when?" She set in front of her a plastic tray of sushi picked up from Safeway at the last minute. "Fish is meat."

"Wrong. Fish is fish. Beef, pork, chicken – they're meat."
I have no patience for such self-serving semantic rubbish.
"That watch means a lot to me," I said.

"Don't you have chopsticks?"

"Didn't you bring any?"

"Never mind." She speared a piece of California roll with a fork. "He was my father, you know."

"I know."

"I gave him that watch."

"I said I would think about it and I am."

"How long are you going to think about it?"

"What's your hurry?" I said. "You're going to get it eventually, when I die."

Her fork clattered to the table. "Well, congratulations. That's about the most hurtful thing you've ever said to me."

"What?"

"I loved him, you know. And it's not like I'm sitting around waiting for my own mother to kick the bucket."

"I know you loved him. I loved him, too." I picked up my utensils. "And I'm glad you're not counting the days to my funeral. Just forget about it, okay, and enjoy your meal. I'll let you know."

"You know what your problem is? You're greedy."

I laughed. "I'm greedy? God, Surinder, cut me some slack."

"It's always about you, isn't it?"

"Look. Let's talk about something else. How's your sushi? Have you seen any good movies?"

"You are a pathetic communicator."

"Yes. It's always about me, isn't it?"

"Does it please you to throw it right back in my face?"

"I promise you: I'll let you know. But I won't stand for any more talk of it tonight."

She huffed and speared a prawn butterflied over a mound of sushi rice. We finished the rest of that meal barely speaking. So much for my Sunday dinner plan.

So when, in the middle of November, I noticed the watch was missing from the old, satin-lined jewellery box I keep in a bureau drawer, I knew exactly where it was. "You have to give it back," I said, over the phone that evening.

Thankfully, she didn't pretend she had no idea what I was talking about. "Why? Let it go. I never ask you for anything." That was true, and had been since puberty through which she flew with barely a tear or pimple.

"Because it's not yours."

"It's not yours either. It was Dad's. And I gave it to him."

"I'm not going to argue. You bring that watch back."

"What are you going to do about it if I don't?" She hung up.

But her question got me thinking: what was I going to do about it? I couldn't live without the watch. Not yet. I needed to know it rested in that box, in that bureau. I needed to know that Graham was somehow still accessible. If Surinder wouldn't give it back, then I had no choice but to go get it.

Rachel, her roommate, answered the door. She was a big girl with a jowly bulldog face, helpful in a way that you knew meant she was really just plain old meddlesome and needed to get a life. "She's not here."

"I know." Her weekly three-hour lecture on constitutional law delivered by a retired supreme court justice who mumbled, the one she'd been moaning about all term, had just begun. "I'm here on a secret mission." I told Rachel I was planning a surprise party for Surinder, and needed to get a few of her friend's phone numbers. Rachel oozed delight. She not only let me in, she led me to Surinder's room and helped me find her address book.

"Why didn't you call? I would have got the numbers for you."

Is it possible she didn't know Surinder's birthday wasn't until April? I thought girls knew these things about one another. The only other explanation – that Rachel was gullible enough to believe I needed five months to organize a party – said more than enough about the mental capacity of prospective lawyers.

"That's very sweet, but I was worried Surinder might pick up the phone." I began writing down a few numbers so Rachel wouldn't become suspicious.

"Oh, Sue's at the library all the time. She's never here to answer the phone."

Sue? This was the first I'd heard of that.

Rachel continued. "I love a surprise party, though my cousin's wife in Calgary organized one for him and it completely back-fired. He got laid off from work the very same day, so when he came home, he –"

"Rachel, could I trouble you for a glass of water?"

"Would you prefer tea?"

"That would be lovely."

And in the time it took for her to boil the water, steep the bags and come back, I found the watch. A mother knows the nature of her child's preferred hiding places.

I gulped that tea and burned my tongue. "Gotta go."

"Call me if you need anything else."

"Not a word. Remember." We sealed our pact with a small hug.

I imagined Rachel there, anticipating the party, gleeful and a little smug about her involvement, until Surinder found the watch missing. She came to my house as soon as she figured it out.

"This is the worst thing you've ever done to me." Even in the dim glow cast by the porch light, I could see tear stains.

"You shouldn't have taken the watch without asking."

"I did ask."

"And I said I'd think about it."

"You never gave it a second thought. Anyway, what right do you have to waltz onto my private property and take things?"

She forgot that when it comes to waltzing onto people's private property and taking things, she is not the only one with talent. "I took what belonged to me."

"You're so nasty. Making up that stupid story for Rachel. Do you have any idea what you'd get in court for that performance?"

"So sue me. You're the one who took my watch."

"Well, I never broke into your home to take it. Besides, I have a legal and moral right to that watch."

"A moral right?" I would have laughed if I wasn't so angry.

"He was my father."

"He was my husband."

"Blood is thicker than water."

"Oh come on."

"I will sue you then. Don't think I won't. If nothing else,

I can prove your negligence as a mother, and your complete abrogation of your parental responsibilities."

"What are you talking about?"

"Come to court and find out."

The hollow sound of her feet pounding down the front steps – *doom-doom, doom-doom* – is with me still.

I asked myself then as I have so many times since if I was a bad mother. A breed of woman with a piece of genetic material missing from her DNA, otherwise, why wouldn't she be sweet, loving, kind, nurturing, giving, forgiving – all the so-called natural things that are a squeeze for me to manifest? What mother steals from her child? Not even an animal mother. A wicked mother.

I took the watch out of its place in my bureau. But all the rubbing I could do along that cracked crystal made no difference. My charm did not work when it came to my child. I cried into the early morning, and sleep, when it came, was flat as death.

❦

If I had my time back, what would I do differently? When Surinder asked if she could go to gymnastics camp in Oregon that spring, would I have said no, not this year, wait until you're sixteen – instead of nodding my head, procrastinating, thinking she'll never go? When she came home selling magazines and chocolates to raise money to pay her own way, could I have taken one less subscription, bought one less box of almonds, and said, good effort, try again next year? When her teacher came by the house one afternoon to discuss the situation, could I have pleaded a long-planned family vacation, a pressing medical problem, anything – except what I did say – that I would never allow my daughter to go to the United States of America?

"I'm very sorry." Her teacher shook her head sadly. "This is a lost opportunity for her." I closed the door, angry at the interfering teacher, and no less certain in my principles.

"You can't tell me what to do!" Surinder shrieked from the bathroom that evening, where she had locked herself in. Behind the door, water ran. Things thrown hit the wall. With a rattle and a thump, something collapsed on the floor.

"Surinder, please try and understand." I hit the door with the heel of my hand.

"Don't touch that door again – or I'll go and I'll never come back."

From another teenager, it would have been an idle threat. From her, it was a distinct possibility.

She calmed down enough to listen to Graham when he arrived home an hour later. She let him in the bathroom. I tried to listen, but their voices were indistinct, and I couldn't bring myself to squat beside the keyhole. Thirty minutes later, she went to her room and he came downstairs.

"What did you say?"

"I just tried to tell her about the Vietnam War – and the draft." He shrugged. "I don't think I did such a hot job."

"Well, your audience is not exactly receptive, is she?"

He took the lid off a pot of soup and inhaled. "Sometimes you're a little hard on her."

"What?"

"I just think you should lay off her a little."

"That's so unfair," I cried. God, I hated it when they both ganged up on me. "Don't you hear the way she speaks to me?"

Graham ladled soup. The subject was closed. But more importantly, the gymnastics team went without Surinder.

"Did you and Dad live under a rock or something?" she said three years later. In her final year of high school, she was working on a history project. She had spread a file of newspaper clippings from the library across the kitchen table. "How could you just turn your backs and walk out?"

"It was important to your father," I said. "And, by extension, important to me. It was a matter of principle."

"Principle? Principle is staying back and fighting for what you believe in. At least, that's what you and Dad taught me."

"Dad could never go to war. He could have never killed anyone."

"I'm not talking about that. Look. It's all here. Here's a guy from Minnesota who went to jail for three years. Here's a guy from Florida who got elected to the state legislature and fought to change the law. Here are three women who started their own lobby group in Washington. *The New York Times*, *The Washington Post*, *Time* and *Newsweek*, and even the frigging *Vancouver Sun*. They're filled with examples."

"Don't say frigging."

"You had a choice. You make it sound like you didn't. That's cowardice."

"Your father was not a coward."

"And then you skipped Grandpa's funeral. Unbelievable. Nothing would've stopped me from being at Dad's. Nothing."

Surinder's accusation hit a nerve. For I had many doubts still about missing Dad's funeral, about having never again seen any of the rest of my family left in Michigan. Though, at the time, it seemed the right thing to do, as every year passed, I wondered if my fear had been misplaced, if I had misjudged the situation. The voices inside me veered back and forth, until I couldn't stand it anymore, and I'd dismiss them – until the next time something raised that memory, and I had to once more deal with my misgivings. How could I explain to that angry face when I myself didn't even understand, when I didn't have an explanation good enough for the voice of judgment that confirmed I had failed my father?

"I'm sorry about that," I said. "I wish I had gone."

"Sorry? That's the best you can say after fucking up so majorly? You're not fit to be anyone's mother." She swept the papers to the floor and ran from the room.

※

When Mac gets back, he and Fee have a private conversation. Together, they decide he will bunk in with Jason for now – and they will loan me $5,000, no interest, repayable by the time their son enters university or college. That gives me about eight years. It is a stretch for them, and a far cry from the amount I need, but I accept. Perhaps it will get Ed Malone started.

For the rest, I try the bank. Under its tasteful clock tower, Saltspring's version of a skyscraper, an equally decorous loans officer conjures up impossible figures. The payments will leave me with less than fifty dollars a month for food, taxes, clothing and other expenses. Though I am accustomed to living off very little, this will never work. Even if I could find some new students to tutor. So I have no choice. I must ask Surinder.

It is incredible to fathom that my not-yet twenty-eight-year-old child may have this kind of money. But then, I never imagined I'd have a daughter who'd buy into the corporate world so uncompromisingly, though heaven help me if I should ever say such a thing to her. I also never lost my father at such a tender age, only to have him, inadequately I admit, replaced by a life insurance policy.

If I call Surinder, she will most definitely hang up. So Fee suggests I write. As I do not have her home address, I decide to write to her plush office in Toronto. Of course she still works there.

Dear Surinder,

Don't throw this away. At least, please read it through before you do. I'm in a lot of trouble and need help, and I don't have anywhere to turn except you. I'm sorry this is the case, but I must face the reality of my life.

About a week ago, the roof of my house fell in. The repairs will cost $35,000. I don't have that kind of money. And I didn't have insurance. I don't need to tell you why. My financial situation has always been a problem.

A bank loan is impossible because no matter how they calculate it, I can't afford the monthly payments.

If there is any way you can help me, I would be grateful. I could handle a very long-term loan if the interest rate was low enough. We could arrange this through an intermediary if you still do not want to talk.

But I hope you will. I am very sorry about our misunderstanding. It is not natural for a mother and daughter to be so distant, whatever their differences. Please write soon.

Love,
Mum.

I don't mention the watch. It is, I presume, somewhere in the rubble of my home. It crosses my mind that I should find it and send it. But the gesture seems shoddy. What would be meant as a peace-offering would be taken as a sort of bribe that would cheapen what I hope is a straightforward and sincere, though painful, request for help, and an attempt to meet her halfway. Besides, I am still not ready to surrender the watch.

My hand shakes when I seal the envelope. It has been shaking since I wrote 'Mum,' pondering whether I had spelled it that way always, or with an 'o' so long ago. How quickly we become unaccustomed to our names when there is no one to use them.

I think about it over the weekend. On Monday morning, when Fee heads to town, I ask her to post the letter.

※

On the morning Ed Malone is supposed to begin, I wait twenty minutes. Thirty. After an hour, I know he is sitting on a deserted beach with a couple of cases of beer and a bottle of whiskey, drinking away my five thousand dollars. He tosses empty bottles onto barnacle- and limpet-encrusted rocks, laughing at the way the shattered glass glints in the tide pools. I hope the fool started his binge above the tide line so he won't get swept out to sea when he passes out and the waves come in. How stupid of me to ignore the rumours. But then his lopsided form turns up ten minutes later. He has brought two men and a truck loaded with lumber.

"I thought you said eight-thirty." I sniff, but nothing smells suspicious.

"I got held up by the waste disposal people. Everything needs a permit these days." He lifts a corner of his t-shirt and scratches his ribs. He leaves behind a gritty smudge before the worn cotton falls back down. "First dumpster's coming tomorrow morning."

I sit on a piece of firewood. They unload the lumber, bow their heads together and discuss what they are doing. They measure, saw, hammer. And assemble a complicated structure of braces meant to hold up what is left of the roof and walls. When the workers are constructing a brace across the front door, Ed examines the foundation. He digs down a few inches and prods with a pointed tool. He stands, steps and bends his way along, a funny, crawling sort of dance in which his skinny butt features prominently. Despite myself, I almost laugh.

Neighbours I know to see but not by name, drive up the lane to witness the spectacle. I suppose they've heard the hammering, or at least, the news. When they find me there, too, they quietly slide their cars and trucks into reverse and back away.

Ed's idea is to make the structure safe so I can retrieve my belongings and he can haul away the debris. "How much will that cost?" "Depends on what you throw out," he says. "One, two grand?" "Maybe." "More?" He shrugs. "Hard to say."

"I'm wasting money," I tell Fee and Mac as we prepare supper that night. "It's all destroyed anyway."

"Perhaps you shouldn't be so hasty," Mac says.

"Perhaps I should fire Ed Malone and hire a bulldozer."

Tutoring seems irrelevant, yet how can I ignore anything that produces money? Unless I tutor on top of her sewing machine, Fee has no space whatsoever. So I call the school. They offer a vacant classroom two afternoons a week, from the time school is finished until the janitor goes home. "Just until you get straightened around," the principal says. "The board won't like it, but I can fend them off for a few weeks." I call my students. All seven agree to the new meeting place and schedule, though the girl who got the last slot mumbled something about missing the bus which I ignored.

It takes three days before Ed's crew lashes together several blue plastic tarps, and fastens them to tree trunks, and to pegs hammered into the ground. My home looks like a gift-wrapped skeleton. Ed pronounces the site safe. "But I wouldn't throw a square dance in there, if you know what I mean." He promises to come every day while I am cleaning to make sure nothing shifts.

Still no word from Surinder, though she probably hasn't even received the letter yet. When I sit on the toilet at Fee's, I count the squares with first-aid tips on the Red Cross calendar that's hung beside the medicine cabinet. Although it should take less than two weeks, it may as well be two years. The wait is excruciating.

I obsess over her reaction to my request. I do the calculations over and over in my mind. How much does a corporate lawyer make these days? What's her rent? She couldn't have much of a student loan to repay after all those scholarships. I urged her to reject the one from Mobil Oil but as usual, she refused to listen to reason.

And what's she done with the life insurance policy? She dismissed it, angrily, at the notary's office, though Graham and I had expected a much different reaction when we had planned for that moment – never expecting his death would arrive so soon. "I don't need money," she sniffed. "I can take care of myself." "In that case, I can recommend a suitable charity," the notary said through half-moon glasses without once looking up from his desk.

When Surinder and I were out on the street, I started. "Your father meant that money for you. You! So you could start your life on the right foot."

I knew what it was all about. Her rejection of the money was a rejection of Graham and his values. She should have been proud her father was a draft dodger, not shamed into making stupid decisions.

"I can 'start my life on the right foot'," she answered, "without help."

"What's wrong with you? It's –" I struggled to find the word I wanted. "– *peculiar*. This idea that somehow you can make your way in life by yourself."

"So what do you want me to do? Give up? Do exactly what everyone tells me to do? That is not, in case you haven't noticed, how you and Dad raised me."

And it struck me, suddenly and with great force, that I had had this same conversation years ago with Amma. Though who had turned the table? Who had put Amma's words in my mouth? I fell silent not wanting to betray myself further by repeating even more of Amma's antiquated ideas.

In the end, I have no idea what she decided. It's been nearly seven years since I've seen her during which time she could have spent the entire amount on designer handbags or lottery tickets.

I deliberate in solitude. I would love to ask Fee her opinion of my daughter's financial situation, but my reckonings seem crass. Even if Surinder has the money, there is no reason why I should expect her help. Though the issue weighs heavily, as heavily as my discoveries in Dhaka – for those feelings do not fade, but flourish instead, as Luna, Shaheed, Hasan and Amma become part of a mountainous backdrop looming over my present situation – I decide to stop thinking about all of it, and get on with what I can.

Fee and I dress in ragged clothes. She ties a red bandanna around her hair. I push a metal wheelbarrow; she totes a couple of shovels on her shoulder. Together, we look like depression-era vagabonds in search of work, bumping over potholes damp with rain from a couple of nights ago. Thankfully, it is a mostly clear day, the air saltwater fresh, the spring sunshine warm. Blotchy clouds form a thin line that bends to the horizon. Our shirttails flap in the cool breeze.

Where I once grew vegetables, the dumpster squats, military green and monolithic. All things damaged beyond use or repair will go inside. As for whatever is salvageable or questionable, organized Fee points out corners of the yard, still dewy, where we will put them. Although she makes sense, there are too many piles, too many instructions, and before she finishes, I forget everything.

I open the front door, squared off now by the brace. It squeaks. The air inside, trapped under the tarp, is already humid and mildewy, much like my hotel in Dhaka. The covering gives an eerie bluish tinge to everything, as though we are looking through a dim black and white television screen.

Lethargy settles into my hips. I doubt I have the energy needed to step over the threshold. "Let's get rid of it all. I don't need anything."

Fee steps around me. "You take your time."

"But I just said I don't want any of it."

She picks up a greenish moccasin, its fringe raggedy as though chewed by a teething mongrel. Is it mine? I don't recognize it. I shake my head and she throws it over my shoulder. It flops into the wheelbarrow.

"Good shot," I say.

"Don't just stand there. Get a shovel."

❧

I start with the table where I once tutored because it is closest to the door. It's hard to recognize under all the plaster, dust and other unidentifiable debris. I locate a corner and pull. It's stuck. I jiggle it. Nothing budges. I pull harder. Then something cracks, and rubble slides down. "Oooh, careful," Fee says. I need her to help – the table's impossibly jammed – but she's busy in the kitchen, so I look for the chairs instead. I spot a tell-tale leg. A slab of layered shingles, rusty nails protruding like quills from the back of the lumber that binds them, pins it to the floor. I search for another, less dangerous chair.

As I pick through the waste, my thoughts drift to my last night with the Chowdhurys. When Luna's rickshaw had disappeared onto the busy street after I had said good-bye to her, I never thought it would be the last time I would ever see her. I knew it was risky, and so did she, but we never imagined she would vanish. How different my trip to Dhaka would have been had she appeared at the event where I was speaking, or answered the door at the Chowdhury home, or been having tea at Beth's place when I turned up. How different if she had come back after the war. If she had never run away with Razzak in the first place.

I move one broken item aside, place another on top, fill the space I have created with still more junk. I accomplish nothing. Fee, on the other hand, that industrious whirlwind, has found a drawer, which she fills, then empties outside in the designated piles, then fills again. She moves like a worker bee, removing load after load of debris.

Amma was so upset that night, and all I did was argue with Hasan. It seemed so important then to defend Luna. Besides, I always believed she would come back, and the family would accept her decision to marry Razzak. When did Amma's fears that night transform into the realization that something was amiss with Luna's story? How unfathomably horrible it would have been when Hasan also failed to return.

What happened to him after we parted? We had been so careful all the way to the airport, and though we had heard much, we had seen almost no one. If he had just retraced our steps, he should have made it home. The timidity of the rickshawallah which I had found so exasperating that night surely would have helped. He certainly wouldn't have dared to venture anywhere near even the slightest danger. But perhaps they, too, had parted. I had no way of knowing.

I shake the memory from my mind and pick my way over to a heap of clothing. "Yech."

I gather soaked, droopy clothes – jeans, shirts, jackets. Sour, cold water needs to be wrung from them. Then I expose the sleeve of a tie-dyed peasant blouse. A black and purple diamond design repeats itself on eggy yellow.

Surinder made it, years ago, in one of those infernal clubs she was always joining, or a summer camp she insisted on attending.

Instead of sewing the usual apron with pansies embroidered on a pocket, or table cloth with fussy lace trim, or whatever outlandishly useless thing those counselors and leaders forced the kids to make, she tried to create something I might actually like. She gave it to me, her thirteen-year-old face alternately shy and defiant.

"Oh, wow," I said, after a moment. Even the most thickheaded parent could see the love in each stitch, in every burst of colour. I hardly breathed as I held the garment, fearful any movement would spoil this fragile encounter, for she was at that age when the slightest twinge of muscle on my part could provoke a major argument. But wow was not the right thing to say, nor apparently was it appropriate to be so still. Surinder interpreted both as aversion. The flood of disappointment on her face is as fresh today as it was then. "You don't have to wear it," she said.

"But I want to. I like it."

"Don't say what you don't mean."

"No. I really like it."

But it was too late. I'd already messed up.

I rarely put on that blouse. I didn't want it to wear out, but its appearance also reminded me strongly of my dismal ability to reach my only child. Even now, soaked and smelly, it equally embarrasses and moves me. I pull it out of the tangle. Water trickles to the floor. I put it on a window ledge until I decide what to do with it. Everything between me and Surinder is a waiting game.

꙳

Fee has to go to the bank and then grocery shopping – Mac headed back north yesterday – so I am alone this morning. We are almost finished, thanks to my willingness to part with nearly everything. In my to-keep pile, I have the bed frame, a dresser, one chair, which I later found propping up a fallen bookshelf, the fridge and the propane burner, though the old tank is dented and unsafe. There are kitchen utensils, pots and pans, the big plastic box that holds the hammer, a few screwdrivers, two or three odd-sized wrenches, and gardening tools, and a mismatched set of margarine containers filled with nails, screws and other fasteners. I'm keeping the photographs. Though they are spoiled, Fee has promised to ask a photographer friend if the negatives can be rescued. The clothing in the dresser also escaped the deluge, as did some tinned goods. But I have no more books, carpets, bedding or linens. The textbooks I desperately need for tutoring are warped, torn and soaked. Anything ornamental that hung on a wall or rested on a shelf is not worth saving.

A gentle rain fizzes against the tarp like little bubbles. The shop light Mac hooked to a nail a couple of days ago is indispensable in today's gloom. I angle it toward the corner where I used to sleep, so I can begin work under its harsh crescent moon.

How tranquil this corner once was. How thoroughly it allowed me to withdraw into it. I would sink into the silence, the darkness, and fall asleep. When I awoke, I would feel disappointed, as though I had lost something along the way. Once my refuge, I can no longer even rise in this unrecognizable corner.

I move stones and some plaster. Underneath lies a small cabinet where I placed my lamp and reading materials. Another keeper. Somehow, it has not been crushed. When its door resists opening, I force the tiny hinges. One snaps off and leaves a jagged metal edge.

There's not much inside, but what's there is intact. Some magazines, an open packet of Christmas cards, two jewellery boxes.

In the turmoil, I have forgotten.

Graham's watch, heavy and pliant as a sleeping child, still fits my palm. I run my finger down the crystal again, and find comfort in the constancy of the sad memories it invokes. What would Surinder make of this watch now? Surely she is too engrossed with her own importance to be as attached to it as she once was. Surely she has new amulets to remind her of her success and ambition.

"Hallo? Anybody home?" Silhouetted against the front door frame, lopsided Ed Malone pulls me out of my reverie. Faithful as a St. Bernard, he hasn't missed a single day. "There you are."

I tuck the watch under a splintered board whose former purpose is unclear. "Hi." I know his routine: he'll look up, down, and leave for another job. I have only a minute to wait.

"Everything okay?" Because of the drizzle, he's pulled his hood up and I cannot see his face. His outline is bulbous like he's been inflated. He saunters in a circle, alternately looking overhead, then down, as predicted. His wet boots squeak. Just one more minute and he'll be gone.

He steps crookedly over a thick beam, and strikes one of the new braces with the heel of his hand. *Thump.* "Yup.

Solid as a grizzly's chest. No worries here." He pulls his hood down, and hands on hips, he surveys the line where the walls meet the tarp. I still can't see his face, lit as I am by the lamp, he in the dusky shadows. The rain continues to mutter. Graham's watch calls my name.

Why isn't Ed leaving? Tension mounts, but he's still studying the walls. Doesn't he have somewhere to go today? He better. He must. The watch glows, hums, sings out, until I wonder that Ed cannot hear it.

He kicks the floor with his heel. *Tap, tap, tap.* "You girls are sure working hard," he says after a moment, to what's left of that section of sub-floor. He walks to the wall and raps at a joint with his knuckles, preoccupied. "Think you'll be done tomorrow?"

I will the watch to silence. Does he see something? A problem unforeseen? A construction quandary he has not taken into account while preparing the estimate? But I'm too afraid to ask – not before I've heard back from Surinder. "Maybe. We're close. Which reminds me – better get back to it, huh?" So, I pull an old Maclean's from the stack and study the cover as though the decision about what to do with this issue requires all my concentration.

He clears his throat. "I been meaning to ask you something."

He needs more money, wants more time. No doubt now. Though I am generally proficient at pain avoidance, I put the magazine down and face my fate. "Go ahead."

"Why did you take so many support beams out of your house?"

It takes me a moment to shift gears. "What do you mean? I didn't."

"I been looking over the debris here and there isn't nearly enough wood here to support a roof this size and weight. Didn't the building inspector tell you?"

"What building inspector?"

"When you bought the place."

"There was no building inspector."

Ed seems puzzled. Like I've just told him I don't have a liver or a heart, or that I don't need oxygen to breathe. "Mighta been a good idea under the circumstances – considering the age of this old girl and all."

How can I explain? My grief, my desperate longing for Graham, my falling out with Surinder and the resentment and sorrow I subsequently harboured. The solace when I saw the house, the overwhelming sense that everything would be all right now – these will make no sense to a logical man like Ed Malone. I struggle to find other words that might.

But before I can open my mouth, a gust of wind comes up. It lifts the tarp, and though it's overcast outside, for an instant, the room floods with new light. It is then I see his face. Used to the shadows, he hasn't had a chance to adjust it. The look is pure compassion.

The tarp falls. Ed's face slips back into the gloom.

"Thanks for the advice. Next time," I say, praying he cannot see my red cheeks, though of course he can, illuminated as they are by the work light.

"All right then." He nods. "Better make a move." The floor creaks again as he heads for the door. "When I said working hard, I meant you were good folks. I can tell. And I'm sorry about your troubles." His silhouette slips away.

Alone in the harsh light, I wonder if I have imagined the whole visit. I am not accustomed to sympathetic looks. In fact, I am not accustomed to any looks at all, for, as a fifty-year-old woman, I have become invisible. Clerks, cashiers, librarians, bank tellers – I waltz through their transacted days barely noticed. I challenge any of them to describe the colour of my hair. My eyes. Estimate my height or weight. Not one will be able to.

And I prefer it. I cherish and protect this anonymity. Many times in my life – in Dhaka, silently renouncing my birth country at the border, moving to this little island, I have longed for the freedom of invisibility. I am a pariah by choice.

So I don't want Ed Malone's looks, kind, compassionate or otherwise. I don't need his pity. It distresses me to think he has feelings for me and my situation. The idea drains so much energy I stop working and forget about Graham's watch hidden under the lumber.

※

Less than four months after I left Dhaka, I decided I couldn't stand being back in Lansing. Everything annoyed me – the lights and signs, the absence of people on the streets, the shimmering opulence of the A&P, the ragged beggars, whom I'd never even seen before. No one but me saw the hypocrisy knit into the entire society. My vision had blurred or cleared, I didn't know which.

When was Luna going to write? I hungered for word of her well-being.

I didn't return friends' calls. I stayed home, avoiding movies, shopping, bars and coffee shops – all the meaning-less activities that had once filled my days and nights. To placate my troubled father, I sometimes went for a walk, but only at night. I wandered the streets of our neighbourhood until I was sure Dad had gone to sleep. I couldn't bear the expectant look on his face when I came home.

I didn't lose my year at university, though there was much discussion when I arrived back in the final weeks of the semester. Michigan State could not reach Dhaka University. After the night of March 25, when the campus was attacked by the army, professors and students slaughtered in their residences, steps to the buildings stained with the blood left behind as their mangled corpses were dragged outside, everyone else disappearing and living under assumed names, there was no one left on campus to answer the phone, return a telex or receive the mail. No one could confirm I attended the university.

The school administration's decision was tempered by the climate of the day; all that interest in conflict and peace manifested in a compromise in my favour. They would review the papers I had written in Dhaka. I would complete summer coursework and write a significant essay. I quickly pulled together a thirty-page comparative study on student political movements in the United States and East Pakistan. I contrasted the role American students played in the Vietnam War crisis – enriching national dialogue – with the role played by East Pakistani students in their independence movement. For they seemed to be responsible for escalating their conflict, taking up arms, perhaps even causing the deaths of many intellectuals and villagers. I used Hasan, name changed of course, as a prime example of the type of student I meant, whose energy would have been better directed to the cause of peace.

My adviser wrote across the top: "Fascinating. But unsuitable for a language degree. Try again."

I wrote beneath her words, "I don't have anything else to say," and resubmitted.

But in the end, I dropped the topic and wrote something benign about Tagore and nature. I graduated with the rest of my class.

My adviser, without my consent, tempted perhaps by the tidal wave of interest in both Vietnam and the Liberation War, and the hunger for more firsthand accounts of both tragedies, submitted my unsuitable paper to an editor she knew at *The Journal of International Student Affairs*. My adviser's pleasure when they accepted the paper knew no bounds and though I protested angrily at first, eventually I was flattered into acquiescence.

That article created a minor stir in academia, which eventually spilled into the mass media. Excerpts of my paper were re-printed, most often out of context and carelessly edited. No one asked me about it – apparently, I signed over my rights to the journal. A flurry of letters to the editor was followed by bomb threats to the journal's office in Washington, Michigan State University, and the offices of anyone else foolish enough to reprint it. I had no stomach for all that sensation. Most of the people stepping into the debate were nitwits, the rest hypocrites.

In Lansing, I plunged even deeper into myself. And when my skin began to take on the pallid look of subterranean fish, my aunt, Adele, came up with a solution. A holiday. In Canada. "We'll lie on the beach, swim when it's too hot. Maybe you'll meet someone." She was my father's youngest sister, only two years older than me. We were more like cousins, though I found her overbearing at times. When she wanted something, our age gap expanded to fill an entire generation, and we would assume our familial roles: her aunt to my niece.

"Adele –"

"Come on." She held out a blinding armful of fashion and women's magazines.

The prospect of a week like that horrified me and I wouldn't have contemplated it any further if my father hadn't intervened. "I keep telling you – you need to get out," he said again over dinner. "Sunshine – air."

"What? Like I'm a flat tire? A moldy sneaker?" I poked sullen holes in my mashed potatoes. "Speak English, Dad. You're the schoolteacher."

"Give yourself a break, hon. What harm will a week on a lake do?"

He had to be joking. The shortlist included an obscenely clean beach, icy Lake Huron water, bland, white Canadians in swimsuits, Coca-Cola, cotton candy, minigolf and shrieking speedboats driven by middle-aged men in sun visors and aviator sunglasses.

I couldn't think of anything I wanted less. Unless – and I had to be honest with myself – it was more time alone.

So I packed. Adele went on a crash diet and did something to her hair just before we left.

"Do you like it? I can get my hairdresser to do yours if you want. It's called a shag."

I wanted to tell her that she looked like a date palm, bushy locks springing out from the top of an impossible thin and scaly trunk. Rather than replication, the new look deserved a quick demise.

We crossed the border and checked into a cabin on the fringes of Grand Bend. "Isn't that charming?" Adele cooed about the pine table for two in the kitchen, and its scarred surface. "All this – rusticity!"

And that was almost the last I saw of her. She latched onto a group of girls ripe with tans, who hung out with boys who wore nothing but cutoffs – "they're locals, you should hear their accents," she said, as though she'd discovered a rare, exotic species – and while they invited me along, I preferred my own company to their silly flirtations and nonsensical conversations.

I stayed in the cabin most of the time. I washed my hair with Adele's shampoo. I read all her magazines. When I finished, I bought a news magazine, but it was Canadian, and there was nothing in it about Mr. Chowdhury's beloved Bengal. I went to the ice cream shop and ordered a strawberry milkshake and after one sip, I threw the pink slop out.

"You're no fun," Adele pronounced.

"Why should you care?" I was on my second read of an article about improving your skin – oatmeal, cucumber slices, teabags. Mentally, I was marking off the passages I thought would most puzzle or horrify Kamala.

"We're going surfing in half an hour. Glen's bringing an inner tube from his uncle's tractor. Surfing with a tractor tire! Can you imagine? Come with us."

On the next page was a question and answer column about clothing. One of the answers was a step-by-step guide to putting on nylons with cotton-gloved fingers. I pictured Kamala and the grace with which her coarse fingers pulled open the string on Amma's medicine bag. Somehow the prospect of reading that again seemed more daunting than an afternoon with Adele's dim-witted friends.

"I love New York. Do you know New York?" one of the cutoff boys asked me on the beach. He was carving a woman's body in the sand.

"I'm from Michigan," I said flatly and rolled over on my stomach. I thought about Shaheed and what he would say if he was here right now.

"I'm going to the George Harrison concert at Madison Square Garden next month," the cutoff boy offered. "Clapton'll be there, Dylan, Ringo – I heard from a very reliable source Paul and John will show up too. The Beatles are reuniting for one last concert. But it's all on the q.t., eh?"

I looked him over, wondering at his cluelessness. "You're talking about the benefit for the Bangladeshi refugees, right?"

"Huh?" He slid his hand down the sand woman's hip.

I picked up my towel and left.

I walked as far down the beach as I could. I sat on the sand at the water's edge and looked up. I counted seagulls, pointlessly spinning as though caught in a whirlpool that refused to suck them in and end their misery. When I reached one hundred, I decided I needed to go further down the beach.

Right beside me though, barely ten feet away, someone else was carving in the sand. I hadn't even noticed him arrive.

"Funny things, aren't they?" he said, not looking away from his work. "Rather dumb. But they sure have perfected the art of making a spiral."

I looked right down then, to the circular blob he was molding. "Is that what you're trying to do?"

"Nope." He heaped two handfuls of sand on top and patted them into place. "I leave that to the experts. Experts with wings."

"What are you making then?" The mound remained shapeless.

"Just watch me." Leaving me no choice. I still suffered from the residual good manners that would not allow me to walk away without just cause. I sat back down, and realized something about the way he spoke struck a chord.

"You're not from here," I said.

"I'm from Michigan." He looked at me then and dropped his voice. "But don't tell. The big index finger of Uncle Sam hath pointed at me. Good thing all you Canadians are sympathetic."

I laughed. "Actually, I'm related to your uncle. I'm from Lansing."

"Aah!" He squawked like a gull. "You're not FBI?"

"No, no. My god."

"No, you are indeed. I see it. FBI. Foreign Beach Interloper. Do not lope any closer."

"I'll let you finish your work before I arrest you."

"Thank you. Never let it be said Uncle Sam doesn't have the most courteous Gestapo."

"Thank you. We like to think we are supportive of the creative arts."

He collected, dumped and shaped sand. I again imagined Shaheed here – what he would say about the expanse of water and sand. What he might carve on the beach. With no conscious effort, I found my hands had assumed the curl I spent contemplating so many nights while lying in bed in Dhaka. His touch outside the banquet hall had remained with me. I was suddenly aware of my breathing and, somewhere on the other side of the planet, Shaheed's. I missed him. Where was he while I lolled by the waves? Why was it taking so long for someone to write?

The pile of sand grew longer and thicker in this stranger's hands and when finally he started working on the tail, I understood.

"Moby Dick."

"Dickie," he corrected. "Or is it Dickette? You shouldn't assume she's a he."

"Whatever she is, she's going to die, beached like that."

"Oh no she won't." He smoothed her bulbous forehead as though caressing it. "She's not what you think, not exactly. She's somewhat evolved. She actually prefers land now. Grown used to it, I guess."

"Then she should be up there." I pointed up toward the grass that fringed the beach, behind which rose a grove of scruffy spruce. "One big wave and she's going to be wiped out."

"Never. Look at her size. She's built to withstand storms. And just about anything else. Adaptation is a wondrous quality to possess."

Surprised that until that moment I had not yet noticed how it smelled here, I breathed in the air off the lake. Though part of the same chain, Lake Huron smelled nothing like Lake Michigan.

The impulse was squeaky as a rusted hinge. Still, I blurted out, "My name is Robin Rowe."

We talked some more. Then it was dusk, and we were still talking. Graham was the first person I had spoken with like that since returning from Dhaka. I was a drifter in the desert who, having traveled from mirage to dried up puddle, had finally found water. I never expected to find it here.

He took me home in the dark. He knew the cottages where I was staying. "Thanks," I said. Outside the cottage, the shuffleboard, bathed in yellow light, was deserted.

"Anytime. By the way, you haven't arrested me yet."

"What?"

"I'm about to escape and you haven't arrested me yet."

I smiled. "Tomorrow then. It will have to be tomorrow."

꥞

That afternoon, as I sort through the mismatched contents of a cutlery drawer on my lawn, a courier brings the envelope from Surinder's law firm. I wait until the taillights on the delivery truck disappear. My hand shakes as I tear open the flap.

Dear Mrs. Rowe,

With regard to your recent letter to Ms Susan Livingstone, formerly Ms Surinder Livingstone of Toronto, Ontario, please be advised we have been engaged as legal counsel for Ms Livingstone in all future matters involving you and our client.

Our client has requested us to inform you that a bank draft in your favor for the sum of CAD$35,000.00 will be forwarded to your solicitors at the earliest possible date. Our client has fixed one condition on this transfer of funds. You will agree to no further contact with our client on this and any other matter in future.

If these terms are acceptable to you, please sign the attached, have it witnessed by your solicitors, and instruct them to contact us with the necessary information to facilitate the transfer of funds.

Trusting these instructions are clear, I remain,
Yours truly,
John Randolph Anderson, Esq.

I throw the envelope and letter in with the cutlery. But it's not enough. So I flip the whole works over. Forks and knives spill onto the lawn. I kick the overturned drawer as hard as I can. And when the clatter stops and silence explodes, I run. Down the road. Through an opening in the blackberry canes. Along a muddy tire track, the ground spongy beneath my feet. Over a broken cedar rail. Like a forest fire, I do not know where I am going, where or how I will stop. I've been dry so long, everything ignites, and promises to turn to cinders and ash.

※

I'm blinded by the late afternoon sun that reflects off the chrome handle of Fee's refrigerator. I shift until I can see again – our cups of tea, our curled hands, all overcast with a glare lodged on my retinas. Fee's spoon clatters a discordant tune against the side of her mug. "Little snip, isn't she?"

She is. I'm so angry, I could spit shrapnel. She's always been direct, my daughter, never one to leave people guessing about either her feelings or intentions. But this time, she's gone too far. Her words, her tone – I can only presume she has no idea what she is doing or saying. But a small voice inside reminds me Surinder always knows exactly what she is doing and saying.

Snip. Brat. She's a toddler armed with a power saw. She's Hasan Chowdhury. When it occurs to me that I now sound as conventional and as controlling as Amma talking about Luna, I back off. "It's her money. She has a right to her opinion."

"Opinion? That's not opinion, that's treachery." On the other side of the house, a door opens, then slams shut. Feet pound along a wooden floor. Jason's home. "What will you do?"

The answer is obvious. How can I consent to severing my relationship with Surinder? Surely this is just a temper tantrum, a rogue storm to be endured until it passes. But what if it's not? What if she truly intends to break off contact forever? What is the correct way to respond? "What would you do?" I ask Fee. She must know something I don't. Her son comes home.

"Dunno. But I wouldn't give in. Impudent pup." She's on her feet rooting through a cupboard. Cellophane crinkles and a sea blue package of crackers lands on the table.

I help myself. Salty, like Fee's invective, the cracker soothes. We sip tea and let the afternoon settle. I wonder about Surinder. She needs a good talking to. Graham is the only one who could ever get through her thick teen-aged skin and, even then, rarely. But she's older. And Graham's gone. Perhaps I should send the watch. But no. That's giving in to treachery, too.

"It's not like I raised her to be this way," I finally say.

Fee's mouth opens, but she stops before anything emerges. Instead, she pulls her hand over her lips and looks to be contemplating something fragile, like a porcelain doll or a glass bell.

ᴖᴇ

I have indistinct memories of my own mother – most of them involving the churning of her strong thick legs as she moved in and out of the realm of my young world. She had tiny hands that smelled light and lemony, one slightly larger than the other – features which demanded my six-year-old notice when she nursed my father through the Asian flu in the spring of 1957. When she came down with it, no one was surprised except her. "It's nothing." She would have wrung out a floor rag made from a worn flannel nightgown, then crawled beneath the table. She would have cleaned until it glistened. Until she could no longer hold herself up. She was that way, keeping rituals intact, no matter what.

The June funeral passed in a blur of coconut macaroons and tuna casseroles. People chucked me under the chin and said how brave I was, or hugged me so hard, I thought my insides would spill onto my mother's spotless floors. I was more interested in three black puppies who played with a greasy paper bag in the empty lot next to the funeral parlour.

There were a few changes around home after that. I stayed with a neighbour once school was out, and until Dad returned from work. But he never failed to pick me up on time. He continued to devote weekends to the family, such as it was – we picnicked, played catch, camped, rode our bikes – after a few weeks, my mother's memory began to fade. Though this disturbed me – I wanted to hold onto something as solid as her form – I did not mention it to my father, who I believed would have perceived my yearning as a lack of loyalty, and been wounded.

I revived memories when I looked at old photos – images I haven't seen in decades, not since I left home, but even today are easily conjured up. With her gardening gear and a bobbing crop of black-eyed susans, squinting into the sun. Hair pulled back in a kerchief, behind the wheel of our new 1955 Oldsmobile, a badge of patriotism for all loyal Lansing residents. Then, holding me in a soft blanket when I was half the length of her arm. The mottled afternoon light on the porch made the image appear like an old, cracked oil painting. But in the end, I do not know if my memories were real, or something accidental, constructed by the collision of detail and desire.

It doesn't matter, I suppose. They are just memories.

೭६

Two more days, and we finish clearing out my schoolhouse. Fee and I cover the rescued furniture with plastic sheets. My bagged clothing will go to the laundromat tomorrow, except for the peasant blouse, which will go to the dry-cleaner. Perhaps when it's pressed and smells less mildewy, I will be more decisive about its fate. Everything else is in cardboard boxes in Fee's basement. My things add a distinctive odour to her cellar.

While I put the laundry into the bed of Fee's truck, Ed appears for his regular inspection. I don't know what to tell him. We are ready to proceed. I am sure some of the five thousand dollars remain unspent – perhaps enough for a deposit on roofing materials. He should order them if we are to avoid further delays. But why bother? I probably won't ever be able to pay for them. Though I know I should say something, my nerves are raw and I cannot stomach the pity he will dole out once he hears about Surinder's ultimatum.

"Give me a hand with this, would you?" I help him re-tie a plastic sheet which has flapped in the wind all morning. He then circles the house, picks up a stray piece of splintered wood and tosses it into the almost over-flowing dumpster. He slams the tailgate when I've loaded all the bags.

"I'll tell them the dumpster's ready," he says. "The site looks good." He says nothing about what's next.

That night, Sunday, everyone except me goes to bed early. I can't sleep. The quiet that blankets the house disallows rest. I get up and go to the living room. I pace between the television and front door. Then I eat corn flakes. I watch the second hand creep around the clock, three, four, five revolutions. Underneath a book – *The Pet Goat* – awfully juvenile, even for Jason – I find one of Hayley's discarded magazines. A quick flip through proves nothing has changed since I was her age. The article on how to recognize love is a duplicate of one I read in 1965.

Not that it helped me. I refused to recognize it with Shaheed, and instead spent so many months avoiding naming the feelings that had taken root between us.

And then when I fell for Graham, love was nothing like what any of those infantile magazines promised. It was so much bigger. I felt both a part of the universe, and as though the universe was inside my body. I was consumed by the belief that he would help me carry my burdens through life, because in some wonderful, coincidental way, they were his burdens, too. I would never let him go. I would follow him into the sea. Into the sky. Across the border to Canada. I felt powerless – and relieved.

I still miss him more than any vacuous article could possibly describe.

What does Surinder know about love? Stupid question, Robin Rowe. Your daughter is nearly thirty. I haven't thought of her love life since she was a teenager and I drove myself crazy wishing she didn't have one. Not that I wanted her to be unhappy. I just didn't want her to get hurt.

Such a soft little baby. Ghostly white, almost translucent. Touch her then, and her skin would turn red as a plum. Her wise eyes and aura of serenity that enfolded her form right from the moment of birth prompted a hospital nurse to describe her as "an old soul." She never pulled my hair, bit my nipple, and when she explored my face, she did not plunge her fingers into my nostrils or mouth. Slow and tender, her touch was a soothing kiss.

When she slept, Graham and I watched, giggled and hushed each other. She would sigh and shift, one fist sliding back behind her ear, tiny lips reflexively nursing on air. Her night waking, heralded by a cry as soft as a kitten's, never alarmed us, so gentle it was, so yielding her reentry into sleep.

I loved to watch the stretch that possessed her entire body when she woke, the way the muscles and bones unfolded, then refolded. The flesh on her chest would tighten around her ribs, her stomach would almost disappear. And then she'd relax. It was like air rushing back into a balloon. Her body knew how to work without anyone ever having taught it. She was a miracle, no less.

Just as she is a miracle now, though she is distant from

that small being that curled into my chest at night and breathed with me, like me, so much so that I wondered sometimes if she was the source of my own breath, not a child at all, but a channel that kept me alive. I cannot give up this connection. I refuse. Before the sun rises, dizzy with the enormity, I know what I must say. She can do what she likes, but I will sell my home and live on the street before I will cut myself off from my daughter.

⁂

After breakfast, rain begins and I write two letters. In one, I employ the formal language of lawyers and kindly advise them right back that the offer they broker is not acceptable to the party of the second part, and that they may wish to inform their client thusly. The other letter I address to my daughter. I desperately want to sound mature and parental. She needs to know that despite all that is happening, I love her and want the chance to reconnect. But along with the ink, anger leaks out of my pen.

Dear Surinder,

This morning, I am posting a letter to your lawyer to let him know I cannot accept your offer. I have thought about it, and the consequences, but there is no way I can volunteer to permanently sever our connection. I will now lose my home as you know. As enormous as this is, I will somehow get through it, which would not be the case if I agreed to never contact you again. That would kill me.

Your offer was not surprising, and yet, I ask myself: how

could you? No need to answer. I know you move in a world where such silliness and self-centredness are not only a way of life; they are qualities of those who emerge winners. And that is what matters in the legal arena, isn't it, no matter the cost? The end justifying the means, and all that...

But I was very disappointed, just as I suspect your father would have been had he lived to read your words. I hope one day you will seek professional help for the bitterness which has clearly consumed much of your core.

I don't expect to hear from you anytime soon, but rest assured, when you are ready to reconnect with your mother (and you will be one day, trust me), I will be ready.

Much love,

Mum.

PS Surinder was such a beautiful and original name for you. You don't understand what you have done by changing it.

I seal both envelopes, put on Fee's raincoat and walk to the mailbox. When I push the letters through the slot, I settle my fate. It is 9:00 am. I am ready to face the rest of my life. My next task is to tell Ed he must stop work immediately. I call him on his cell phone and we arrange to meet in town.

Twenty minutes later, we are surrounded by trendy boys in baggy pants and girls with nose rings. They chatter like birds. The cappuccino machine goes full tilt, as though it could burst under all that pressure. Coupled with the babble, it's raucous in here. We sip coffee and while I struggle to gather my thoughts, I watch the rain on the window. Rivulets, wide and narrow, converge and separate. The window could be a map of Bangladesh.

Finally, I lean in and nearly shout my story – the revised version I see fit to tell, because now that I've made up my mind, I don't want to share the sordid details. So I mention "a family member", vaguely refer to a gene for stinginess and leave it at that.

"So we have to stop. How much more do I owe?" I reach for my purse, as though I might perform the impossible trick of pulling the balance owing from its innards. I fear his answer.

His gnarled fingers play a nervous guitar on his paper napkin. This time, no fingerprints. He's washed his hands. He waits what seems like a long time. "There's still a little left in the pot."

"Great. Can I – you know – get a refund?" At least I can pay something back to Fee right away, and after the house is sold, I can settle with her and Mac.

"Well, actually, I've already ordered the trusses. Sorry." He frowns, then sighs. "I don't understand. The bank's throwing away money…"

"To anybody with the means to pay it back." It pains me to admit the full extent of my penury. I won't look at him. I want no more of his compassion.

We sip our coffee. I wonder how we appear. A couple contemplating a sick child; a pending lay-off; a move off the island. Heads bowed, foreheads furrowed, lips shut tight as though there is still time to stop the words that confirm their impossible situation.

"There's something," Ed says suddenly. "Just an idea." I look at him politely, I have to, but there are no unexplored avenues. It costs money to fix a roof. I have no money. End of story. He clears his throat. "I've seen you – you do good work. I could use an extra pair of hands these days."

"Use?" And it is like being underwater where the waves strike the shore. Sand swirls, pushed and dragged. The bottom falls, everything shifts, images flow. And when your sputtering, sand-coated self finally emerges from the surf, you are surprised that a mere instant has passed, not an entire lifetime.

What is this strange man talking about?

"I'll pay decently. You could start right away – on your own place. We can work out a scheme like – you know – some part of your wages goes toward the balance owing. And you get weekends off, unless you want the overtime. There's plenty of work besides your house. Whaddya say?"

I say the first thing that comes to mind. "But I'm a tutor."

"Oh."

"I have students. Commitments." My palms sift the air for excuses.

"No one's saying you have to quit. Like I said, you can have your weekends, and probably most evenings. Hope you're an early riser though. We like to get started about 7:30."

In all my ruminations, I never once contemplated a return to full-time employment. If I go back to work, I can get my house finished. I can get a bank loan. But I have no interest in working alongside anyone, especially grimy-fingered, work-booted men like Ed. I know who I am: a semi-retired middle-aged widow with little income, whom it pleases to manage on her own, thank you very much.

If I accept his offer, perhaps I won't know who I am anymore.

"I'm not very nice to work with," I say. "I'm not really a people person."

"You'll be working with whatever you find in the tool box in the bed of the truck. Plus these." His hands flop at the wrists. "It's not the kind of work that requires people skills."

"I don't like to talk much," I warn.

"Suit yourself. It's not required for the job."

I work at the flaky arborite on the edge of the table, with a finger nail that is equally chipped and wonder. Graham and I did re-do that whole house by ourselves. But it feels like several lifetimes ago. Like it happened to someone else.

"And another thing. What makes you think I could even tell a socket wrench from a pair of vice grips?"

He laughs. "We'll go slowly. But it's not hard. There's nothing like a good dose of common sense when it comes to working on people's homes, and I already seen you got that." As if to mock his words, an arborite chip flicks off my nail and hits his cheek. It sticks to his stubble.

"Sorry."

He brushes it away and waves to say no matter.

I wonder then about his motivation. I look at his face for pity, which I do not need or want, then for signs of drunkenness, which would do in both of us.

"But why?"

He shrugs. "I told you. There's too much work. I need someone reliable. It's a *bona fide* offer." He speaks the Latin words like they are a cut of meat or a new fast food. Surinder with all her legal accoutrements would be scornful.

But worthy of scorn or not, he is offering me a way out. I will not have to sell, move, break off contact with my daughter, give up tutoring. Just go back to work. For awhile.

It may be the noise in the coffee shop which is building, it may be the caffeine urging me on, a kind of intoxication, it may be the lightness I have felt ever since posting the letters this morning, who knows what happens in the mind and body when a quick decision is needed?

I nod yes. His smile is both welcoming and relieved.

※

The war in East Pakistan ended just before Christmas 1971. By that time, Graham and I were married and tenants at a drafty Baldwin Street rooming house in Toronto, the unofficial ghetto for draft dodgers and other war objectors. After nine cruel months, independent Bangladesh was born. The news stories of victory emerged, grainy, out-of-synch pictures on the TV that sat in the dining room. Graham held the rabbit ears while I watched parades and parties on stations from Buffalo, scanning, always scanning for a face I recognized. These stories were gradually replaced with more analytical pieces – including a series in a fat newspaper I found at the public library on the widespread collaboration that had taken place between the army and its supporters in East Pakistan. The journalist, Mohammed Atta – was he Bengali? West Pakistani? – said the much-maligned Biharis were not the only collaborators. Religious leaders, government officials, even some college students were identified by name. Though one interviewee speculated that the war would have lasted mere days, not months, and would have been much less brutal in the absence of the collaborators, in general, the reports themselves drew no conclusions. But I didn't need details to imagine how difficult life must have been for Razzak and his family in that climate. I hoped that he and Luna were safe.

I still hadn't heard from Luna. She was taking so long to write. Amma, too, was taking her time, but I was more anxious to hear from Luna herself, to hear everything about their escape, their return and the inevitable open arms Mr. and Mrs. Chowdhury would have offered their new son-in-law.

I finally became so exasperated with the silence that I gave up waiting. It had been more than nine months since I'd left. If I wanted to know what had become of the Chowdhurys, it appeared I would have to be the first one to write. That first letter would necessarily have to go to Amma as I had no mailing address for Luna, wherever she was.

It would have been so much easier to compose the letter had I known what had become of Luna and Razzak, and how the family had fared during the war. So I decided to keep it brief.

Dear Amma,

How are you? What news is there? I pray you are all well in Dhaka. What a terrible time you have had with this war. I have been watching the news since I arrived back in America. I've been so worried.

Please send me word, however brief. It's a terrible thing not to know what's happened to people you care about so much.

Please let me know also if there is anything I can help you with. I feel so helpless being so far away.

I send my love to you all, especially Luna. Tell her I would love to receive word from her.

Best wishes,

Robin

PS Everything is fine for me, though I will worry until I hear from you.

I folded the fragile blue sheet of air mail paper in three, put it in an envelope on which I had already written the Chowdhury's street address, and took it to the post office to mail. I expected Amma to write back as soon as she could. She was dependable.

From my new home in Canada, I waited for a letter. But nothing came. Perhaps mail service was disrupted. It was easy to imagine a letter lost in the post-war chaos. Then again, maybe no letter had been sent – yet. Maybe the family needed a couple of months to regroup and get over the trauma. What had happened to Shafiq in all the ruckus? No doubt he was back on the job, scowling and slopping soup once more on the tablecloth.

When no letter came, I thought maybe Amma had sent it to my father's address instead. So, I called him. Every week, I called him to ask. But the answer was always the same. By the time the lilacs bloomed alongside the rusty wire fence that demarcated our unkempt backyard, Dad's words were predictable. "Sorry, Roo, not yet." I tried to be patient, but restlessness dogged me. I would not feel settled until I heard from someone in Dhaka.

I thought about going to visit Dad. The muddy spring air in Toronto smelled just like Lansing's. But I was nervous. There was no way Graham could have crossed the border. As for me going alone, no one knew the risks faced by a draft dodger's wife trying to re-enter the United States. American immigration might stop me at the border for questioning about Graham, and then it was hardly far flung speculation to say I could be detained for the sole purpose of luring him back. In those days, the authorities stooped low as slugs. All summer, I delayed the trip, unable to make up my mind.

A year had passed since I'd left Michigan, and still I had no firm plans to return. "I've half a mind to come up there myself," Dad said. "Have to wait for the next school vacation though."

"Love to see you, Dad, but be careful. The FBI is probably tracking you, too."

Graham landed a regular, full-time job at a bakery, and we were able to move out of the ghetto and into a cheap one-bedroom apartment. I became pregnant. Graham wept, the bakery owner sent a coffee cake whose cinnamon made me nauseous. I thought about Shaheed. Had he married, too? Maybe he was expecting a child of his own as well.

When I told Dad he said, "Good work, Roo. Now I've got to come. I'll ask about a ticket at Christmas."

But there was a huge snowstorm that December. The wind sculpted magnificent drifts around whatever stood in its way. Roads and airports were closed throughout Michigan, New York and southern Ontario. "We can hardly get out the front door of the building, Dad. The whole city's shut down. You better wait."

"Easter then. Is Easter too late?"

"We'll count on it then."

Hormones raging, I had the strangest dreams throughout my pregnancy. In one, my mother, decked out in my father's favourite track suit and cleats, was selling shoes from a street stall in Dhaka. Overjoyed, I hugged her and cried, "What are you doing here?" She, however, could not understand me. She spoke a language I knew was Bangla, yet the words made no sense to me either. She kept thrusting a pair of yellow rubber chappals under my nose. I kept pushing them away. When the frustration became too great, I awoke.

By January, I was very worried about Amma and Luna. The war had ended a year ago. Why hadn't anyone written? I knew about the casualty figures from the Liberation War. But, I reasoned, Luna and Razzak would have left before the mass exodus following the March 25th massacre. They'd be across the Indian border before most people had a chance to pack. Besides, they were smart, and in possession of good, hard cash; if caught in a tight situation, they could buy their way out. As for Amma and Mr. Chowdhury – even Hasan – I eventually convinced myself they were okay, too. With Hasan's street knowledge, Mr. Chowdhury's political connections, and Amma's instinct for avoiding even the slightest danger, they would be all right.

I simply didn't understand why they hadn't written to say so.

I let the Chowdhurys fade from my conscious memory when my swollen belly became too big to ignore. At the end of my second trimester, I planned for Dad's visit which, with any luck, would coincide with the birth. "You'll love Toronto," I said. "But please be careful. I'd hate for anything to happen." I dreaded the thought of the FBI somehow holding my father responsible for our decision. Who knew what those thugs might do to him?

As it turned out, something did happen, but not what any of us expected. Dad disappeared a week before his Easter holiday. He didn't show up for an evening softball game in a small town about forty minutes outside Lansing.

The team played on regardless, won, and returned home. It wasn't until he also failed to show up for work on Monday morning that alarm was raised.

Adele called. "All of the hospitals have been contacted. The police have started looking."

"Keep me posted," I said. It was not like Dad. I pressed the baby with my palms and she kicked back.

He was found the next afternoon, about twenty miles outside of Lansing, behind the wheel of his half-submerged car concealed in a creek lined with willow trees. The police guessed he had swerved to avoid a deer on the roadside, but there was no way to tell for certain. The paramedics thought he had been dead about two days, but the hospital assured me, no, he had been killed instantly, his neck snapped on impact.

The baby was due in ten days.

"The funeral's Good Friday," said Adele. "Practically the whole city's going."

I ran to the doctor's office, though I fully understood my options. If I went, there was the obvious risk that I would go into labour on the road. There was, for me, the bigger risk that my child would be born in the US – and I had no idea what chain of events that might lead to.

"Go," said Graham. In our bed, he held me, one arm around my shoulders, the other encircling my belly, while the weighty silence of the neighbourhood threatened to swallow us. "Screw those fucking officials."

But we were so paranoid then. Anything, especially if it was unthinkably brutal, seemed possible. I wept. I cursed. I packed my bag not once, but thrice, thinking those bullies will never catch me, and, if they do, they will never make me stay, Graham is right. But I unpacked each time I remembered that while they might have a hard time making me do anything, it really wasn't me they were interested in. The possibility existed that I could end up giving birth without Graham. Then, in some sickening application of law, I'd be charged with some criminal act related to protecting Graham or withholding information of his whereabouts – and held – as a lure to bring my husband back for punishment.

After twenty-four hours of wavering, I called Adele and told her to go ahead with the funeral. I would send flowers.

And then I swore I would never again, under any circumstances, set foot in the country of my birth.

Labour was fast, as though little Surinder was a tadpole who'd just lost her gills and tail and discovered the sweet taste of oxygen. I cried when she was born, the wrenching inside like a part of me was being torn away, the simultaneous yet not at all contradictory sense that I was at the centre of a miracle. The tears were also a release. Like a lopsided tower of child's blocks, the world I knew had collapsed. I clasped in my arms both the red, wrinkly body of my child, and the fragile power of my own singularity. Ready or not, now I was a parent. A parent without parents. An orphaned nomad lost in a swirling universe.

Adele asked me what I wanted to do about Dad's house. Rife with memories, the only place where I had hope of connecting with either of my parents, where perhaps my loneliness could be abated, it was now an exoplanet. Cold. Oxygen-deprived. Unreachable.

"Sell," I said. I did not cry.

Of course, the sale of the house also meant Graham

and I came into a little money. At the end of the fall, when Surinder was six months old and the Christmas decorations were beginning to appear on the streets downtown, we packed up and left Toronto the Good, as it was known in those days, for the west coast.

⁂

Ed Malone gives me thick leather gloves and a worn pair of boots which require me to wear two knoppled pairs of wool socks. I will buy better fitting boots once I get my first pay cheque.

My first pay cheque. Money in my hands every two weeks. Independent of forgotten cheques, parents' overdrawn accounts, students' colds and flus, last minute cancellations. No more explaining to a sniffing loans officer at the bank how irregular my income can be. No more need to produce six years' worth of tax returns to prove how it usually evens out – and still see skepticism flash across her face. When giddiness leaves, I luxuriate in the idea of finally being flush.

Ed says we will clear the building rubbish while we wait for delivery of the trusses, sheathing, tar paper and shingles. To help, he hires Andy, an all-round handyman who lives near the pub at Fulford. "This is Robin," Ed gestures from beside the lightning-scarred tree stump. "And this is her house."

" 'lo," says Andy. He looks down and scrapes his toe in the grass, so I'm not certain whether he's addressing me or my house. His leather boots are soft with creases. He wears a once-black Metallica t-shirt and equally faded khaki pants. His mouth opens and closes like someone who is not used to speaking much, a trait I already appreciate.

"Let's roll," Ed says.

Ed and Andy begin on what's left of the roof. They loosen, then fold back a corner of the tarp. Wielding sledgehammers, they attack the section which remains aloft. Less than a dozen hits, and it crashes down with an earth-shaking thud. In the silence that follows, dust rises.

"Clean break," Ed says.

Tarp reattached, we enter my house together. Time to sweat. We lift sheets of half-rotten plywood, heavy with layers of shingles. We break apart splintered lumber that once supported the roof. It cracks, dry bones in our hands, on our knees, under our feet. We haul out ceramic shards of sink, bath, toilet. Then we tear at the sub-floor. Though nearly unrecognizable, I can remember the location of each of the soft spots I used to avoid. Nails bend and screech. When the big stuff is outside, we shovel. The scrape on the concrete slab is as rhythmic as a cat's purr.

My thoughts wander back to Luna. Why hasn't she contacted her parents? She should have. She could have explained exactly what happened and made them understand that all I did was help. Beth should have intervened as well. As a person with a foot in both worlds, she has an unbiased opinion – at least, she would if she spent any time thinking about the whole story. If only someone would step in and make things right, I would go back there tomorrow with their box. I would have to rob a bank, but I would do it. Just so long as everything was as before.

I feel terrible about Shafiq's suicide. One part of me can't even believe he did it – he was so slow and feeble. He used to take hours to do even the smallest task. Even something as minor as setting the table would require an hour or two.

How did he muster the strength to tie a noose and climb a tree? He never should have done it. There was absolutely no need for him to have gone so far.

Fee arrives with coffee and cookies, and watches for twenty minutes. Before she leaves she says, "Purge away, boys and girl. Does wonders for the constitution."

After she leaves, I tackle a stubborn piece of wood in a corner beneath the place where we've just collapsed the roof. It's a very secure section of the floor – two layers of tiles under vinyl all firmly fixed to plywood. I try to wiggle it, bend it, pry it off the sub-floor, but it won't move. Ed hands me a crowbar. I ram the tip underneath, and lean into it. Something gives. I reposition my hands and push again. The nails release with a slow creak and finally, a pop.

Satisfied, I hold the crowbar in two hands.

"Hey," I say. "This is really nice."

Heavy and tough, yet smooth and well-balanced. It rests in my palms. It's a familiar feeling, and yet nothing has ever fit quite so well in the palm of my hand.

Nothing.

At least not since –

I run across the room. To where I last held it. I look. There is nothing to turn over. There is nothing there but concrete slab.

"Robin? What's wrong?" Ed says.

I run outside. The dumpster almost overflows. But is this the first load? The second? I can't remember. I haven't paid attention. Damn, I haven't paid attention. A piece of lumber juts out at an unnatural angle. I grab it. A nail punctures my glove and hand. I don't care. I pull with all my weight. Nothing moves. I roar as if to amass strength.

I will empty this entire dumpster if I have to. The wood moans and cracks. But nothing happens. I can't dislodge it. I pull harder. My feet leave the ground. I swing by my arms, kick the dumpster. *Boom.* I swing away, then back and kick again. *Boom.* And again. *Boom.*

"Lord, Robin, what is it?" Ed pulls my arm. Grip lost, I crash to the ground. I look at my hand. Blood, dark and thick, seeps through my gloves. A deep gash spans the distance from the base of my thumb almost to my wrist.

"What are you doing? Andy, get the kit." Ed falls to his knees and takes my bleeding hand. "Look what you've done to yourself."

He presses on the wound. It should hurt. But chemical relief has kicked in and I don't feel a thing. Except despair. I have to find that watch.

"Let go." I struggle but he holds me down.

"Tell me what's going on."

"I've lost something – a watch. Have you seen it? I had it last week. It was there on the floor." I point, as though there might be a clue, a lingering shadow of its shape. "I have to find it."

Ed stills. "I'm sorry. It must be gone."

"What do you mean gone? I need to find it." Andy's back with the first aid kit. He lays it before Ed like an offering. I twist. I have to get back to the dumpster. "Let go of me." But Ed holds fast. The gnarly fingers of his other hand root through the box at the same time.

"Can you see the peroxide?" Ed sifts through paper-wrapped bandages and plastic bottles. Andy's hands plunge in there, too. He finds and holds out the peroxide.

"We have to empty the dumpster." Ed and Andy look

up at the heap beside us. "I'll go through it myself if I have to."

Andy opens the bottle. Ed shakes his head, and removes my glove. "She doesn't realize that's the third load," he says over his shoulder. The gash is jagged and deep at one end. It screams septic. Andy grimaces.

"Who cleared out that corner? Was it you?" I ask Andy. "Did you see it?" He shrugs. "What's that supposed to mean – yes or no? Did you see it or not?" I know I make no sense, but his puzzled face, his careless shrug, his reticence drive me wild. "You threw it out, didn't you?"

"It could have been any of us," Ed says. "In fact, it might've been you."

I collapse. I give in. My tears flow alongside my blood. Graham's watch is gone. Worse still, I might be responsible.

Ed takes me to the clinic in Ganges while Andy stays, ostensibly to look for the watch. But I can tell they are trying to appease me, so I will go to the clinic without a fight. They think the watch is history.

Ed and I are asked to sit and wait in metal chairs with unnaturally angled backs and seats too high for my feet to reach the floor. These are the type of chairs offered by people who don't want you to get comfortable. The other people waiting read magazines and drink coffee from paper cups. One man snores. Ed waits a respectful few minutes, then lowers his head close to mine. "So what's the big deal about the watch?"

"It was my husband's. He passed away eleven years ago this summer."

"Family heirloom?"

"Not really. I was just sort of attached to it, I guess."

And so was my daughter – but painful throbbing in my hand pushes the memory aside. I wince and swallow a moan.

"Give me your hand for a sec." Ed massages tiny circles around the knuckle of my baby finger until suddenly, the ache fades.

"Hey, what are you doing?"

"There we go." He stops moving his fingers and presses down, firm and steady. "Acupressure."

The throbbing disappears entirely. I'm relieved – and incredulous. "Where'd you learn that?"

"Detox," he says casually. "The second time." He drops my hand.

I look around the waiting room, expecting everyone to have fallen off the disagreeable chairs. But no one even glances our way.

"There are dozens of pressure points on the hands and feet that can relieve all kinds of pain – physical and psychological. I just took an educated guess about this one. Worked, eh?"

"Oh." I force a smile. Sit up. Blink quickly. Ed speaks of being treated for alcoholism like it is a common cold. Like an idiot, I ask, "So – how was it?"

Ed laughs. "Awful. Words alone cannot describe it. It's the only thing that keeps me from drinking again." He slouches back in his chair, still smiling, and shrugs. "Once an alcoholic, always an alcoholic."

"But aren't you cured now?"

He leans in. "Not a day goes by when I don't crave a rum and coke. Hold the coke."

I'm aghast. "How long has it been?"

"Nine years on September 4. Seven fifteen in the morning."

The exactness of his knowledge touches me. I have the same precise recall of Graham's death. We fall into awkward silence. He probably regrets having said so much. The quiet becomes overwhelming when, at exactly the same time, everyone stops turning pages and coughing. Even the snorer stops.

The tension is broken by the swish of a glass panel that separates the receptionist's desk from us. I pray she will call me. "Adams?" she says. The room settles again after a man enters the inner sanctum of healing.

The throbbing returns. Ed should do the acupressure again. But first I ought to say something to let him know he shouldn't regret his confession. Alcoholism isn't the big deal it used to be. Every day, the news is replete with stories of people going in and out of clinics. I won't take it any more seriously than he does.

"You know, when you were late for work that first day? I thought you took all my money and went on a bender on the beach." I laugh. I want him to laugh, too, but his face flares, his lips struggle around a sentence that can't quite find its form.

Finally, he says, "But you don't know how dreadful it is – wanting so badly the one thing you can never have."

Another wound opens – one I have been trying half a lifetime to heal. Longing for Graham spills out. Endless yearning like a summer drought. Loneliness that drags like a hot sun across a hazy sky. The passage of time. The way memories nurture you for only so long before they dry up and blow away like dust. I want to tell him I do know what it's like. I know exactly what it's like.

Instead, this pain beyond bearing, I hold out my hand.

He nods, and presses my flesh where he believes it might make a difference.

꙰

Less than a day on the job, and already I need sick leave. Ed tells me not to worry, and to take it easy while the wound heals. But I am at the house the next day. When I reach for a splinter of lumber, Andy and Ed jump. "It won't get better if you don't let it," Ed says. "Give it time."

I stop then, and contemplate returning to Fee's, but I cannot bring myself to leave. So I sit on the damp grass and watch. When Ed is outside, Andy's in the house. When Andy leaves, Ed goes back in. It's like a ballet. At noon, Ed tightens one of the tarps. "Going into Ganges for a bowl of soup. Wanna come?"

"No thanks." Ed eyes me suspiciously. "Don't worry. I won't touch a thing." Hands up, I smile. I just don't want company today.

After the truck's taillights disappear, I sit down where the watch last lay. Emptiness hangs, symmetrical garlands of loss. A void fills the space in my hands. I conjure up the watch, see the hands settled so comfortably at 4:18, the crack across the crystal and the way it distorts the numbers on the face. I feel the crack on my thumb, the edge I know like my own skin.

A gust of wind stirs, then lifts the tarp. Light slivers into the room. The fabric flaps overhead, snaps crisply, and an instant later, I fall back into my darkness. There it is. My sign. If I once doubted it, now I know there is no need for denial. The watch is gone – thanks to my negligence. I've lost the only piece of Graham left in this world – and the only means of reconnecting with my daughter. In the empty shell of my house, the whole of the rest of my life rears its lonely head. Surinder, Luna and the Chowdhurys – everything I've touched is a mess. My sorrow is too deep for plain tears, the commonplace weeping of mortals.

੭੬

Amma's box is old, dusty, but still intact. It was stamped in black by the airline the night I left. I imagine I remember the thwack of the stamp as it hit the cardboard, though I was nowhere near it when the stamping took place. The imprint has faded, but I can still recognize the shape of Bangla letters. The date of my departure is scrawled on the mark: 25/03/71.

I work by lamplight in a cool, shadowy corner of Fee's basement. I slice open the jute twine and brittle tape with paint-stained box cutters, then turn down the flaps. I don't remember the last time I opened it. Now, I need to see what is inside. I think it will help me figure out what I must do with it. I am certain of only one thing – it should not see out the remainder of its days with me. I do not need further reminders of my inability to fulfill promises.

. Everything is there, as though Amma packed it just last night. The posters are faded, naturally. The misshapen balloons are stuck together at the edges. The record sleeves have parts missing. Lacy layers remain. Earwigs? Silverfish? I really don't know what creature eats cardboard.

A corner of the box that contains the reel-to-reel tape jabs my wound. I pull back, use my other hand instead to open it. The spool is thick with recording tape, but delicate as pastry. I expect edges to flake off. I close it before anything can happen.

I open the book. "To Motiur-bhai and Salma-bhabi, Long live good friends and our Bangla Desh, Affectionately, Mohammed Elias." What had he been thinking when he signed this? Had he known about the ban on his works? Was this the gesture of an angry rebel? Or just the warm, innocent wishes of a good friend?

The intimacy suddenly overwhelms. I feel it, an extra throb in my wound. I am going through someone's underwear drawer, reading someone's diary. Though I lack the clear answer I am seeking, I will close the box until another day when I am more prepared.

Then I see the envelope.

The colours on the snapshots are faded, the images, clothes and hair circa 1970, are blurry. Me in the saree. Luna and me. Hasan, Shaheed and another boy whose name I don't remember. And Amma, two arms around me, leaning her heavy form into mine. God. I look happy.

I close the box. The envelope I take upstairs.

I lean the photos up against the wall and begin my draft. *Dear Amma* – no, she might not like that. *Dear Mrs. Chowdhury* – too formal. She might not like that either. Maybe I should address it to Mr. Chowdhury. He's probably sorting Amma's mail. Finally, I write, "Dear" and leave a space. I can decide later.

It was very nice to be back in Dhaka. No. That's silly. Evasive even. *Sorry.* No, too abrupt. *I'm very sorry.* That's better, but they're never going to read on. *I was shocked and sad to find out about Luna from Beth.* That's true. But again, why should they read it? *Please let me help you find Luna.* But if they really believe she's dead, I may only be torturing them. Besides, how am I ever going to follow through on such a wild promise?

I throw down the pen.

Though it would be the coldest course of action, perhaps I should mail the box without any letter at all. Let them make of it what they will.

❦

Five days later, I have a hand well enough to return to work. The house, cleared of debris, is a stone shell cemented together and covered with blue tarp. Now we wait for the delivery of roofing materials. In the meantime, I remain a full-time employee, so Ed and I go off to build a deck.

"Good opportunity," he says. "Pretty basic, but you'll see how a structure is put together and supported. It's a not-too-distant cousin of the roof."

In their designer jeans and Birkenstocks, the older couple who have hired Ed are a recognized part of the island oligarchy, but seem nice enough. They move a coffee maker and supplies outside for us. I can't help but scrutinize her face to determine just how much older she is than me, and why fate has allowed her husband to exist while spiriting mine away before his time. Where are her children? Do they speak to her, call on her birthday, send flowers for Mother's Day? She smiles a lot, has good skin and colours her hair. She reminds me of Amma without the overwrought emotions. After a careful examination, I decide she is one of those women of indeterminate age, her preservation the product of a rare, uneventful family history.

She smiles conspiratorially when I ask to use the bathroom, then ushers me to a room where not a single item is out of place. On the wall, there hangs a photo of a young couple with two babies – twins – from a photo studio. From the look of the young woman, I presume she is the daughter and this is her family. They look impossibly happy, as perhaps I once did, with Graham and Surinder. I am relieved when I see a small spider and cobweb by the toilet roll.

Outside, we work with cedar. It smells good enough to eat. I learn to use the circular saw. Ed shows me how to ease it through the wood instead of pushing it. I experiment until I find the right amount of pressure to apply. I learn to listen for the change in tone, and feel for the shudder, which tell me the cut is almost complete. Before long, I stop fearing the machine.

Then Ed and I assemble the pieces. I fetch and hold, he hammers, then I hammer and he fetches and holds. Ed measures and marks the next batch of lumber for cuts.

There is no plan, no blueprint – just a tattered piece of paper that Ed pulls out of his shirt pocket and checks from time to time, those fingers scratching at a place on his temple where the hair is thin. But I understand. Ed was right about the need for common sense.

On Surinder's twenty-eighth birthday, I am faced with a platoon of two-by-sixes to cut. On one, I see two pencil marks, and I am not sure which one to cut. But I look at the others, lay the pieces out in my mind, and make a sound decision. I wish in matters of family, it was this easy to solve a problem.

A hydraulic truck crane, a huge, mythical beast whose engine roars, delivers roofing materials to my schoolhouse. On the laneway, it leaves deep tracks, which means cars might bottom out now. I imagine frustrated drivers leaving their corroded mufflers in the tall grass, orange fossils, tailpipes periscoping through the blades as though pleading for more air. I must remember to warn people. But then I remember I don't really have anyone to warn.

The truck stops before my schoolhouse. The engine idles. Diesel fumes fill the air. Andy climbs the back of the truck. He scoots across the lumber like a mountain goat, looks over the load and nods to Ed who, in turn, nods to the driver.

Bundles of lumber and plywood are hooked to steel cables, winched off the bed of the truck and manoeuvred onto palettes in my yard. The crane operator handles every load with such delicacy and precision I am reminded of setting a table. Each pile is massive – thick and white and strapped together with tense metal bands that will spring open when we snip them. The lumber is stamped with meaningless words and codes. We will cut through these symbols in the coming weeks, reduce them to sawdust.

Ed walks around each pile as it is released. He pokes at the knots and cut ends of lumber, taps along the length of each piece, checks to make sure everything he ordered has arrived. As a novice, I don't know how he can tell one pile from another. It is a mysterious reckoning.

Shingles and big black rolls of tar paper are next. Chemical smells waft by as each bundle flies through the air and is stacked near the lumber.

Finally, it is time for the trusses. Earlier, on Fee's kitchen table, Ed had sketched out a dozen options of rather confusing frames of 2x4s and 2x6s that looked like letters from a foreign alphabet.

"But what's the difference?" I said, comparing the 'W' with the 'scissors.'

"It depends on what you want," Ed replied. "If you want the ceiling open as it used to be, you could choose this one." He points. "Or this one." He points again. "Actually, you could pretty much choose any of them, but the point is – "

"And if I want an attic?"

"Then you could try this." His finger snarled over to an 'A.' "That would be easy. But come to think of it, I could do something like this," he said and started another sketch.

Reeled back to the early days of my return from Dhaka when I found choice nauseating, I held up my hands to say stop.

"I want the space. I don't need an attic."

"Okay, then," he said. "There'll be extra stress on the walls. They'll actually get pushed out by the weight of the roof. We have to check if they can bear the load. And what are storms like at your place?"

"Storms?"

"When the wind is strong, it puts upward pressure on the roof." He demonstrated with his hands. "We have to plan for the fact that under certain conditions, nature wants to lift the roof off your home." He chuckled.

"Isn't this your job?"

He nodded. "I just need to know what you want inside."

I examined the drawings as though some truth was

going to emerge, as though the answer would speak itself. But clarity evaded me.

Ed broke the silence. "Frank Lloyd Wright always put his living spaces right underneath the roof. It became a kind of signature. He had no time for flat ceilings or storage spaces, though most of his clients had more than a few words to say about that – but I suppose it made it easier to fix the leaks, which also became common with his designs. Do you know what he told Herbert Johnson when water started dripping on his head during one of his famous dinner parties?"

I said, "I'll take this one." I closed my eyes and allowed my fingers to decide.

So today 'scissors trusses' will be winched off the truck.

Ed, Andy and the crane operator have a discussion. I walk over to listen.

"What's wrong?" I say.

"We're going to stack the trusses on the walls," Ed says. "Easier to install that way."

The trusses – all thirty-four of them – are mammoth. "Can the walls hold that much weight?"

"Well, they'll have to. I mean, they have to once they're installed. And they'll have to bear even more once the sheathing goes on. And the shingles – well, we may as well find out now if this is going to work."

"You don't sound certain."

He laughs nervously, though he also smiles. "Well, we could knock a wall down – that's not likely. If there's a weak spot in the foundation, the weight could cause a crack to open up." He counts on his fingers the number of possible catastrophes, but stops when he sees my face. "Those are worst case scenarios."

"I should have torn the whole thing down," I grumble.

He shakes his head. "Don't worry. Stone, even when it's as old as this, tends to be pretty reliable."

Andy climbs a ladder propped against the house. The crane surges into action again. Ed hooks the first truss. The cable tightens, the load is lifted, the boom swings. Ed guides it until it is out of his hands. He then hollers and points, but Andy and the crane operator both know what they are doing. In a minute, it's up. I wait, but nothing crumples or even shifts. Ed looks relieved. The hook swings up and away, and then back down to the truck.

The second truss is cinched into place. It, too, goes up and is stacked atop the other with the same precision. Ed gives the crane operator a thumbs up. The stack grows. And grows. When we're about halfway, I have a premonition the whole thing will collapse. But no one else appears the least bit nervous. So I force myself to stay quiet.

Finally, we're down to the last truss. I hold my breath, certain that this one will produce the final blow that destroys my home. The boom rises, then turns and the truss rotates slightly. When it finally slows and stops, the crane operator lowers it. Andy's gloved hands reach for the truss as though he is trying to latch onto a piece of the sky. He gets a grip, guides it into place and unhooks it. Thirty-four trusses balance on the walls of my schoolhouse – and nothing has collapsed.

The job done, the guys are all reassured smiles. The crane truck rumbles in the background. They stand around and talk, again. Ed finally calls me over.

"He can haul out that stump, too," he says, referring to my lightning-struck fir tree. "No charge."

But I shake my head. What might be precipitated by the stump's removal? A shift in the ground that causes the house to collapse. A hole, impossible to fill. Ants, earthworms and termites which, brought to the surface and rendered homeless, will burrow beneath my house and terrorize me until the day I die.

So the crane disappears in a cloud of exhaust. Andy pops into his mouth the crust of the smelly tuna sandwich he's been eating since he came off the ladder, and pockets the plastic wrap. "Time for the humans to get to work," he says. From him, that is the closest thing I have heard to a joke.

We are blessed with yet another fine day. The wind blows in the direction of Crofton, so even though it's still morning, and the pulp mill's huge digestors are doubtless chugging away, the air smells fresh for a change. After a few minutes, we take off our jackets. The air's cool but feels good on my bare arms. This spate of weather is unusual for this time of year, but I refuse to waste time wondering why. If it's the result of climate change, okay. Today, I'll take it.

Ed consults the dirty paper in his pocket more often than he did with the deck. Again and again, he and Andy go into or behind the house, come back outside, point and nod, bow their heads and consult in a language I am just learning.

Andy climbs the ladder yet again, this time standing on the narrow cap plate that tops the walls. Calmly, as though walking down the road, he goes to a corner of the roof, hammers in a nail, hooks a measuring tape on it, then pulls it to the next corner. He inches along the cap plate and marks it at regular intervals with a stubby pencil. The consummate acrobat, he surprises, never stumbles.

Then it's time to right the trusses. "I think Robin, it would be better if you sit this one out," Ed says. Reduced to the role of observer, I am annoyed, but do as he says. The truth is that the ladder leaning against the house seems gargantuan, Andy's acrobatics intimidating, and all I can think about is Graham's tumbling body. I know eventually I will have to climb the ladder, but I have an unrealistic hope that my fear will be gone before I absolutely have to.

Andy pries each truss from the stack, while Ed, inside the house, guides and supports it with a lumber brace. Andy pushes, pulls and adjusts without the least bit of hesitation. He calls out when the edge of the truss meets his pencil x-marks. It is a miracle when each cumbersome form reaches its resting place. He nails rafter ties into place. The heavy old hammer sounds good.

It takes the rest of the day to raise the wooden structures. Ed climbs constantly up and down another ladder toting a level long as a baseball bat, to ensure the trusses are aligned from all angles. Well before the sun sets, an upside down ribcage juts into a darkening sky. It sits, fragile, awkward, much the same way an unbidden anticipation has perched itself on my shoulders, a large bird with sharp, clingy claws whose intentions are not patently clear.

❦

The next day, plywood sheathing will go on. I try not to think about how close I am to having to climb the ladder.

We begin trimming the rafter tails. "See?" Ed says. "The walls are slightly crooked. Typical of a building this old." I don't see, but I nod nonetheless. He climbs, measures and ties a string embedded with chalk across the rafters where they poke out at the eaves. He plucks it with his knotty index finger. *Twang.* "Try that," he says to Andy. When the dust settles, I see what he has been talking about.

Andy cuts with a circular saw. One by one, irregular ends of shorn lumber tumble to the ground. The remaining ends of the rafters are uniform, like dentures, or freshly-trimmed bangs.

"Why don't we do this after the sheathing goes on?" I ask as I pick up the scraps.

"Appearance. This building line is the most important one. If it's crooked, you'll notice."

Finally we are ready for the sheathing. Time to climb the ladder.

"It's pretty easy with a roof like this," Ed says, "no hips, no valleys. You just work your way up from the eaves to the centre ridge." Yet, when he explains how the panels should be staggered and meet in the centre of each rafter, I hardly hear his words.

The aluminum ladder creaks. I climb, past the height of my hips, then my shoulders. No problem. I'm fine. This is easy. I pass the windows. Then it hits me. I'm going down. Fingers reaching, arms clutching, eyes open, trying to focus on something, trying to grab anything, the world accelerating by my body until –

My knuckles whiten. I wait. The moment dissolves. I pull myself onto the roof trying to imitate Andy's ease.

The aluminum ladder teeters as my foot leaves it. A second wave of panic rushes in. I push my chest into the rafters. Wrap my arms around their boniness. The wood is unyielding to my small grasp.

If I look anywhere except at my fingernails, which are turning purple, I will fall as Graham did. If I say a word, I will fall. I will fall, not once but a hundred times, and each time, I will experience the thud when I hit the earth, both as myself, a falling woman, and as an onlooker, powerless to stop the fall.

"Uh – did you bring a hammer?" Ed says, over his shoulder. He's ahead, surveying the situation, and doesn't seem to notice my immobility.

My pores have opened to release the excess adrenaline that floods my system, short-circuiting the tangle of nerves that make up me. I'd happily descend and get the hammer, but the only thing worse than going up is going down.

So I ignore Ed and shinny up a quivering rafter. The floor of my schoolhouse yawns below. I am a fly watching myself move in that world underneath. I decide not to look. I push myself higher with my booted feet, a mixed blessing – true, they grip the wood, but they are heavy like cement. If I could, I would kick them off, just to feel again the bend of my ankle.

Until I am as high as I can go. My hands, fingers wrapped around the ridge, look like scaly bird's feet.

"Robin?" Ed calls from the cap plate where he is comfortably standing. Holding onto nothing. "We start the sheathing from here, and work up to the ridge."

I peer over the ridge. The slope down goes on forever, then plummets to the earth. I feel my heart drop with it. How did Graham fall? Head over heels? A straight slide, maybe. Or, like an Olympic diver, a single roll. I close my eyes.

It's always quiet at my schoolhouse, but it's even quieter

up here. The voices of Ed and Andy seem to emanate from another world. A ship's whistle calls distantly across the water. The sounds of wind chimes mysteriously find their way to me. I open my eyes at once because I cannot bear the memories that multiply, fed by this stillness. Between farmhouses and barns, St. Mary Lake is edged, the cottages around the shore like pieces of a board game. And off in the distance, like a footnote, the ocean.

I can see the ocean from my roof. I never knew that before.

I experienced my first night sky in East Pakistan on the roof of the Chowdhury home with Luna. She and I were seeking relief from the sweaty chambers below. Dhaka was so poorly-lit then, stars glittered in abundance, even from the middle of the city. It was a monsoon night, windy but not raining. High clouds whisked overhead, obscuring the moon and stars one moment, then revealing them the next. Warm, fishy smells were carried from the lake nearby. Despite the odour, we turned our faces into the wind. Our sweat evaporated. Luna untied her hair and let it loose. I pulled the elastic from my own hair, and set it free with my fingers. We opened our mouths as though we could swallow whatever wild thing the wind bore.

I expected Amma to appear, Hasan with a reprimand, Shafiq sent to call us to tea, to a meal, to study, anything really to ensure we were not behaving wantonly. But that was the only time I ever remember Luna and I finishing our fun before someone else decided it was over. When we'd filled our bellies with all the wind had to offer, we scampered down the stairs, our laughter diminishing as we drew close to the ground again. It took a minute to comb out the tangles and re-tie our hair. But the red in our cheeks took much longer to fade.

I wonder where beneath this sky Luna is. Whether she is alive. Whether I will ever know.

In a brush of wind, Graham's ghost manifests. I let him flow to me, through me – it's the first time he has appeared unbidden. The first time it has not been me initiating contact, seeking him so desperately. His presence both defines and fills the spaces between the pulses of my heart. I understand then what pulled me so purposefully to this house. All along I thought it was the stone, when really, it's been what's up here. It's taken six years and a catastrophe to discover the truth.

Something moves in my line of vision: I look down. Andy smiles.

"Good view from up there, eh?"

"Yeah, real good."

"Robin?" Ed calls from behind. "What are you up to?"

I slither back down the rafters, look over my shoulder from time to time to see how far I've left to go. The view disappears first, then the sounds revert, finally the wind is lost. Graham is gone, too. In the natural order, everything must regress to its earthly essence.

I reach the eaves finally, my grasp firm on the house. My trembling is residual. What will remain is less clearly named.

Slowly, I pull myself to a standing position on the cap plate beside Ed. Up, up, up – and I'm taller than I was ten minutes ago. Taller and leaner.

Let the sheathing begin.

❧

In my newly covered home, I inhale the scent of fresh-cut wood. My eyes adjust to the light and when I taste something of my previous life, I understand how hungry I have been these past weeks. "When will I be able to move back?"

Ed scratches his chin, dirty, gnarly fingers leaving prints around a tiny razor cut. He stopped the bleeding with a scrap of tissue that's miraculously stayed in place all day. "Depends on the weather."

But this business is erratic. Andy goes off to drywall a family room at a home on Musgrave Road. Ed and I stay at my place, work on the trim, then tackle the soffits, but without Andy, we are slow. We're ready for the roofing felt – tar paper – but Ed needs Andy's help to carry it up the ladder. Nevertheless, when Andy's available, Ed has some business with the regional district and has to run to Victoria for a day. Then there's a weekend.

On Sunday night, it rains. Until the sheathing dries, we can't apply the tar paper. So Monday, we wait for the sun and wind to do their work. In the meantime, there are other jobs. Back at the house with the deck, Ed and I install French doors. We cut an opening through an intact wall. I fight the impulse to resist such destruction. Finally, Andy and Ed's schedules coincide. We spend a half day applying roofing felt. But in the afternoon, Ed and Andy go back to the family room to do the trim.

"Don't worry," Ed says as they leave. "We're making good progress."

At the end of my first pay period, Ed hands over the cheque, which I try not to snatch. His trademark fingerprints are all over it. I am learning to live with my own black fingerprints, which now adorn my purse, jacket cuffs, boots and the light switches at Fee's. "I know it's not much –" he says with embarrassment.

"It's fair," I say, doing my best not to show how moved I am.

※

We're all back on the job on a grey Monday morning. Andy and Ed carry two bundles of shingles to the roof. They grunt. Their bodies stagger – the chemical stench of the asphalt burdens as much as its mass. Up on the roof, Ed peels shingles apart and shows how they fit. "This is where architecture meets nature. Just remember – tabs down, four nails per shingle, stagger the joints, and don't forget the gap." He gets me going with the starter strip at the eaves. As with the sheathing, we'll work up to the ridge. Eventually, I get the concept, but am happier once I figure out how to nail the gritty things together without them buckling.

This huge jigsaw puzzle comes together quickly. And when, halfway through the day, it still hasn't rained and the picture emerges – a black roof, smartly pointed and better proportioned than I remember – I am impressed. There's still the ridge to shingle, the chimney to flash, and nails need to be coated with roofing cement. But once that's done, we can begin work inside. And then I can go home.

Mac's called and plans to return again in two weeks. It would be nice to give him back his bed.

"When will we be finished?" I ask Ed.

"Well, the inside's not habitable yet. We'll need to finish a little work in there before you can move in."

Ed, Andy and I work together on the new windows.

It's awkward to work around the bulging stone – and we find several openings lack the trouble-free ninety-degree angles that would make the installation proceed smoothly. "Predictable considering the age," Ed says, "but still a bit of a nuisance." Andy curses often. But by the middle of the second day, they're installed, and my house is sealed.

Wind and rain finally shut out, warmth has a chance to develop. Despite the cold stone and concrete, it swells to fill the space. Though much more remains to be done, Ed tells me I can go ahead with finishing the frames – and the underside of the roof and rafters, if I wish. Indeed, I do. The emerging warmth, and the way the sun falls though the windows gives me an idea.

The stain I've chosen for the inside is tinted the soft colour of silt on the banks of the Jamuna River. I last saw this riparian shade from the window of my airplane, a river's edge in constant flux, traced across the land like a scar. I run my brush over a freshly caulked, sanded and cleaned windowsill. Stain – it implies damage. Imperfection. The reverse of what I am actually doing. This colour looks even better than it did on the chip at the hardware store.

Ed and Andy have gone to Saturna Island for the day to install a hot tub at the home of another of the half-famous painters of which these islands are so full. It's a job that's been put off since the trusses arrived. But I make good progress on my own, and today in particular, I am happy to share the company of my house with no one.

My brush is a superb tool – such fine bristles, though they are dense. I soak them in the can, and then squeeze off the excess on the rim. I brush back and forth, back and forth, my whole body into the rhythm. The wood drinks the stain. My house is thirsty.

I reach up. A drop falls on my new boots. It spreads, fine fingers of pigment seeking their limits. Like the black fingerprints that trail me, the chipped fingernails and callouses, it is a sign of my experience, a crown I have no choice but to bear, dignity being the only option.

Earlier this week, I received a second pay cheque from Ed. Used to frugality, I neatly divided it into four: the loan that enslaves me to the bank until I'm sixty-three, the loan to Fee and Mac, my living expenses and savings. But then Fee proposed a celebration. "Shakespeare in Victoria. There's a matinee on the weekend. But it's your decision. To be or not to be?"

"To be," I said. Insane as such a decision is for someone as poor as I am, one luxury will be permitted.

My arm aches from reaching, so I take a break. Outside, I walk around my house. The neat shingles, the fascia, the evenly-spaced soffits. The gutters are rather poetic. All the lines are clean and straight as they must have been a long time ago. The trusses and joists feel sturdy even though they cannot be seen. Ed was right. There was enough integrity left to work with, to rebuild.

Back inside, I wet the brush and look around for somewhere to begin again. There are so many surfaces.

❧

The production of *Much Ado About Nothing* is superb. The manic woman who plays Beatrice steals the stage. Fee and I laugh a lot. When the curtain falls, we choose not to rush for the next ferry, which we could just make, provided the lights are in our favour and we break the speed limit all the way down the Pat Bay Highway. Fed by Beatrice's spirit, we are tempted. However, we opt for procrastination. We follow an alley bounded by dumpsters that intersects Pandora and enter Chinatown. We choose a dark, aromatic cafe where the hot drinks menu, written in coloured chalk, is longer than the food menu.

It is bright and warm outside, so the place is almost empty. Fee and I can actually hear one another talk. The afternoon stretches ahead, lazy as a sun-drenched cat. After coffee, we decide to miss the next ferry, too, and instead join the rest of the sun seekers outside.

We follow Wharf Street, tourist-occupied restaurants on one side, and parking lots that dip down to the sea on the other. We follow stairs to the apron of the Inner Harbour. Sun sparkles on the waves. Boats knock restlessly against one another and the wharf. Seagulls call out when someone throws a hotdog bun or a piece of doughnut into the water. Pigeons and crows whirl overhead looking for leftovers.

The combination of the laughter, coffee, sunshine, and the luxury of time loosens my tongue. "I've been thinking about Surinder."

"Really? What about her?"

"Just that this has gone on too long now."

Patient Fee. She neither changes the pace of our stroll, nor says a word. This is exactly why I spend time with her. She lets me unwind at my own speed.

"It's embarrassing – having to cover up all the time." I cough. "And anyway, it would be nice to get a mother's day card – a phone call on my birthday – that sort of thing –

have a half-decent intelligent major argument about politics again." When I force a laugh, I feel less desperate.

But Fee knows me well. She has heard every single word and more.

A gas-masked man makes alien landscapes with spray-paint and sells them on the apron. The air reeks of solvents. He shakes his can, the ball bearing rattling inside and loosening up the paint. When he sprays, Fee speaks over the hiss. "What's your plan?"

I wait for him to finish painting the moon silver. "I always thought I'd have the watch to fall back on – you know, that I could parcel it off to her and mend everything. Not an option anymore."

"Have you a plan B then?"

"I can't think of another idea I haven't already tried."

Fee and I walk on, a grassy bank at our left, the water to our right. First Nations carvers, bent over miniature totem poles and masks, line this part of the walk. The smell of cedar lightly masks the heavy fuel odours from the harbour. "Speaking of plans – A, B and C – I've news of my own," Fee says casually. "Mac's met someone."

Met someone? It seems unthinkable – I didn't know he was looking. I thought he and Fee were – well, if not a couple, at least content. Why hasn't she said anything earlier?

"She works at the hospital in Kitimat."

"Is it serious?"

She breathes in, exhales long and loud. "He wants to bring her home to meet Jason and Hayley."

I need to catch my own breath. Try not to jump to conclusions. "What do you think of that?"

Fee resembles a tightly-wound dervish unleashed in a

crystal shop. "She's a baby. Only two years older than Hayley, and plays guitar in a rock band on weekends. Can't you just imagine the tattoos? And holes pierced all over that taut body like she's a bloody sieve. Hayley's old enough to make up her own mind – mind you, I don't want to be anywhere near when that happens – but Jason – he's a child – what am I supposed to say to him?" She sighs. Clearly, she's been thinking a lot about this. Five steps later, she continues. "But all this means naught. For I've realized that I still have feelings for the bugger."

This news sits heavy, though I must admit I am not surprised. "Sounds complicated."

"The truth is – and I must face it – it's been over for a long time – but the way we live, I guess I've been thinking all along it was going to turn out different. Like we'd end up sharing a porch swing and pots of Earl Grey one day.

"One lump or two, my lover?" she simpers. "Ooh, I'll give him a lump he'll never forget."

"Are you going to say anything?"

"What's to be said now? Fiona Burns knows as well as anyone things in life don't turn out how we expect. No matter how many years' worth of lying we're willing to do to ourselves pretending otherwise. I feel such a fool."

"Sorry. That's dreadful. He's acting like a jerk. Maybe you could try to talk to Jason instead. Even Hayley. Prepare them."

"The question now is not what to do about Mac and Jason, Mac and Hayley, not even Mac and me; the answer to that being rather obvious now, don't you think? I hope he enjoys the hospitality of that flea-pit hostel in Ganges. But how'm I going to forgive myself for being so thick-headed? And what'm I going to do now?"

I might join her wail. This being human – disorder, randomness, innumerable caprices, and the acts we take (or do not take) in good faith, the blunders that dog our every good intention – is nearly unbearable. I cannot get through another minute of my life without answers – about Surinder. About Luna. About the Chowdhurys, Shaheed, Shafiq. Dad. And Graham. Loose ends are the contorting limbs of a mythical octopus destined to strangle me. In such a short and uneventful life, how could I have created so many?

"Come on," I say instead. "We'll miss the ferry again." We trek back to the parking lot, tense and uncertain, as though answers might jump out from behind parking meters and bus stop benches and bite off our heads.

⁂

After the third pay cheque, I give up tutoring. No more uncooperative kids, their forgetful parents, the erratic income. There's no time anyway. Work with Ed is steady, and he's right. I could work weekends if I wanted. Most of the kids betray no emotion; they shrug it off with a "What? Oh. Okay." Their shrugs remind me of Surinder's at that age, and I wonder if any will go on to have a skyrocketing career like hers, if any will estrange themselves from their parents.

One parent calls to thank me and wish me good luck, another to beg me to carry on just until the end of the school year – and I do agree to continue French with her daughter, though she will be the only one. A third wants me to recommend someone new. From the rest, there is silence. One of them still owes me for six sessions. It irks, but I write it off as a bad debt.

At my house, we're going to rebuild the sub-floor next, a job I probably should have done when I bought the place.

"Think of sheathing the roof," Ed says. "It's much the same. We'll frame with 2x6s, and cover it with – say – 5/8 inch OSB. That should be strong enough for you." Blessed stars, I understand what he is saying.

On the day we plan to cover the place where Graham's watch last rested, I am jumpy. Regret – for all I have lost, mistakenly, deliberately, everything snatched away from me, everything I ever stupidly offered up – hovers, a rank cloud which Ed and Andy must sense. But no one says more than is necessary. A little to the left. Give it another nudge. Got another nail? Mundane questions ramble on and on.

With the strike of his hammer, a last blow to a nail holding the frame together, Andy announces he needs to go into town. The blade of the table saw needs replacing soon, and he'd better buy one or at least, place an order. Ed and I carry on what we are doing, on opposite sides of the room.

I study the grey concrete slab before me. I want to burn its impression into my mind so I can recall it whenever I want, because I will probably never see it again. I wait a few minutes for the image to coalesce.

Ed interrupts. "Robin, I need a hand over here." When I do not respond, he looks over and stops. I can sense his breathing across the room.

When the image I need is fixed, I speak. "You once said I could never know how dreadful it is to want the one thing I can never have." Ed nods when I meet his eyes. "Well, that was wrong. I know all about it."

He nods, more slowly this time, like he's not sure which

way this is going, what revelation may come, but trouble seems possible.

"Eleven years, and nothing has changed," I snap, annoyed that I have to witness Ed's trepidation, that he's incapable of keeping his feelings to himself. This is my moment. I seize all emotion in the room as if it belongs to me. "I still miss him. I cry all the time. I dream of him so often, I hate to wake up and find he's not there. At this rate, I'll soon have spent more years mourning him than I spent living with him." The words fly up into the rafters, borne by a fountain of despair, and bounce right back between us. "So you can't have a rum and coke. Big bloody deal. I will never see Graham again. Never. Do you understand what that means?"

Neither of us moves until the fury dissipates. The air lies still.

The floor squeaks as Ed crosses it. He sets a sheet of wood carefully on the frame, butting it up against a sheet that's already nailed into place. The spot is covered.

Business-like, he presents me with his hammer and a handful of nails. "Whenever you're ready. It's your house."

I accept the tools. And when the last swing of the hammer has made the last nail head flush with the new floor, the image of the concrete slab vanishes from my mind. I'm shocked and stunned at my own stupidity, as I suddenly realize that the watch is not the last piece of Graham left in this world.

Surinder is.

࿐

I promise Jason a frappuccino and with the clues I have, put him to work on the Internet at the café in Ganges. It takes him a minute.

"Look, Robin," he points to a pop-up window on the screen. There's an obscenely tumescent bronze acorn mounted on a stand. "She's going to get a trophy."

Surinder is one of thirty North American lawyers under the age of thirty being recognized for their outstanding contributions to the legal arena. We click on the photo of a young woman from Mexico and find out she performed more than a thousand hours of pro bono work with an indigenous group, which resulted in the closure of a multi-national battery manufacturer polluting their water source, and a UN resolution to protect environmental rights of indigenous people in Mexico and three neighbouring countries.

Surinder, on the other hand, is being recognized for her contribution to interprovincial procedural law. While representing a brewery in Alberta that wasn't getting fair access to markets in Quebec, she helped clarify and re-define the court's evidential requirements. In certain cases, there would be a shift in the onus of proof.

"What's 'ozone of proof?'" Jason asks.

"Onus of. It means responsibility." I wish I could feel happy. On one hand, I do, happy for her, even proud she's my child. But I cannot silence the part of me that wishes she had done the pro bono work instead.

Her bio tells me nothing I don't already know. Same law firm, I was right. She's not married. No children. What else is happening in her life? Why do I have to find out from a computer?

There'll be a ceremony in Seattle in July. And ceremonious it will be, if the pictures of past events are anything to judge by. I see somber lawyers on stage, posed group photos, a few of the proud parents, arms entwined with their children. Everything they wear is sophisticated, classy and achingly alike. Clearly they all shop at the same store.

Even if she wanted me there, I would never be able to afford the shoes to attend such an event.

Besides, there's the issue of the border. Going to America is simply out of the question.

¿€

Ed and I are installing an old, claw foot bathtub at a home in Long Harbour. It's a huge, graceful beast which, once it's taken out of its packaging, reveals insides that have been reglazed to a finish so perfect, it begs to be scratched or chipped. Ed cautions me to be careful when we shift the tub into place, extra careful with the pipe wrench which I need to hook up the new plumbing connection.

I know how slippery a wet pipe wrench can be. I know because I did this once before, put in a bathtub, stopper and tap set at our old house in East Vancouver, the spine of the do-it-yourself book pressed open, an upside-down tea cup containing hardened plaster holding down the pages against the slight breeze that blew in the window. It was the first project I tackled on my own. Graham was working on something else that day.

"My son's coming next week," Ed says suddenly, casually.

I stop only for a half a beat, then continue with the wrench. "I didn't know you had kids."

"Kid. Singular." Ed's bent over a pile of parts which will come together to make the pop-up stopper. I can't see his face. He sorts with his curled up finger. There's the striker rod, an adjusting nut, a spring which will hook into the middle link. He lays the flange next to the rubber o-ring and the stopper, and lines them up with the rocker arm. "Not many people do. I myself haven't seen him in twelve years."

There were big pictures beside the instructions in the book. I had read the whole thing over about fifty times the night before, but still, I finished each step completely, checked and re-checked it, before I moved on. I twisted the book up and down, around and around, like it was a map, and I didn't want to lose my way.

"Why not?" I ask Ed.

"He left with his mother – my ex. Things were pretty bad. I was drinking a lot back then." *Clink, clink.* Ed attaches the striker rod, then checks the lever on the over-flow plate. "That's when I made up my mind to get sober. But by the time I did, there was too much water under the bridge. How are you doing over there?"

I nod, okay. "What made him get in touch with you now?"

He shrugs. "He's on his way overseas for a few months. Some exchange or something. Has to fly through Vancouver." He sits back on his haunches. "He writes poetry. In Spanish."

Despite all my care, when I finished the job and called Graham, hot water came out of the cold tap. "But I did everything exactly the way they showed," I complained. I picked up the book, turned the page, turned back, as if the answer might lie there. "It's these pictures. They're useless."

Graham laughed and pulled his t-shirt over his head. "What are you doing?" "Having a bath," he said. He unzipped his jeans and pulled them down. "Come on." "But it's filthy." And indeed, the tub was, filled with dust and bits of caulking. But he climbed in anyway. His feet squeaked. "Ooh, this feels great. Do we have any bubble bath?" And when the taps were turned off and I was lying in his arms immersed, little bubbles popping in my ear, still sulking a little, he said, "Never mind. We'll get used to it." I felt his smile against my forehead. "We can get used to just about anything."

I look over at Ed. "You're okay with this?"

"The poetry?" Then he grows serious. "Truth be told, I'm scared out of my wits. I don't know what he's expecting from me, but I'm no saviour."

"No – but you're his father."

He laughs. "Sometimes that's the problem, isn't it? I only hope he's not too disappointed with his old man."

"I'm just about finished here," I say. "How's the stopper?"

"I'm ready," he says. I make room for him to work. "Really, I admire him for taking the initiative. I didn't have the courage – all I said and did back then. I was one sick puppy." He positions the flange and gently taps it into place.

"I have a kid, too." It seems the right time to reveal this. Still, I blurt it out because I'm hardly used to talking to anyone about her. "A daughter."

"Really? How old?" He takes the news mildly.

"Twenty-eight."

He looks impressed. "What's she up to?" He slides the rocker arm into the drain.

"She's a lawyer in Toronto – as far as I know."

Ed's got the inside mechanism in place. Now he's screwing on the overflow plate.

"Kids, eh?" He sighs.

"We're like chalk and cheese," I say lightly and shrug. "I never could understand her."

Ed grows serious. "At least you know that much about her. My son's a total stranger. I don't know what he likes, what he hates, what he eats for breakfast, when he gets up and goes to bed – "

"Don't worry. You'll find out. At least he wants to see you."

"We only get a few days together. He has to be at his new job beginning of next month."

"Where's he going?"

"Bangladesh – I think that's the name of it." He says it *bang*, like an explosion. "He's going to work with orphans. Or maybe it's a hospital?" He finishes with the screw. "Sounds interesting whatever it is, though I wish we had a bit more time together."

I am grateful he is not looking my way. Grateful he does not see the expression on my face, have the chance to witness the muddle of feelings there until I have a chance to sort them out. Part of me wants to tell Ed unequivocally to do whatever he can to prevent his son from going to Dhaka. Another part wishes it was me going.

"Speaking of which –" Ed gets up, wipes his hands on the back of his jeans. "Having courage, and spending time together, and all that I mean – how'd you like to go for coffee sometime?"

I redden; though his tone is casual, his intention is perfectly clear. He doesn't mean a coffee break with a work buddy. No one has asked me out since Graham died. The words sound strange, and the idea of sitting across a table from Ed Malone and talking seems –

I nod, yes, before I know it. "OK. That would be nice."

Robin Rowe, you fool.

You just agreed to go out on a date with your boss.

⁊

I stop before Fee's home, as afternoon turns to evening, as her house becomes a silhouette against the streaky sky to the west. Someone turns on the lights inside. Windowpane-shaped beams fall then stretch across the yard. The colour of the grass and trees changes. I look away. I don't want my vision distorted.

Up above, the sky is clear. The moon is a broken boat. The first stars float around it. I count two, then a third, then two more, though I think they have been there all along, and it's just now I have noticed. I trace the shapes of the constellations I know, where I think they will appear: the dippers, Orion, Cassiopeia and Cygnus.

I'm not expected inside – not yet anyway. A walk to clear my head would do me good. So I take the road to the sea. It curls over and down hills, past a real school, a bed and breakfast, the fire hall. I step onto the gravel shoulder for the one set of headlights that disrupts my train of thought. I am alone the rest of the way.

I'm certain Luna did not lie to me. Certain Razzak was not a spy. And yet, what good is my certainty? It did not change the course of their escape, neither has it brought them back.

And Shafiq. The final act of the loyal servant – the shameful part Luna and I played in his fate. How willingly we sacrificed his honour. Surely to live without forgiveness, as I do now, with memory, without a way of making reparation, is the only just punishment. I try to swallow the guilt, but there is more. Infinitely more. An ocean full, and still more.

Luna on my mind, I seek the parts of her I loved the best – her spontaneity, her spirit, her capacity for both loving and being loved. It seems natural, at the edge of the sea, barnacles of the low tide crunching under my work boots, to enter the water. I drop clothing and inhibitions. This island *is* crowded now – but crowded with people who'd think nothing of a solo swim at night in the nude.

At the far edge of the bay, lights rim the ferry wharf. Their reflection shimmers in the sea, creating the illusion of underwater torches. The wharf remains otherwise deserted. The ferry won't be in for another couple of hours.

The chill halts me before my thighs are wet. Arms wrapped around my breasts, hands on my shoulders, I have the sense someone is watching. I turn. No one's on the beach. My invisible spectator remains so, but the feeling of being observed does not lessen. Only one way to stop the show. I churn forward and when I think I really won't be able to take it any longer, I plunge. I imitate the arc of a seal, a dolphin, a whale. I become liquid as the medium around me. I dive until my belly scrapes the stones, then, arching my head back, I rise to the surface.

I'm still in very shallow waters. I squat, immersed, reluctant to feel the jagged edge of evaporation on my wet skin. The water I've displaced surfacing merges with the waves bound for the beach. Always for the beach, unstoppable, forevermore. No one hand can alter their path in any but the most superficial way. I am no different. I will leave no mark here tonight.

I push off and stroke out to sea. My body slips through the water, against the flow of the tide. With tough, dirt-embedded hands, I part waves. They fold back behind me, obliterating any indication that I have passed this way.

I wish it was such for my time in Bangladesh. Luna should be presenting great-grandchildren and complaints about her too busy and too absent adult offspring to Amma and Mr. Chowdhury. Shaheed should be taking his son to Ramna Park, Bangabandhu's house, the banyan tree on campus – all the places where he himself took part in changing history – and then to the monument erected in memory of his own martyred father. Shafiq should have spent years resting his skinny legs in the comfort of a family he was not bound to serve, except perhaps as a raconteur of familial history, or an arbiter of small disputes.

The water seems warmer out here, though this defies logic and biology. With my next stroke, a flash in the water. My heart pounds. I collide with the memory of my night exodus from Dhaka, the rockets that flared overhead. Then I remember something else about biology. The plankton that light up when agitated. Bioluminescence is a natural part of this world. The shimmer that surrounds me is not a rocket, a bomb, a grenade. Not a chemical. Not a violent rage made manifest. Just microscopic organisms going about their lives.

When I have recovered somewhat, I stroke on out to sea. Fear has passed, but leaves a new chemical energy. I do not turn around to see how far I have come.

My protector that night, Hasan – am I anywhere near making peace with this man? What might I wish for him? Certainly health – and perhaps less of the misery than I have experienced so far with my own life. Dare I wish him peace? Certainly a restfulness that may allow him to recognize what I cannot seem to – that which is important.

Not a flash of lightning then. No thunderbolt from the wispy clouds. No scorching baptism. Instead, grace moves in like a tide. Gradual, persistent, inevitable. Stubbornness and denial cannot withstand its force.

A splash ahead. I suspect a harbour seal, fishing, playing, whatever it is that people anthropomorphize into "cute" behaviour. I stroke twice toward the sound, then turn on my back and float.

Overheard, the constellations have emerged. It gives me a sense of order to be able to find the ones I know. The water licks my ears. I let my body rise and fall with my breath, moving limbs as little as I can, enough only to keep myself from sinking.

I curse war for what it has done to all of us. Loss and injury. All in the name of the pompous notions of liberty, independence, and security. Settling things. As if war ensures any of that. As if combat has no consequences other than the ones we seek. I contemplate my part in these wounds. All the time I thought I was not part of the war; I was not involved. Such delusions. As if having the best of intentions is always enough. As if doing the right thing is so obvious. As if involvement is something one can choose. I know its face now, its jaws. It is a hungry animal, devouring first those who claim to be above it all.

I roll over, exhale, and stroke further out to sea.

Hasan and the others got what they wanted, didn't they? The right to manage their own affairs. Dignity. Freedom. But then, there are the ghosts – ghosts that wander the rice paddies at night, trace the rivers with feet that leave no prints in the sand, cling to the silty, shifting chars. The living ghosts are worse – doomed to eternal anguish even two generations later, driven by fantasies of revenge, finding collaborators in every corner of the country.

The darkness flows, and what life remains in motion is being lulled into sleep. I list my own wars. With arrogance and domination. Injustice and violence. With Hasan, the American government. The Chowdhury's rigid social rules. With death's inept sense of timing. And with my own daughter. Those are only the major ones. There have been many more skirmishes. More than thirty years of wars, and what have I to show for all that bloodshed?

The casualties of my war are still being counted. Relationships have fallen, some only injured, others mortally wounded. While violence, brutality, bungled foreign policy-making, social conventions that stifle, early and accidental deaths continue. And so do longings – longings seared into the heart, irrefutable and never satisfied. I have gained nothing.

Loss is one constant in these wars. The other? Me.

I know one trick in the water, taught by my father when I was only six. How to sink. Once more, I plunge. Trace an arc, until I am completely submerged. Head down, I release air. It bubbles up along my cheeks, my ears. I imagine the trail of it leading to the surface. It knows only one way to go. Not me. I kick, and push myself further down.

Not deep enough, not yet, Roo. Dad always told me I

could go even further if I wanted. I push air out – what is residual in the third of the lung humans supposedly never use – and with my arms and legs, dive even deeper. My hand hits something. A rope of kelp. I sense the bottom near. I pull myself all the way down to the kelp's root.

The world's best breath holders clock in just under nine minutes. They're relaxed, meditative – aware of and trusting the mammalian dive reflex. It slows their breathing, their heart rate, too. Their bodies divert blood away from their extremities. These adaptations, nearly forgotten, mysteriously resurface in water, putting to rest any questions about our origins. Most people can manage a minute or two. How long have I been? Thirty seconds? Forty? I have much further to go. I summon the reflex; demand it conquer my urge to surface.

Graham went down too, but not with this resistance. His body accelerated effortlessly. God I miss him. God I will never get over him.

The sea bottom is sludgy. But I expected stones, like the beach. I am startled. Thrown off track. The flow of my concentration flickers for an instant. Then a disobedient nostril – or perhaps it is my diaphragm tightening to a different impulse – disobeys the dive reflex. Opportunistic water fills the hole. I release the kelp and choke. This is not the dive reflex. This is a survival reflex – and I cannot stop my body from wanting to breathe any longer.

I fill with, and am in danger of becoming water. I must rise. But I have no air left to buoy me. I thrash. But the kelp has metamorphosed into a jungle of ropes that wrap around my ankles, or is it my wrists, my waist, my neck? Then I forget where up is. I open my eyes, thinking I will see light. But there is none. And my eyes become another opening into which water floods.

Graham, Graham, I am coming to you. All the years since you left, I have longed for this, prayed for it, and now the moment is here. Where are you? Come out of the murk.

My mouth opens – voluntarily or involuntarily, no part of my brain can figure it out – I scream no. I am not ready for you Graham. Not yet. Water rushes in, just as into the murkiness flows a stunning alabaster cliff face that I have seen once before and I know one thing for certain. I am dying. In one minute, I will be dead.

⁂

On the beach, a girl's voice calls. Luna. I open my eyes to a spinning universe, and when I am able to roll on my side, water trickles out my mouth onto the barnacle-covered rocks. I become conscious of their sharpness cutting into my back.

How did I get here? A lifeguard? A passing boat? Dolphins? Mermaids? Who or what was my rescuer?

Foolishly I sit up and look around. But I am alone. Not a soul in sight. There is no boat. No lifebuoy. No ambulance on the road beside the beach.

No one rescued me.

If no one rescued me, then I must have brought myself back to land.

I dress slowly and wonder how my lost, fragile, death-seeking body managed this miracle without the participation of my memory.

✿

Alongside the road back to Fee's, the trees exhibit an extraordinary density I know has always been there, but that has eluded me up until now. When I reach her yard, I stop. Something needs to settle before I step back into my world, something unearthly restored to its netherworld.

Fee's door opens with a flood of light. Fee's body, hands on hips, throws the shadow of a giant that nearly touches me. "Why are you doing lurking out there like a bandit? Come in before some militant from the Neighbourhood Block Watch calls the police."

"Give me a minute, would you?" She closes the door.

I have stuck to my convictions like a barnacle to rock. But all this time, my war has been with myself, on my own turf, dragging innocent bystanders into it, assigning them the ammunition to take me down.

"Shit," I say. I kick the earth and the steel toe of my boot digs up a divot. I fall to the ground and nudge it back into the hole with my hands.

I find the fit. Which is more than I can say about the hostilities that have preoccupied much of my adult life.

Hasan's parting words come back. Sometimes drastic measures are called for. Drastic measures like surrender. Only I'm afraid my war's gone on for so long now, I haven't got the foggiest idea how to surrender. Or to whom.

✿

The pick-up rattles down the lane. I hear the familiar clunks, with my new kitchen window open. The rain is misty, pours through a golden light emerging from the patch of clear sky in the distance. My schoolhouse still smells of new carpet, paint and other chemicals, and the cool air flooding through the open windows is a necessity. It will take a few more months of living here for these smells to disappear completely, but when they do, I will remember them fondly. How they signify the freshness of nearly everything in my home. How it feels to be starting anew.

Mac stops the truck and he and Fee open the creaky doors. "Morning," Mac calls. "Got a delivery here for a Robin Rowe."

"You've come to the right place," I call.

I orchestrate the movement of boxes from beneath the truck tarps to my home. We scoot through the rain, so it takes barely five minutes. There are two for the bathroom, five or six for the kitchen area. My suitcases go beside my bed. For now, Amma's box goes on the mattress. I don't want it misplaced in the confusion.

I make a pot of tea for us on my new, used stove. While the water boils, I walk from window to door, from sink to fridge. Breaking trails in the new carpet. Automatically I avoid the places on the floor where the sub-floor was rotted through. I must learn the new shape and feel of my home.

Mac and Fee remain on the small, covered front stoop. He arrived back in town yesterday – alone. Fee and I have yet to debrief on the subject that hangs heavy between them, but there's no sign of the pierced nurse. I note their voices are friendly enough. A familiar ease fills their space.

The rain taps softly overhead. Its whisper on the shingles is the only voice inside. I scan the rafters, look for telltale globules of water forming, hanging precariously.

About to fall on my new carpet. Surely I created at least one significant leak when I shingled the roof. But I see nothing up there except rafters. Perhaps the roof is good, though as Ed said, no roof is really done until it's been tested by a storm. I will have to wait for the windy, rainy weeks of winter before I know for certain.

A second truck approaches. I know the sound of that engine, too. It's Ed and a load of furniture – the things I bought second-hand in Ganges. Cast-offs from another family, or families, perfectly worn and used just enough, their dents and scratches an antidote to my unsullied floor and ceiling. There is a bookshelf, a table and chairs. An old-fashioned bed with an iron headboard and a heavy, squeaky · set of springs. And a sofa. Big enough for me to lie down on. It's worn at the arms, but no springs stick up through the upholstery.

All this luxury can't be good for a person. But I dismiss this austere thought. Too much thinking can also do its share of harm.

This is Ed's day off. He is helping me today as Fee and Mac are. As a friend.

I go outside when Ed pulls up. I confess to being excited to see him. Fee and Mac know this, judging by the way they remain seated, cast significant glances in my direction, then whisper and giggle when I head toward the truck. Ed and I have not had our coffee yet, such as it is. We've not set the date. But there is a softness to the way he looks at me now. And though you'd have to drag me across Montana behind a pair of wild buffalo before I'd admit it, there's a fondness to the way I watch him, too. I am almost always relieved now when Andy's not around because I don't have to try so hard to hide it.

This morning, contrary as always, I try not to smile. But it's pointless.

"Where's Lawrence?" I ask. His son's been here three days – I've met him twice already. They've been spending most of their time walking – beaches, trails, little-used roads – and talking. His son is guarded, but not unfriendly, and apparently thinking of staying a few extra days. "Lots to work out," Ed says. "The jury's still deliberating." "You'll get there," I say. I try hard not to think about Surinder.

Ed climbs out and slams the door behind him. "He's asleep. I didn't wake him." He walks around to the back of the truck. "Good day for moving."

"Isn't it?" We reach for the tailgate at the same time, and I feel foolish and insanely happy when my dirty hand brushes his gnarly one. "Oh. Sorry."

"No problem." Is his hand shaking? I can't believe it. We are like teenagers. I can't believe this is happening. I glance at Fee and Mac, but have to look away once I see how hard they are trying to conceal their laughter.

Then I slip on my conductor hat once again. The bookshelf goes over there, against the wall, its empty shelves crying to be filled. The table and chairs are moved into the house, close to the old pot-bellied stove, where perhaps it will be warmer to sit. I can't decide exactly what to do with the sofa, so they just set it down and wait while I try to picture where it will look best. When I turn back, Ed, Fee and Mac, damp hair, ruddy cheeks, rain drops staining the shoulders of their shirts, are sitting on it, side by side, looking expectant. They're like an audience at the turning point in a drama that's spilled off the stage. I laugh. This companionship fills me up. "Leave it for now. I can't make up my mind."

"One more piece," Ed says. He and Mac go outdoors. I whirl around. What's left? Everything is here, isn't it? I run through the inventory – this was it, I am sure, but then Fee's at the front door. "Careful of the top, boys," she says, "okay, all clear. Watch the fingers on your right hand, Ed Malone."

A huge, wooden wardrobe is being squeezed into my house.

"Hey. That's not mine," I protest.

"It is now," Ed grunts as he sets his end on the ground. *Thud*. Mac bends and gently sets his end down. *Thud*. The piece comes to rest, imposes itself on the room like a rainforest tree.

It's dark and beautiful, the kind of wardrobe a child might like, weaving fantasies and dreams from its deep recesses and secret compartments. I push on it, half afraid it's going to tip. But it sits solidly, sure of its place on my floor. I open a door. The smell of old wood rushes out – and takes me all the way back to Amma's, and the almirah I used all year at the Chowdhurys.

"I don't get it."

"It's a housewarming gift. For you. Remember Saturna? That artist did a barter. I didn't mind, it looks better on the books. But what am I gonna do with a locker like this?"

My dupattas, the two sets of shalwar kameez Amma had made for me, my pink saree. All those clothes I brought from Lansing and then abandoned. The Michigan U. sweatshirt that eventually grew mouldy in the monsoon and had to be thrown away. The flannel pyjamas that the moths devoured because I refused to use the stinky mothballs Amma offered. In my mind, I flick along the bar of hangers and remember.

"Thanks, but it's too much. I can't take this."

"You'll be doing me a favour."

I glance at Fee. She about to burst. Mac's scratching the back of his head like it's a long-neglected duty, studying the floor like it's the most interesting thing he's seen in weeks.

"Lawrence might like it. Didn't you ask him?"

"Lawrence is twenty-one. He lives out of a backpack."

I look inside again, as if the answer might rest there. But I'm really just biding my time. Breathing in the old woody scent that is almost my Dhaka. Trying to find the right words, understand the circles of my existence, the loops that bring me back to where I was before, only to find, much to my surprise, I now know it differently.

I close the door, the click of the latch a quiet *tak*. I have exactly what needs to be put in here – at least temporarily. I fetch a tea towel from a kitchen drawer and wipe the rain off the grainy surface. The wood is smooth and still warm from wherever it was.

"Put it there," I say when I have finished. "By the window. And thanks."

Ed says, "You're welcome."

The rain continues into the evening. I shine a flashlight up into the rafters every ten minutes looking for a leak. In between, I unpack, heat up the dinner Fee brought over earlier, eat, make my bed, and finally wash in the bathroom. There's no mirror yet. I don't have to have everything in place before I sleep in my house again.

When I turn off the light, I listen for the drip, but there is still none. The roof continues to hold. I go to sleep in my innocent little corner, no longer the place it once was, but that's for the best. Tonight, I am alone but not lonely, filled with a longing but not for the impossible, expectant but not anxious, a little troubled but not afraid to let it be for tonight. The unresolved parts of my life will be there when I awake. Like old friends. I look forward to seeing them in the clear light of day.

Epilogue

The cool ocean wind should temper the hot July sun, but today, it's not powerful enough. My skin burns and crackles. I'm queued up on a scorching sidewalk, and for the past forty-five minutes, I've been waiting to get into a shed that masks as a ferry terminal. There's a problem with the immigration desk, the computers are down, they've overbooked – rumours fly up and down the line. "Oh really?" I say to each one, then forget it. I refuse to repeat the hearsay. It will just make me more anxious, and I really need to focus now, to turn within myself and extract whatever strength I possess if I am to actually get on this boat.

The harbour reeks today. Fuel overpowers the scent of salt. But all I smell is fear. Pungent, messy panic wafts up from my every pore, hangs like a cloud over me, so heavy I am certain others notice.

I glance at my watch. We are scheduled to leave in twenty minutes, though that seems impossible. I won't even have checked in by then. There is time for me to back out. There's no way Surinder would even have the slightest idea that I had failed. No one except Ed, Fee and Mac will know of my cowardice.

But I do not leave the line. Not yet. For I understand this much now: staying hasn't protected me. Venturing out at least offers possibilities.

I try to visualize the ceremony. I'll be dressed improperly. My shoes will be all wrong. But Fee only laughed when I told her, then said my work boots, if I chose to wear them, would be good enough, and heaven help the child who rejects a parent come to beg forgiveness based on footwear.

The theatre will have walls of a colour so plain as to defy description. It will be unnaturally lit, there'll be a glittery chandelier hanging from the ceiling, an observer to good taste from on high.

I will enter like it is my business. I will be proprietorial. I will sit behind the row reserved for VIPs, in a chair whose upholstered seat gives, and shake out my hair, which almost reaches the nape of my neck now that I've decided to let it grow out. I will force myself to forget about my shoes, ignore the whispers of the people who think a hand-made tie-dyed peasant blouse is inappropriate attire. I will remember what Ed said on our last date. As much as anybody, I have a place in that room. I have a responsibility to be there.

There's movement in the line. A few people applaud. One woman bellows, "Hallelujah." A strident man grumbles, "Incompetent ninnies – it's about time," in a voice that we are all meant to hear. Again, I am reminded of yet another reason for staying away from the country of my birth. The national sport, sanctimonious demand-making, is hard to stomach. But I don't duck out of the queue. I move ahead with the others. I have promised myself that for this one trip, I will look the other way and swallow my distaste. When the line comes to a stop again, I am mercifully under an awning. It's a bit cooler in the shade.

There will be a huge screen at the back of the stage. Ornate but serious lettering will spell out, "Top Thirty Under Thirty 2001." It will fade, then one by one, slowly, the thirty portraits will appear, proud parents whispering, "There he is," when their child's picture is shown. As we wait for the ceremony to begin, there will be no one on stage, but an officious man, single-minded with his business; he will cross it twice, oblivious to the rapidly filling auditorium and the fact that we all have nothing to look at besides the pictures and his ungainly waddle.

The applause that begins the ceremony will, like everything else, be tasteful. Loud enough to exhibit parental pride, but with restraint. The master of ceremonies will be handsome and mild, his suit double-breasted and so excessively expensive-looking, he may as well have left the price tag dangling from the cuff. Although I suppose with such expensive suits, they don't use price tags.

"Ticket please." *Thump, thump.* A woman stamps my ticket. "Take a seat inside, after immigration. We'll be boarding in groups." She writes a big three on my boarding card and hands it to me.

Through a Plexiglas window, I see a desk ahead – three burly people, so alike in hair, uniform, manner, even from this relatively short distance, it is impossible to say whether they are men or women. What's crystal clear is the fact that they are immigration officers. What startles me are the tiny stars and stripes badges on their shirts.

What is American immigration doing on Canadian soil? Why am I apparently the only one disturbed by this? Leave it to the nation of hypocrites of democracy to find a novel way of occupying a foreign territory without anyone raising the slightest objection. Leave it to the nation of somnolent mice to let it happen.

I didn't expect to have to pass by this officialdom until my journey was almost over. This surprise is more than enough reason to reconsider my trip. I shake while I dig in my bag for my ID. I don't know what I'm going to say if they start to question me. How does one prepare to be abused in the name of authority? I should leave before I find out, but then, I remember my mission.

What will Surinder say when we are finally face-to-face? I haven't come that far in my imagining. Fear of a confrontation chokes me. But I know I have no choice but to make this trip. To lay to rest the ghosts that have kept me from the country of my birth, away from my child, absent from much of the past decade of my life. It is the only way ahead.

"Next," calls the immigration officer. She's young and businesslike. She doesn't look up until I am before her desk. "Where you going?" she asks, as she looks over my ID.

"Seattle."

"Purpose of your visit?"

I hesitate. What would she say if I really told her? Told her what a mess I've made of my life, all the doors I thought

I'd closed, which in fact were left unlocked and open to the elements. How I let some imaginary internal war distract me from the real business of living, so I'd neglected everything that had meaning. That I have one chance left to stop fighting and re-enter the world, and this tiny crack of an opportunity is it. Told her that today, I am nothing more than an insect hatching from a tiny, viscous egg, into a world I know almost nothing about.

"Tourism," I say.

"Where were you born?"

"Lansing, Michigan."

I wait for her to blink, to check a computer screen or clipboard where surely my name has been written under the heading, "Draft Dodger's Wives." "Enemies of the State Living in Exile." Or "Traitors." But she doesn't move a muscle. "Where's home?"

"Saltspring," I say and nod in the direction of the Strait of Georgia.

Will this trip unmake some of the mess of my life? Ed thinks so. But I don't know. Sometimes I look back and shudder. Surinder's only one unfinished chapter. Luna and the Chowdhurys are another, and though I'm thinking about sending the box to Lawrence, in the hopes that he will have greater success with the Chowdhurys, or, at the very least, be able to donate the box to a museum or library. It possesses a meaning beyond my own personal archive and has earned the right to a destiny in Bangladesh. But there remains also the unanswered question of Luna's whereabouts.

Luna. Lately I've begun to picture her resting in an unmarked grave, somewhere in Bangladesh. The image is unsettling – until I remember that it is her own grave, where she lies with her arms around her beloved, and I feel some solace. But I still prefer to see her in another land, still with the man she loves, thriving, remembering her mother, thinking: this time I will pick up the phone; this time I will get a passport and a plane ticket and go. When I see her this way, I urge her on. Don't wait Luna. Don't wait until you can't. Don't let boundaries, real or imagined, stand in your way.

"Go ahead," the immigration officer says. "Next."

The waiting room fills with people like me. We're definitely late now, and the tension in the room is palpable. I could go back. Feign the onset of a sudden illness, a need to go to the hospital. But the idea of passing back through immigration, facing that woman again, keeps me seated.

In the end, I was no better than Hasan or Amma when it came to Luna. The woman is as much a mystery as is her whereabouts. Though I loved her as much as any of them, the heaviness of her absence rests on me. And Shafiq dead, Hasan's war wounds. Shaheed a martyr before he even had the chance to have a son of his own. How stubbornly I believed I was the only one serving justice. Can I live with that guilt? Have I any choice?

"Group one," a bean-pole shaped boy calls out. "Everyone else remain in the waiting area." There's relief now that we're actually boarding, though the jostling of people and luggage has a tinge of nastiness. I'm glad they haven't yet called my number.

They'll call the kids – young lawyers – up one at a time, in alphabetical order. The young woman from Mexico will be nearly first. Her last name is Alvarez. I will applaud her too loudly and make some of the audience glance my way, smelling a troublemaker. As if the peasant blouse wasn't warning enough. Let them stand guard.

Surinder – rather, *Susan* Livingstone – will be the fourteenth one called up, sharing the exact centre with a boy with the last name Mallory. She will stride across that stage in her own perfect suit, graceful in heels that would make me stumble. But she will move as she always has – with the confidence befitting someone of her accomplishment.

She will take her trophy.

Again, I will applaud too loudly, too long. The VIPs will turn around, people down the row will lean over to see who's making all the racket and behind me, I will feel the stir I have created.

I smile. "Group three," I hear. I let the anxious ones stampede over one another to the front of the line. When they're through, I pick up my suitcase and walk unhindered up the gangplank.

My picture dissolves. I try to conjure up an image of my Surinder looking up startled, then running off the stage, into the audience, into my embrace. But no. That doesn't work. Then I try to picture a shy smile from her, after which I wait impatiently for the ceremonies to end. But I can't see that either. I have to accept the truth – I don't know what will happen.

The high speed catamaran powers up like a child's toy. It pulls away from the wharf, gathers speed in the Inner Harbour. We are told where to find lifejackets. Life boats. Muster stations. But people are drawn instead to the bustle of the harbour. The float planes landing and taking off. The ferry from Port Angeles thumping against the wharf. Kayakers, sailboats, the tiny harbour ferries that carry